"He was murdered, and one of you is responsible."

Luc Trahan's announcement as he walked up behind the sheriff caused CoCo's midnight eyes to flash. "I'm sorry for your loss, but you have no right to accuse anyone in my family."

"Are you sure about that?" He nodded toward her grandmother and little sister, both glaring at him as if he were pond scum.

CoCo followed his gaze. "I'm positive. And you should be, too, Luc." Her voice softened a beat.

His heart tripped in remorse. Traitorous little thing, his heart. He *thought* he'd gotten over CoCo LeBlanc.

"Do you have any proof of your allegations, Mr. Trahan?" Sheriff Theriot asked quietly.

"That *old woman's* a voodoo priestess," he replied.

And so are you, Coco LeBlanc, he found himself saying quietly inside.

What was wrong with him? He'd finally come to terms with his father's death and how wrong he'd been to partially blame CoCo. And now he'd just accused her of shooting his *grandfather.*

And, besides, if they were to line up everyone with motive enough to kill Beau, Luc himself would be at the head of the pack.

ROBIN CAROLL

Born and raised in Louisiana, Robin Caroll is a Southern belle right down to her "hey y'all." Her passion has always been to tell stories to entertain others. Robin's mother, bless her heart, is a genealogist who instilled in Robin the deep love of family and pride of heritage—two aspects Robin weaves into each of her books. When she isn't writing, Robin spends time with her husband of eighteen years, her three beautiful daughters and their four character-filled cats at home in the South—where else? An avid reader herself, Robin loves hearing from and chatting with other readers. Although her favorite genre to read is mystery/suspense, of course, she'll read just about any good story. Except historicals! To learn more about this author of Deep South suspense mysteries to inspire your heart, visit Robin's Web site at www.robincaroll.com.

Bayou
Justice
ROBIN CAROLL

Steeple
Hill®

Published by Steeple Hill Books™

STEEPLE HILL BOOKS

Steeple
Hill®

ISBN-13: 978-0-373-44264-5
ISBN-10:   0-373-44264-5

BAYOU JUSTICE

I waited patiently for the Lord; He turned to me and heard my cry. He lifted me out of the slimy pit, out of the mud and mire; He set my feet on a rock and gave me a firm place to stand. He put a new song in my mouth, a hymn of praise to our God. Many will see and fear and put their trust in the Lord.

—*Psalms* 40:1–3

To Case. . .
for believing
for supporting
for encouraging
for loving.
Love Always,
RC

Acknowledgment

A book is a wonderful collaboration of many
people. My heartfelt thanks to my editor,
Krista Stroever, who used brilliant insight to make
this book shine, and to my agent, Kelly Mortimer,
who pained over each word with me and used up
all her red pens in editing. Thank you both for
giving me the chance to attain my heart's desire and
believing in this story.

My eternal gratitude to Colleen Coble. Without
you, I wouldn't have had the endurance and the
"p" word to keep on. Your brainstorming, support,
love, encouragement, and opening of doors in the
publishing world for me kept me on the straight and
narrow. I love ya!

I thank my wonderful critique partners for their
help—Dineen Miller, Heather Diane Tipton,
Ron Estrada, Camy Tang of the Story Sensei,
and Ronie Kendig. The book wouldn't make sense
without these "slice and dicers"! Y'all are the
absolute best! Thanks to Cheryl Wyatt for walking
the journey with me.

Special thanks to my bestest bud, Tracey Aaron, and
my sister-in-law, Lisa Burroughs, for reading every
single word I write and not being afraid to tell me
it's not working. I love you!

Without the love and support of my family, I
wouldn't even be writing. My love and thanks to my
parents, Joyce and Chuck Bridges—for all the times
you've watched the grands so I could go to writing

conferences, and for your encouragement; my sisters and brother, Cindy Pittman, Rebecca Harden, and Charles Burroughs—for commiserating with me and celebrating my successes; Krystina, Brandon, and Rachel—for thinking it's cool their aunt talks to the voices in her head. I love you all so much and I thank y'all for coming on this ride with me.

A very special thanks to some of the most awesome prayer partners in the world, who have lifted up my writing and my life before the throne so many times. You ladies bless me daily! Big thanks to the members of ACFW, whose support and encouragement is the absolute best!

Finally, my most humble thanks to my daughters—Emily Carol, Remington Case, and Isabella Co-Ceaux—you girls are the reason I get up every morning and write. Each of you inspire me with your love and personality. I love each one of you so much—you are my most precious blessings from God.

All glory to my Lord and Savior, Jesus Christ.

ONE

Humidity, the South's great oppressor, seized the Louisiana bayou firmly by the throat. Late afternoon heat washed through the air in waves, turning and mixing to make the region downright sticky. CoCo LeBlanc wiped her brow and squinted, scanning the grassy shores. A living bulk shifted on the lush embankment, then the alligator stretched its mouth, his jagged teeth glistening in the late afternoon sun. Moodoo appeared healthy. CoCo stared, smiling at the twelve-foot reptile. She let out a long sigh. It'd been a rough couple of weeks, nursing the prehistoric beast back from the brink of death. Stupid poachers—would they never learn they couldn't hunt alligators anytime they got the notion? If she ever caught them…

Moodoo waddled along the banks, then surged his large body into the bayou. CoCo marked his location on her tracking sheet and then fired up the airboat's engine. She settled into the single seat before turning the steering wheel to head back to the house. Picking up speed, the airboat skimmed over the murky bayou. Drops of water jetted up, spraying CoCo's face and arms. She leaned closer to the edge of the boat, welcoming the cool mist. July in Lagniappe meant misery, no matter how you chopped it.

She banked the airboat and tied off on the knotty root of a live oak tree that had survived for several centuries. Stepping to the ground, she let the air pockets bubble up around her feet before striding toward the house with sure steps. Her hair was plastered to the nape of her neck, and her thin cotton tank top clung to her back. Too bad her tan lines were so messed up because she couldn't wear the same style shirt to work every day.

A man's angry voice burst through the cicadas' chirped song. "You get out or I'll have the sheriff force you out."

"You get on, now, Beau Trahan. Before I put a *gris-gris* on you," her grandmother replied, her voice quivering.

CoCo recognized that tone and quickened her pace. What now? She rounded the corner of the old plantation home to find Mr. Beau and Grandmere facing off on the veranda. She took the stairs two at a time, the wood creaking in protest. "What's going on here?"

The businessman in slacks and shirt, complete with power-red tie, faced her and glared. "Your grandmother seems to think she's above the law. As usual."

"Get off my land, you old goat." Grandmere's deep green eyes narrowed to slits and she took a step in his direction.

"It's not your land, *vielle*." He wagged his finger in front of Grandmere's face.

Not a good move on his part to call her an old woman, not good at all. CoCo shifted between the dueling elders, popping her hands on her hips. "What's this all about, Grandmere?" She turned to her grandmother, but kept track of Mr. Beau from the corner of her eye.

"He says he owns this house." Her grandmother waved a crumpled piece of paper. "Says he's evicting us. Just threats. All little men like him can do is threaten."

"Read the notice, you bat. Marcel signed this land over to me years ago when he couldn't pay his gambling debt. It's all legal—I drew up the papers myself." Beau Trahan, tall and distinguished as a retired politician should look, crossed his arms over his puffed-up chest.

Sounded like something her late grandfather would have done.

CoCo and her sisters had moved in with their grandparents thirteen years ago when their parents had died in a car accident. Grandpere died five years ago, after CoCo had returned to Lagniappe from college. The last years of his life had been littered with gambling and depression.

CoCo pried the paper from her grandmother's fist and scanned the eviction notice, chewing her bottom lip. Thirty days, that's all they had to save their home. She squared her shoulders and set her jaw, piercing him with her stare. "You've served your notice, Mr. Trahan. I'll contact my attorney immediately, and he'll get back to you regarding this matter."

"Not going to do you any good, young lady. The law's on my side." He directed his words to CoCo, but his eyes remained locked on Grandmere. Even in the stifling heat, not a single strand of gray hair moved out of place.

"The spirits are on mine." Grandmere wore that hazy expression she got when riled to the point of pulling out her voodoo paraphernalia.

Oh no, not the spirits again. CoCo let out a deep sigh and gripped her grandmother's shoulder, digging her fingers into Grandmere's bony frame. "Please leave, Mr. Trahan."

"Thirty days, Marie. That's it. And only because the law stipulates I have to give you that much time." Beau spun around and stomped to his pristine red Cadillac. He slammed the door, revved the engine, then peeled out down the dirt-and-gravel driveway.

CoCo waited until the rooster tails of dust disappeared

before turning back to her grandmother. "Did Grandpere sign over the deed to this house?"

Grandmere's eyebrows shot up over her fading green eyes. "Not that he ever told me. Beau Trahan, that *cooyon* is only trying to cause trouble, *ma chère*. I'll handle him." Her arthritis-gnarled hands grabbed the handle of the screen door.

Shoving her foot against the base of the door, CoCo tapped her grandmother's shoulder. The blue veins were apparent under Grandmere's thin skin. "No voodoo, Grandmere. I mean it."

"Just because you've turned your back on the old ways, doesn't mean the rest of us have." Grandmere shot a look that could freeze fireballs, her jade eyes turning into icicles. "You'll see. You were wrong to drop your training, CoCo. You're a natural."

Biting her tongue, CoCo moved her foot and let her grandmother enter. The argument stayed as constant as the bayou's summers. Ever since she'd come to Christ two years ago, she'd walked away cold from voodoo, black magic and all that her grandmother had been teaching her. Why couldn't—no, wouldn't—her family open their eyes and see the truth? Didn't they realize their eternal lives were at stake?

A breeze stirred the hot air, teasing the edges of the eviction notice. CoCo shook off her guilty conscience and marched inside the house. She'd deal with her family's salvation later. Right now, she had to find an attorney. Preferably a great one.

For a moment she considered calling her middle sister, Alyssa, up in Shreveport. Just as suddenly as the thought scampered across her mind, she disregarded the idea. Alyssa wasn't interested in the pressing issues happening in Lagniappe. As usual, the responsibility fell to CoCo.

The kitchen had always before been a place of soothing with its bright yellow paint on the walls and cabinets adding a sunny glow to the room. Despite the lack of updated appliances, the kitchen welcomed. She glanced at the clock—4:10. She needed to hurry before businesses closed for the day. She grabbed the Vermilion parish phone book, dropped into the kitchen chair and flipped through the business pages. Not much choice of attorneys. All the last names looked familiar, but none of the first names rang any bells. CoCo closed her eyes and jabbed her finger on the middle of the page.

Trahan Law Firm

Oh, but no. This wouldn't do.

Lord, could You give me a little direction here? She flipped to the other side of the page and repeated her random-selection process.

Dwayne Williams, Attorney

That sounded promising. A whole lot better than anything to do with a Trahan. She pushed back her chair and lifted the cordless phone off the counter. Punching with more force than necessary, CoCo dialed the number listed in the phone book.

On the second ring, a chipper female voice answered. "Law offices of Dwayne Williams. How may I help you?"

"My name is CoCo LeBlanc and I need to speak with an attorney as soon as possible." CoCo chewed the inside of her mouth.

"Yes, ma'am. Just a moment, and I'll connect you with Mr. Williams."

Elevator music sounded over the line. Pretty slick, getting to talk to a lawyer on the first call. Maybe because it was so close to quitting time?

"Dwayne Williams." His voice sounded deep, full of timbre.

"Mr. Williams, my name is CoCo LeBlanc and I need a lawyer. A man, Beau Trahan, has just served my grandmother and me, with an eviction notice on our home."

"Did you say Beau Trahan?"

"Yes." She pushed the bangs from her forehead. "Is that a problem?" Great, leave it to her to pick out an attorney who probably sat in Mr. Beau's back politician pocket.

"No, not at all." The sound of papers crinkling rustled in the background. "I can work you in tomorrow morning at nine to discuss your case. Is that a good time for you?"

Fast appointment, too. "That'll be perfect. I'll see you then." She hung up the phone, staring at it, hard and long. Jumbled thoughts bounced off the edges of her mind as she worried her bottom lip.

Did she dare call him? It'd been two years since they'd spoken. Did she want to open up all that hurt and anger? Yet, maybe he could talk some sense into his grandfather.

Jerking the phone up again before she could change her mind, she punched the number she knew by heart, still knew as well as her own. Would Luc Trahan answer?

Luc Trahan strode up and down the length of the front porch, glancing down the long driveway lined with oak trees and then back to the wood planks beneath him.

"You're going to wear out the veranda if you don't stop pacing," Felicia said.

He glanced at his younger sister, sitting properly in her wheelchair. "I'm just ready to get this over with."

"He's gonna blow, you know that, yes?"

"I do. That's why I need to get it over with as soon as he gets here." Luc turned and began the next lap. How could he break the news gently to his grandfather? He shook his head. There was no easy way. Felicia had hit the nail on the head— Beau Trahan would blow a gasket when Luc told him that he had no intention of taking over the managerial reins of

D'Queue Casino. Luc enjoyed his job as a freelance consultant for an accounting firm and had no desire to go elsewhere.

"Luc, look at me." His sister's soft voice never failed to calm him.

He did. Her big blue eyes twisted his heart.

"You're doing the right thing, no matter what Grandfather and Mom think."

"I know. I just hate to disappoint either of them." He dropped onto the porch swing adjacent to her wheelchair. "He wants this so badly for me."

"It's not what *you* want. It goes against everything you believe in."

"And Mom…"

Felicia smiled. "Oh, she'll moan and grumble, only because she's scared of him." She touched the back of his hand, caressing reassurance into his very being. "He isn't going to kick us out like Mom thinks he will."

"What if he does?" His gaze rested on her sweet face.

So sweet, so gentle—so unfair cerebral palsy had attacked her frail body. At only twenty-eight years old, she was confined to a wheelchair, one leg too weak for her to even walk across the room. Would Grandfather kick them out of the house if Luc didn't abide by his wishes? That could never happen—Felicia needed the stability of their home and the care their grandfather's money provided.

"Stop worrying so much, you." She gave his hand a final squeeze before dropping her own back in her lap. "He's threatened Mom with that for years now, yet he's never given us the boot. He's all talk."

"I wish I could be as sure. This just might be what calls his bluff."

Felicia flashed her full-tooth smile. "With all his ranting

and raving over me and Frank, he still didn't follow through on his threats. We'll be fine." She stared out into the yard. "When did he say he would be here?"

"He told Mom he was on his way when he called about ten minutes ago."

His cell phone rang, the chords to "Dixie" playing loud and clear. He snapped if off his belt, flipped it open and pressed it to his ear. "Hello."

"Luc."

Just his name—that's all it took for his heart to stutter. Her sultry voice always did make his pulse race. His memory slammed the image of her curly black hair, dark eyes with specks of green dancing around the irises, and tanned face to the forefront of his mind. Her strong French heritage had blessed her appearance, that much was certain.

He swallowed back the emotions clogging his throat. "CoCo."

"Your grandfather just left here." Her breathing came across the line as ragged, hitching.

"What was he doing at your place?" Luc shook his head at Felicia's inquiring stare. What could the old man be up to now?

"Serving us an eviction notice." His ex-fiancée's voice quivered. He recognized that trait—she barely had control over her emotions.

"An eviction notice? What're you talking about?" Luc stood and paced again.

"Just what I said. He hand-delivered an eviction notice to Grandmere today, right before I got home from work."

His gut clenched. Work. Her *work*. He gritted his teeth. The memory of yet another reason they broke up slammed into his mind.

"Luc, are you listening?"

"Yeah. I just don't understand."

"Neither do I." Her throaty sigh over the line tightened the knot holding his stomach hostage. "I wanted you to know what he's up to, and to tell you that I have a meeting with an attorney first thing in the morning."

Lawyers, already? What exactly had his grandfather done? He ran a hand over his hair. "I'm sure it's just a misunderstanding."

"I don't know what's gotten into him, but I'm not going to battle him without legal counsel."

No, CoCo wouldn't back down from any fight. He knew that all too well. Her personality wouldn't let her roll over and play dead.

"So, why are you calling me?"

"I don't really know." Her voice changed, moving into the confrontational tone he also recognized. "I thought you should be aware. I'm not going to lie down and take your grandfather's bullying. I intend to fight him with everything I can."

"Curses, *cunjas* and hexes, CoCo?" He could have bitten off his tongue for letting that slip out. The pain was still raw, even after two years of not being together.

She snorted. "Some things never change. I made a mistake in calling you, Luc. You're too much like the old man to see reason."

Ouch, that stung. "I'm sor—"

"Consider yourself warned. My family will fight you Trahans."

The disconnecting click cut loud in his ear. He held it a minute longer, not wanting to believe she'd hung up on him. Even when he'd ended their relationship and walked away, he'd never hung up on her.

Lord, why can't I control my tongue?

"Was that CoCo?"

He placed the phone back on his belt clip and stared at his sister. "Yeah."

She practically bounced in her chair. "What did she want?" Hope of his and CoCo's reconciliation glimmered in her eyes.

He hated to disappoint her, but any hope of that had just gone down like the setting sun. Just as it had when his father had died and he'd realized he couldn't marry CoCo LeBlanc. "To let me know Grandfather served her with an eviction notice."

Felicia's eyes, already round, grew as large as Confederate coins. "What? When?"

"Just now, apparently."

She covered her mouth with her hand. "Oh, no. What's Grandfather thinking?"

A rumble on the road caused them both to stare down the driveway. Sure enough, their grandfather's Caddy sped along the dirt road.

"I don't know. I'm guessing we're about to find out."

Grandfather slammed the door of his precious car, ran a hand over his thinning hair and then strode up the stairs. A smile danced on his face, a rare sight. "Luc, Felicia." He gave them a brief nod, not breaking stride as he headed for the door.

Lord, I don't know what to say. I can't antagonize him, yet I can't help him either without knowing what's going on.

"Grandfather," Luc began, staring down at the porch. His grandfather's shoes didn't even have a coat of dust covering them. Dirt ran in fear from Beau Trahan.

"Yes?" His grandfather glanced over his shoulder. "What is it, boy?"

"I just got a call from CoCo LeBlanc. Want to tell me what's going on?"

Chuckling, Grandfather let his hand fall from the door handle and then moved to sit on the porch swing. "Little lady already called you, huh? Trying to sweet-talk you into getting me to change my mind, I guess." He laughed and slapped his thigh. "Hope you told her you weren't buying into her feminine wiles again."

Luc shifted his weight from one foot to the other, despising himself for feeling like a disobedient teenager. "What're you doing?"

"Demanding what's mine, of course." His grandfather's eyes set hard in his chiseled face.

"An eviction notice on the LeBlanc's property?" Luc shook his head. "What's up with that?"

"Marcel LeBlanc signed that deed over to me years ago to cover a gambling debt to the casino. I've been really nice, not making them move. Now that I'm retiring, letting you step into my shoes, I have to move out of the penthouse. Since I don't want to make your momma and sister here move out, I'm claiming my property."

Guilt nudged against Luc's chest, but he picked his battles one at a time. "You can't just evict them, Grandfather. Where will they go? Their family's lived in that house since before the Civil War."

"Not my problem, son." His grandfather studied him. "You aren't still sweet on that little swamp witch, are you?"

"I just don't think it's right to evict them."

His grandfather shook his head as he pushed to his feet. "You're too soft, Luc. You'll have to toughen up to be manager at the casino."

Luc leaned against the porch rail. Maybe he appeared casual, even though his insides had turned as mushy as quicksand. *Dear God, help me make him understand.*

Felicia gave a slight tilt of her head. "I need to get inside. It's too hot out here." She pushed the control on the automatic wheelchair. Luc moved and opened the door for her. She gave him an encouraging smile as she rolled into the house. He let the screen door bang behind her.

His grandfather hit him with a hard glare, his hazel eyes not dimmed by the years. "You got something else to say to me?"

"About being too soft to be casino manager…"

Grandfather let out a loud laugh. "Don't you worry, son. I'll help thicken up your skin."

He took a deep breath. "It's not that I don't think I can do it. I just don't want the job."

"What?" His grandfather's eyes bugged bigger than a bullfrog's.

"I don't believe in gambling, Grandfather. You know that. I never said I wanted to follow in your footsteps." Luc let out a slow breath. "I love being a consultant, and don't want to change jobs."

His grandfather jumped to his feet. "I'm not believing this. After all my hard work, the years I put in there to get you in position to take over, I can't—"

"I never said I wanted you to do any of that. You just assumed. I'm perfectly content where I am."

The shout Grandfather emitted made Luc jump. "I don't care what you want. You'll take over at the casino. And that's final."

Luc drew up to his full six-foot-three, towering a good four inches over his grandfather, and stared into the old man's eyes. "No, I won't. I'm staying as a freelance consultant."

"You will or else." Grandfather stood toe-to-toe with him.

"Or else what?"

"Or else I'll not only kick you all out in the street, but I'll publicly disown you. You'll be dead in this town."

TWO

The morning sun split the blue skies, nearly blinding CoCo with its brightness. She cut her gaze through the Jeep's windshield, over to the front door of the law office of Dwayne Williams for about the fortieth time in the past ten minutes. No sign of activity. She checked her watch again—8:01, still too early to show up for her nine o'clock appointment.

"I don't understand why I had to come." Grandmere hadn't stopped complaining since they left the house. "I told you, I can take care of Beau Trahan."

God, can I get a little help here? CoCo clenched the steering wheel and leaned into the blast of air conditioning. As if that could cool the frustration burning in her. "Because we're going to do this legally."

"My way is legal."

"No, it isn't," CoCo said. "I don't want to hear anymore about the traditions of old. Just this once, let me handle things. Okay, Grandmere?"

Her grandmother huffed and rolled her aged eyes but remained silent. She turned her attention out the window.

Hauling in a deep breath, CoCo closed her eyes and rested her forehead against the steering wheel. Fatigue weighed down her very soul, and keeping up the long-standing argument with Grandmere wore her out even more. Sleep had flickered just out of reach last night. And it was all Luc Trahan's fault.

She'd managed to keep the wall she'd erected around her heart intact for two years. Two years! And with one measly phone conversation, it had begun to crumble. CoCo stared into the blazing sun. She wouldn't allow Luc to worm his way back into her heart. Not after he'd left her dangling in the wind the way he had—right after he'd proposed. He'd broken her heart once…she wouldn't let him close enough to crush it for good.

"It's about nine. What're we waiting for?"

CoCo snapped out of her reprieve and glanced over at the door to the law office. The blinds were now opening. "Guess we can go." She killed the engine and slipped out of the car, rushing around to the passenger side to assist her grandmother.

"I'm not old and decrepit," Grandmere snapped as she shrugged off CoCo's hand. "Despite what Beau Trahan thinks."

Ignoring the challenge in her grandmother's tone, she led the way to the lawyer's office. She'd grown tired of arguing with Grandmere over the past two years—to the point she'd avoid any further confrontation if at all possible. Opening the door, she smiled as the blast of frigid air hit her face. Just the walk across the parking lot had made her hot and sticky. She knew her face had to be beet-red, despite her tan.

"Good morning. Ms. LeBlanc?" the perky receptionist sitting behind the front desk asked.

CoCo nodded. "Yes. I have an appointment with Mr. Williams."

"Yes, ma'am. He's ready for you now." She stood and walked around the desk. "If you'll follow me, I'll show you to the conference room."

Their footfalls thumped softly on the deeply padded carpet

as they followed the receptionist down the hall. Light paneling shone beneath the overhead track lighting. She swung open a door, revealing a long mahogany table and large windows overlooking the grassy area behind the building.

"Can I get you a cup of coffee or a glass of water?" She waved them into the room while she hovered at the doorway.

"We're fine, *merci*." CoCo pulled out a plush chair on rollers for her grandmother.

"Mr. Williams will be with you shortly." The receptionist pulled the door behind her when she left.

Grandmere sat and glanced around the room. "This lawyer looks pricey, *ma chère*. It'd be easier if you'd just let me take care of Beau in my way."

The door swung open, saving CoCo from having to think of a response. A tall man in a business suit strode inside. His hair, black as the bayou bottom, contrasted against the chocolate color of his skin. "You must be CoCo LeBlanc. I'm Dwayne Williams."

He gave her a solid handshake. Her spirits soared—Grandpere had always said you could trust a man with a firm grip. "This is my grandmother, Marie LeBlanc."

Grandmere stood quickly and extended her hand. "Mr. Williams."

"Pleasure to meet you, Mrs. LeBlanc." He straightened and waved them both to the chairs. "Please, sit." He moved to the chair across the table from them and sat.

"Now, tell me what Mr. Trahan served you," Mr. Williams said, steepling his fingers over the legal pad and pen sitting on the glossy table.

Digging the paper out of her purse, CoCo's hands trembled slightly. She set her jaw and slid the eviction notice across the table to him. "This is what he hand-delivered to us yesterday."

Why were her palms sweating? As casually as possible, she wiped her hands on her jeans.

He scanned the paper and then lifted his pen over his legal pad. "Mrs. LeBlanc, is it possible that what Mr. Trahan states is true?" He tapped the pen against the paper. "Could your husband have signed over the deed to your property?"

"Beau Trahan is a lying, two-bit scum. Marcel never signed over any property deed—not willingly. Beau did something underhanded—I just know it. Probably told my Marcel he was signing something totally different." Grandmere's eyes hardened around the edges.

CoCo patted her grandmother's hand. "Mr. Williams, I—"

"Please, call me Dwayne."

She smiled. "Dwayne, I've lived with my grandparents for thirteen years, and this business about signing over the deed has never been mentioned before."

"It's easy enough to check out. If this did happen, there'll be a claim on file down at the courthouse. A matter of public record."

"So, what do we do?" CoCo held her breath and waited for his reply.

Dwayne sat straight in his chair. "I'll be honest with you. The main reason I took this case was because it involved Beau Trahan. I'm investigating him in an unrelated issue." He pressed his lips together for a moment, pausing before dropping the pen. "I'm inclined to believe Mrs. LeBlanc."

"That Mr. Beau had my grandfather sign something he didn't understand?"

"Yes." He held up a hand. "I'm not accusing Mr. Trahan of anything—not yet—but I can see something like that happening."

"Isn't that illegal?"

"Yes, it is. However, I'll have to research it more fully. I'll start by going to the courthouse and filing a motion against this eviction notice. At the very least, that should buy us an additional sixty to ninety days."

"And then what?" How could they prove Beau Trahan pulled such an underhanded scam on her grandfather?

"What we discover will determine how we'll proceed."

"Mr. Williams," Grandmere interrupted, "your words are all good, but what's this gonna cost us?"

He smiled, his white teeth flashing in contrast to his smooth, black skin. "If you're interested in me representing you in this matter, how about a one-hundred-dollar retainer and a balance of nine-hundred dollars?"

CoCo grabbed her purse. "That sounds fine. Should I pay that retainer now?" A thousand dollars to make this whole thing go away sounded a lot cheaper than the fee she'd imagined on the drive over. *Thank You for Your provision, Lord.*

"You can pay my secretary on your way out." Dwayne smiled again. "I'll need to get some more information from you before I can proceed."

Luc ran a caressing touch over his saxophone as he placed it back in its case. Playing the horn always brought him inner peace. Not as much as his daily prayer, but for midafternoon it held its own. Now that he'd finished the big consulting job he'd been working on for the past month, he had two weeks free. Felicia's wheelchair bumped against the sitting-room doorframe. He swiveled to stare at her.

"He didn't mean it." She maneuvered her chair across the gleaming wood floor.

"I think he did." He straightened, lifting his sax case.

"He'll calm down. You'll see."

How he wished he could believe her. "I need to find him, talk to him. Try to make him understand how I feel."

"Luc, when has he ever cared about what any of us feel?" Big tears welled in her crystal blue eyes, and she ducked her head.

"Hey." He set the case on the floor and crossed the room to squat before her. "What'd he say to you?" He patted her bare knees.

"Nothing." She sniffed and wiped away her tears.

"Then why are you crying? Come on, *Boo,* when have you ever not been able to tell me everything?" He crossed his eyes and stuck out his tongue, a trick he'd used to cheer her up since they were children.

She let out a small giggle. "I talked to Frank this morning."

"And?" He waggled his eyebrows.

"It seems Grandfather paid him a little visit yesterday." She hiccupped. "He told Frank to s-s-stay away from me if he didn't want to end up in f-f-financial ruin." Fresh tears pooled in her eyes.

Luc let out a low whistle. "He sure was a busy man yesterday." He held his sister's hands. "What'd Frank say?"

The smile she flashed sparkled and brightened the entire room, even more so than the floor-to-ceiling windows along one wall. "Frank said he told Grandfather that he could drop dead."

"Good for him." Frank Thibodeaux seemed to be good for his sister. He'd never seen her look happier.

"Luc, you know how Grandfather is. He'll set out to ruin Frank if I keep seeing him."

"He can't hold us under his thumb forever." Luc straightened, staring out the large windows overlooking the bayou. The afternoon sun reflected off the water, casting prisms of light and color across the marshland.

He turned back to stare at his sister. The large room appeared to swallow her small form. The white paint on every wall in the house screamed purity, always reminding him of Felicia. "You just keep seeing Frank if he makes you happy. I'll figure something out."

"Frank's so mad, it scares me."

Luc glanced at his sister, laying a hand on her shoulder. "Scares you how?"

"He's so angry over the way Grandfather treats me. He says Grandfather isn't allowing me to get new and inventive treatments that could maybe help me. He says there's a surgery that could let me walk."

His sister shook her head. "I don't know what to think. All my doctors are 'Grandfather selected.' I've never questioned it before because he's paid all the medical bills. If what Frank suggests is true…"

Luc ground his teeth. "We can look into it."

"How? Grandfather controls everything we do, who's in our lives, how we live."

"And it's going to stop now."

She stared up at him with such hope and trust in her eyes it almost physically hurt him. "How? What can we do?" She lowered her head. "Maybe Mom's right. We should be grateful for all he does for us." Her voice cracked on a sob.

"Stop that. It isn't true and you know it."

"I think Grandfather's threats have pushed Frank into making a decision."

"What kind of decision?"

Felicia stared back up at him. This time, her smile twinkled in her eyes. "I think he's going to propose soon."

"That's great, *Boo*." Happiness filled Luc's chest, but a bitter sting of remorse fell like lead to his gut. At one time, he, too, had been thinking of marriage, had even presented a ring. A life with CoCo. The knife in his heart twisted at the thought of what he'd had…and what he'd thrown away. If only he'd been able to forgive….

"I'm scared if he asks me and I accept, Grandfather will retaliate."

"That settles it. I'm going to find him and talk reason to him right now." Luc lifted his case.

Felicia's hand stopped him. "What are you going to do if he won't listen to you?"

"Then I'll think of something else. If I have to, I can move away and get a more permanent job, buy a house for you and Mom. With this last job, my reputation is solid enough now that any accounting agency would be thrilled to hire me on full time."

"Don't be silly. I know you prefer consulting. If Frank proposes, then you don't have to worry about me. I don't want to be a burden anymore."

"You're not a burden. You're my sister, and I love you."

"I love you, too." Her hand moved to squeeze his. "You shouldn't have to fight my battles as well as your own."

"It's high time someone stood up to him."

"And you think that person is you?"

He squeezed her hand back. "Who better?" *With God's guidance.*

The purple hue of the setting sun nearly stole CoCo's breath. She jerked her gaze from the window and laced her boots with haste. Only a few minutes of daylight remained, and she still needed to track two of the gators on her list. If she could prove they were multiplying at a less-than-normal rate, she could get more grant money for research from the

Wetlands Preservation Center. And if her theory was correct, it could reduce the limits during hunting season. If only the *cooyon* from the State Wildlife and Fisheries would listen to her explanation.

Hunters…just the thought of them made her spine turn to grits. They weren't supposed to hunt any of the yellow-tagged gators, yet four were still unaccounted for since a month ago. Tracking these reptiles was her life's work—why she'd gone to college and graduated with a degree in environmental protection. She'd loved the bayous and swamps she called home and felt compelled to do her part to save them. She still did.

CoCo shut her bedroom door and whisked down the hall. Her fingers itched to fire up her airboat and get on the water. She made the turn at the top of the stairs, gripped the banister and then took the first step.

Whispers halted her movement. Coming from her baby sister's room.

She backtracked up the step she'd just taken and moved to Tara's door. Pressing her ear against the wood, CoCo held her breath and listened.

She recognized the mumbled words. An incantation of a *gris-gris*. Icy fingers tickled down her spine.

Jerking the door open, CoCo glared at her sister.

Tara sat cross-legged in the middle of her bed, a voodoo doll held in one hand, red paint dripping from a brush in the other. The doll already had two streaks across its body.

"What're you doing?" CoCo placed her hands on her hips.

Her sister didn't even bother to try to hide her actions. Instead, she lifted her chin and met CoCo's stare. "What you're too scared to do."

CoCo inhaled through her nose, biting back the acidic retort stinging her tongue. "Tara, I've told you not to do this."

"I've told you—I'm twenty-four years old and you can't tell me what to do anymore." She tossed her long hair over her shoulder. Being outside in the summer had lightened it with streaks from the sun. "Besides, you're just mad because Grandmere pays attention to me now."

Guilt at Tara's even being exposed to voodoo nearly strangled her. "That's not it at all. You know better. She's only teaching you because I refused to learn anymore."

"You're just jealous." Tara's words might have sounded angry, but CoCo detected the hurt behind them.

"Oh, Tara." She sat on the foot of the bed, her fingers absentmindedly tugging at loose threads in the pink coverlet. "I stopped learning because I know it's wrong."

"Because the god you found told you it's a sin." Tara leapt off her bed and set the doll and brush on the oak desk. "Goody for you, but you aren't going to take this away from me. I won't let you."

CoCo fought to get her legs to support her. "I'm not trying to take anything away from you. I'm trying to save you."

Tara let out a harsh laugh. "Save me? That's rich." She narrowed her eyes and waved her hands. "Just go. Get out of my room and let me take care of things."

"I've got it under control." CoCo gestured toward the doll. "You don't need to do this."

"Yeah, hiring an attorney gets it all under control. Who're you trying to fool? Old man Trahan has all the lawyers in these parts in his hand."

Her words stung CoCo, just as if she'd been slapped across the face.

Maybe she should have called Alyssa. At the very least they could provide a unified front. Their stance against voodoo was about the only thing CoCo and Alyssa agreed on.

Dear God, show me how to reach Tara. Call her to You as You called me.

"Go, CoCo. Go play with your alligators."

"It doesn't have to be like this." If she could just help Tara see…

Tara shook her head and held up her hand. "I said get out of my room."

When had Tara grown to be so rebellious and bitter? Had she failed her sister when their parents died?

"I said, go!" Tara slapped the blue doorframe hard. A framed photo of their parents dropped to the floor. Tara's eyes widened. "The picture fell off the wall. That means someone will die, CoCo."

"That's just superstition."

"Go!"

Without another word, CoCo turned and strode from the room and then down the stairs. She needed to get on the bayou, to be alone, to find peace. Her steps were quick as she made her way to her airboat. She untied the rope from the live oak stump.

A vehicle rattled down the gravel driveway.

CoCo turned, her heart and stomach switching places.

Luc Trahan skidded to a stop. What was he doing here? Through the windshield, his gaze met hers. Her betraying heart leapt.

She tossed down the rope and marched toward the truck. Luc got out, smiling as if he hadn't crushed her heart and dreams. "What are you doing here?"

"I just wanted to let you know Grandfather's acting on his own with this eviction thing."

He looked good—too good. She stiffened her spine. "Doesn't matter. I've already retained an attorney to fight him."

"Look, I think we—"

CoCo held up her hand. "There is no *we* anymore. You made sure of that, Luc." She crossed her arms over her chest to hide her trembling. "I think you'd better leave."

"But..."

"No anything. Just go. I want you to leave. Now." *Please, please just leave.* She couldn't allow him inside her heart again. It'd taken her too long to regain her emotional footing.

He moved toward her, closing the distance between them comfortably.

She backed up a step. "I said to go, Luc." Her heart thundered. "Please." She hated herself for pleading, but knew the tears would come soon. She refused to give him the satisfaction.

As if he could hear her thoughts, he nodded, got into his truck and slammed the door.

Dirt filled the air as he sped off. It took her a moment to regulate her breathing. Her emotions betrayed her. CoCo narrowed her eyes toward the road, even though his truck had long moved out of view.

You won't keel me over again with a warm smile, Luc Trahan. Not ever again.

THREE

Why, God? What more do You want from me? Haven't I paid enough? Lost enough? Repented enough?

How had she failed so badly? Tara, her baby sister, already graduated to *cunjas* and using voodoo dolls. CoCo shook her head in the darkness.

With Alyssa gone, the responsibility of looking after her baby sister fell directly on CoCo's shoulders. The weight often felt crushing. Hadn't she endured a bad enough day without having to deal with Tara's involvement in their grandmother's old ways? Why didn't they listen?

CoCo's stomach roiled. Grandmere wouldn't even bother teaching Tara if CoCo hadn't stopped her training. She sighed. Being a Christian sure didn't make life any easier—if anything, she'd had more heartache and grief.

And Luc showing up out of nowhere. Calling him had been a mistake, a big one. When the chips were down, why had she gone on auto-pilot and called in her knight in shining armor? She let out a breath with a gust. Some knight he'd turned out to be.

The only reply to her prayers was the tree frogs croaking, blending with the chirping of the crickets, filling the evening with the bayou's own unique song.

CoCo turned off her running lights, killed the engine of her airboat and let it drift. The soft lapping of water against the boat lulled away her frustration. She drew in a deep breath, sucking in the calming scents of the bayou—sweet onion flowers and muskiness. This was her habitat, where she felt most comfortable. It would be over her dead body before she left her home. No matter what deed Beau Trahan possessed.

A bump against the airboat sent it rocking. CoCo flipped on her spotlight and shone the beam into the water. A young alligator, maybe five feet long at most, nudged with his nose again. CoCo laughed. A little bull testing his dominance. She reached for her tagging tool.

Loud thrashing sounded to her left. Pinpricks of dread skittered against the back of CoCo's neck. She recognized the sound—water currents caused by an alligator having something in its death roll.

She jerked the light in the direction of the sound. Illumination reflected off the water, casting shadows into the weeping willow trees. There, a little farther to the left. CoCo shifted the light to the movement.

A flash of fabric. A twist of flesh. Another whooshing splash.

Heartbeat thudding in her ears, CoCo grabbed her noisemaker and pressed the button. The wail, imitating the guttural sound mother alligators made, bounced off the trees. She lowered the device to water level and sounded it again.

The alligator jerked toward her, leaving the body he'd had in his jaws. The young bull growled and grunted, defining his territory. The other gator dove under the water, slipping below her. CoCo kept the light on the older reptile. He surfaced a few feet from the young bull, who continued to warn off the other alligator with his rumbles. Within seconds, the bull attacked. The two reptiles rolled with one another. Waves rocked the airboat.

She sounded the noisemaker again. Both alligators faced her. She let loose another blast. The bull dove deep, surfacing 40 feet away. The other followed. CoCo trolled toward the human body floating facedown. Reaching behind her seat, she pulled out a long hooked pole. Her hands trembled as she jabbed the body with the hook and flipped it over.

The lifeless face of Beau Trahan stared up at her.

Leaning over the edge of the boat, CoCo retched and gagged. Once her stomach stopped heaving, she yanked the radio off its stand. "Alpha Tango Charlie to Vermilion parish sheriff's office."

The static crackled over the radio, followed by a loud blast. "Sheriff's office, go ahead."

"I need the sheriff out here at marker twelve-one-four, immediately."

Again the crackling filled the night air, silencing the frogs and locusts. "Alpha Tango Charlie, what is the emergency?"

She glanced over at Beau Trahan's blank expression. "I found a dead body at this location."

The dispatcher informed her a unit would be on its way shortly. CoCo replaced the radio and then gazed over the bayou, looking anywhere but at the body. She flipped on her night lights, turned on her distress signal and then sat. Her top teeth captured her bottom lip and rubbed.

God, what more?

Long moments passed before a siren whirred off in the distance. She stood and caught sight of the incoming boat. Blue and white lights tangoed like macabre dancers. CoCo engaged the trolling motor, moving the airboat to face the incoming vessel.

Sheriff Bubba Theriot, his thick glasses mirroring the flashing blue-and-white, nodded as soon as they drifted close enough to her. "CoCo, whatcha got?"

She jerked her head toward her shoulder. "Dead body. Heard the death roll, then saw him. Got the gators to leave with the noisemaker before I radioed in."

A deputy killed the engines and directed the boat to where she'd indicated. Bubba glanced over the side, his red hair looking brassy under the boat's lights. "Oh, man. It's Beau Trahan." He glanced over at CoCo, his face paling by the minute.

"I know."

He turned to his deputy. "We need to drag him out and carry him back to shore." His gaze flitted to the body for a second before shooting over to her. "We'll need you to make a statement."

The deputy slipped the retrieval rod into the water, hooking Beau's waist in the curve. CoCo stared back at the sheriff. If she had to watch them haul Beau in, she'd hurl again. "Okay. Can I just meet you back on land?"

Bubba gave a curt nod. "We're closest to your house. We'll put in there. I'll radio the coroner to meet us."

Great. She didn't want to see any more. Her property wasn't where she'd had in mind to meet, but at least she could go now. "Fine."

She fired up the engine and whisked away as camera flashes went off. Shudders wracked her body. Everything about the situation gave her the creeps, but nothing more than the burning question—what had Beau Trahan been doing out in the bayou this time of night?

CoCo banked the airboat, tied it off, then rushed into the house. The screen door slammed behind her.

Grandmere sat up. "*Ma chère,* what's your hurry? You look like a band of demons are after you."

"I found a body in the bayou."

"Oh, no!" Her grandmother's voice bounced off the sunny walls.

Tara bounded down the stairs, the wood creaking and popping. "Grandmere, what's wr—" She stopped when her gaze lit on CoCo. Her eyes narrowed. "Oh, you're riling her up again, aren't you? Come to lecture her about me?" She crossed her arms tightly over her chest.

"Stop it, Tara. Contrary to what you may believe, everything is not all about you. I found Beau Trahan's body in the bayou." Anger shoved out the fear and revulsion she'd felt just moments before. A hum echoed off the bayou, but she ignored it and glared at Tara.

Grandmere struggled to her feet, her curled fingers grasping the back of the torn couch. "Oh, my. Are you sure, child?"

CoCo's stomach knotted. "I'm positive."

Her grandmother gasped, but Tara snorted. CoCo darted her stare to her sister and arched her eyebrows.

"Well." Tara shrugged. "The old man got what was coming to him."

"Tara!"

"It's true." Her sister flung her straight hair over her petite shoulders marked with tan lines. "I'm not sorry."

Boards creaked from the porch. CoCo scrutinized her baby sister, recalling how Tara used to run to her for help and direction. What had happened to that sweet little girl? How could her sister be so cold, so callous? "That's a horrible thing to say about another human being."

"What, did one of your precious alligators get him?" Tara's mouth twisted into a sneer.

"No, ma'am. Mr. Trahan was shot in the back," Sheriff Theriot said from the screen door. "May I come in?"

"Oh. Yes. Certainly." CoCo pushed open the door and waved the sheriff into the room.

He ambled inside, already pulling his little notebook from his shirt pocket. He popped the top off his pen, sat on the couch and then looked at CoCo. "I need you to tell me everything about finding Mr. Trahan."

She wet her lips and closed her eyes. "I was late getting to my run today because I had an appointment in town this morning."

"About what time did you get on the water?"

Opening her eyes, she locked gazes with her sister. "About sevenish."

"Isn't that a little late to be getting on the bayou?"

"Yes. I normally go in the morning and then again in the afternoon, but like I said, I had an appointment."

Sheriff Theriot gave a little huff, scribbled something on his notebook, then returned his attention to her. He looked entirely too casual sitting on her grandmother's floral-patterned couch. "So, you got out on the bayou around seven. Then what?"

CoCo flipped on the lamp sitting on the sidebar. "I went through my normal routine, marking locations of the tagged alligators on my tracking sheet. I saw a new bull gator, a young one, and reached for my tagging equipment. That's when I heard it." She pinched her eyes closed again. The action didn't block out the memory.

"Heard what?"

She stared back at the sheriff, fighting against the stinging tears. "A death roll."

"And then?"

"I shined the light over there and I saw...I saw the gator had a human body."

"Uh-huh." He jotted on his notebook again. "Then what?"

"I grabbed my noisemaker and scared off the alligators."

"Gators? Thought there was just one?"

"No, the young bull decided to defend his territory against the gator that had the body." She hated the way her voice cracked.

"So, you scared them away. Then what?"

She hauled in a deep breath. Bad mistake. The stench of death lay just outside. She could smell it, sense it creeping into the house and settling between her shoulder blades.

"CoCo?" Sheriff Theriot tilted his head to the side, waiting.

"I got my stick out, hooked the body and then flipped it over. I radioed it in immediately."

"I see." The sheriff mustered to his feet. "That's all you can tell me?"

"Yes." What more could she say?

"You didn't hear a gunshot? See any boats in the area?"

She thought for a moment. "No, nothing."

"Uh-huh." He ambled to the door, pushed it open, then leaned outside and spit. He turned back to face her, a bit of tobacco spittle lingering in the corner of his mouth.

Her stomach rebelled. She rushed down the hall, shoved open the bathroom door and bent over the toilet. Dry heaves shook her body.

"You okay?" Tara stood in the doorway.

CoCo leaned her forehead against the clawed tub. "Yeah." She stood and turned on the tap. "I'll be there in a minute."

"Just thought you might want to know, Sheriff said he called Luc."

Marvelous. Just what she needed. The cherry on top of an already lousy day. "*Merci* for the heads-up."

Tara nodded and left, her footsteps echoing on the wood floors. CoCo rinsed her mouth and splashed cold water on her face. She wondered how Luc took the news. This was a tragedy. However despicable he might have been, Beau Trahan was Luc's grandfather. She set the towel on the counter and then walked back to the living room.

Sheriff Theriot glanced at her through the screen. Men's voices filtered in through the door, riding on the beams of headlights. Other law officials and the coroner must have arrived.

"CoCo," the sheriff said as he opened the door and stepped inside, "is it true you and Mr. Trahan had a disagreement yesterday?"

News traveled fast in the bayou. No big surprise there. "Uh, sort of."

"Care to explain?" He cocked his bony hip against the doorframe.

It struck her that he looked an awful lot like that Opie character from the old *Andy Griffith* show. "It really wasn't that big of a deal. He gave my grandmother an eviction notice, and I asked him to leave."

"An eviction notice? And you say it wasn't that big of a deal?" His unibrow crinkled.

"I mean, sure we were upset, that's the appointment I had this morning. I went to see my lawyer."

"Who would that be?" He'd fished his notebook and pen from his pocket once more.

"Why does it matter?" All of a sudden, her stomach lurched again.

Sheriff Theriot gave her a what-are-you-hiding stare. "Just gotta verify it, that's all."

"Dwayne Williams."

He scribbled. His pen scratched against the paper, rubbing her nerves raw. "You say you weren't all that upset with Mr. Trahan yesterday?"

"I was upset, but I didn't kill him if that's what you're implying." Indignation stiffened her spine.

"I said nothing like that. I'm just trying to figure out what happened." He pushed open the door and spit off the porch again. "This is a homicide, Ms. LeBlanc. We have to check out everything and everyone."

"I'm a suspect?" Her palms sweated.

"He was murdered, Ms. LeBlanc."

"And one of you is responsible," Luc Trahan announced as he walked up behind the sheriff.

CoCo's midnight eyes flashed. "I'm sorry for your loss, but you have no right to accuse anyone in my family."

"Are you sure about that?" He nodded toward her grandmother and little sister, both glaring at him as if he were pond scum.

She followed his gaze, then met his stare. "I'm positive. And you should be, too, Luc." Her voice softened a beat.

His heart tripped in response. Traitorous little thing, his heart. He'd assumed he'd gotten over CoCo LeBlanc. Apparently not. She still took his breath away.

"Do you have any proof of your allegations, Mr. Trahan?" Sheriff Theriot spoke quietly.

"CoCo called me yesterday after Grandfather served the eviction notice. She was mad, really mad. Said she wouldn't be bullied by my grandfather." He never broke eye contact with CoCo.

Her eyes widened. The green streaks around the irises glimmered. "I was mad, yes, but I didn't threaten him in any way, and you know that."

"What about them?" He nodded toward her family lurking behind her.

She shook her head, her curly tresses falling over her shoulder like black ink. "An old woman and a young girl?" She guffawed. "Surely you don't mean to imply they had anything to do with his death?"

"That *old woman* is a voodoo priestess." *And you, too.*

"You don't believe all that…wait, what did you call it? Mumbo jumbo. All that mumbo jumbo could kill someone?"

The scab ripped off his old wound. "But they do." *She's still so bitter, God. I pray You'll touch her heart, soften it, bring her to know and love You.*

"Their beliefs didn't kill your grandfather, Luc." There she went again, using her soft and sultry voice against him. His heart reacted.

Sheriff Theriot shifted his weight. "We'll have more information in the morning." He nodded at CoCo. "I'll need you to come down to the station first thing."

"D-do I need to bring my lawyer?"

"Do you need one?" Luc hated the accusation slipping into his words, but couldn't stop it.

Her eyes were steel as she glared at him. "I think you need to leave, Luc. You've already been ordered off my property once today."

"Since this is legally my grandfather's land, it's now mine, wouldn't you say?" Why did he continue talking, instigating the situation and riling her up? He didn't want to hurt her. He'd *never* wanted to cause her pain. Yet, he had…but it'd hurt him, too.

"You need to leave, *cooyon*. Now." Her grandmother took a step toward him.

The sheriff laid a hand on his shoulder, practically pulling him out of the house. "It's been a long day. Just go home, Luc. Be with your mom and sister. We'll meet in the morning."

Finally, logic and reason prevailed. Luc stared into CoCo's

eyes, searching for any sign of malice or deception. He found none—they shined with clarity and honesty. What had he done by accusing her? Again.

"Luc." The sheriff jerked harder on his shoulder.

"Yeah. Okay." He strode off the porch, not looking back. He couldn't bear to see the heartbreak and hurt in her eyes. Once had been enough for that. He didn't have it in him to say any more.

Sheriff Theriot followed him to his vehicle. "What's this about you being ordered off the place today?"

"I came by to talk to her about the eviction notice."

"What about it?"

Luc shrugged. "Just that Grandfather was acting on his own."

"Didn't realize you two were talking." Bubba hitched his single brow.

"We aren't." He ran a hand over his hair. "I just thought it was wrong that Grandfather was evicting them."

"Uh-huh. I see. Just come by the station in the morning. Maybe we'll have some more information available by then."

"Thanks, Bubba. I appreciate it." He got in the car and started it up.

Once on the main road, he slammed the side of his fist against the steering wheel. He'd finally come to terms with his father's death and how wrong he'd been to partially blame CoCo. Now, Luc had just accused her of shooting his grandfather. What was wrong with him? If they were to line up people with motive to kill Beau, *he* would be at the head of the line.

Braking to a stop at the end of the road, he pulled air into his lungs in great gulps. He'd wanted out from under Grandfather's thumb, and he'd gotten his wish. But he'd never wanted the old man killed. If CoCo and her family weren't the killers, then who?

Wanting to avoid talking to his mother, the drama queen herself, Luc steered in the direction of his great-uncle's house. Somebody needed to tell Uncle Justin. The enormity of responsibility sat heavily across Luc's shoulders.

How did one go about telling someone their brother had just been murdered?

FOUR

Exhaustion weighted each limb, but sleep eluded CoCo. She lay in the four-poster bed, the night sounds of the bayou drifting in through the old plantation's air-conditioning units. Visions of Beau Trahan's dead face flickered across her memory. As long as she lived, she'd never forget those lifeless eyes. It brought back the nightmare of two years ago…being called out to the bayou to help capture an alligator who had killed a man. A man who went into the water following a boating accident. A man who happened to be Caleb Trahan, Luc's father. She'd forever be haunted by the horrors of his death, too.

Flipping onto her stomach, she punched her feather pillow a couple of times. Why did her life have to be so complicated? Every place she turned, death seemed to find her. And it always went back to Luc and his family.

Why, God? Again? I don't understand. I'm following You. Why won't You stop this death cloud hovering over me?

She laid in silence waiting for a response. None came. CoCo turned her head and glared at the clock—11:32. She let out a groan and pinched her eyes shut. Luc's face swam in her mind. With ease she could recall the feel of his arms around her…his gentle hands in her hair…his lips grazing her temple…the promise of forever sealed with a ring. She sniffled and turned onto her back.

Her door creaked open, spilling radiance from the hall night-light. Tara hovered in the doorway. "Are you awake?"

CoCo pushed into a sitting position. Her shoulders pressed against the oak headboard. "Yeah, come on in. What's wrong?"

Her sister's steps faltered as she made her way across the hardwood floor to perch on the edge of the bed. "Who do you think shot Mr. Beau?" Her toenails flickered hot pink, a bold contrast to the white comforter.

"I don't know." CoCo leaned forward in the semilight to try to study her sister's face. "Do you have any idea?"

Tara shrugged. "I really don't know, but it couldn't have happened to a better person." She held up her hand. "I know, I know, it's not nice to say. You have to admit Beau Trahan wasn't a nice man."

"No, he wasn't, but that doesn't mean he deserved to be shot."

"I understand that. And I'm sorry because I know it puts something else between you and Luc."

"That's over anyway. This doesn't change anything."

"Are you sure about that?"

CoCo nodded, pressing her lips together.

"I'm not so certain. Luc still stares at you *like that*."

The smile she forced cost her more pain in her heart than she'd ever imagined it would after all this time. "It's been over for two years. You know that."

"If you say so. I just see the way he looks at you. Like a man in love."

CoCo snorted. "You're imagining things, Tara." No, no…she couldn't let hope rise in her chest. He'd betrayed her, the pain he'd inflicted left a scar across her heart that would never totally heal.

Her sister stood. "I don't think so. Hey, it's your life, not mine." Her words were sharp, but delivered with a soft tone.

"Did you want to talk about anything else?"

Tara shook her head. "I just wanted to check on you. I know it's been a rough day"

Now here was the little sister she remembered. She flashed an authentic smile. "I'll be okay, *Boo*. I appreciate you asking."

"Okay. I'll see you in the morning." Her sister turned and walked soundlessly to the door.

"Tara?"

"Yeah?" She glanced over her shoulder.

"I love you."

A smile spread across her sister's face. "I love you, too."

With the door closed, the room sank into darkness once more. CoCo glanced at the clock—12:59. Lovely. Today had already disappeared, and tomorrow didn't look too promising. She scrunched back under the cotton sheet, flipping to her side. Maybe she *had* touched Tara with her witnessing. Could it be?

A screech owl hooted right outside her bedroom. Once, twice. CoCo bolted upright, her heart racing. Old habits dying hard and all that jazz. She slipped out of bed and crossed to the window, pushing back the sheer curtains. An owl perched on the magnolia tree branch just outside. It seemed to stare right at CoCo, before hooting twice more. The moon danced in the sky, catching the stars and washing them in more light, as if they weren't brilliant enough.

Her door swung open. Tara trembled. "Did you hear it? There's gonna be another death."

CoCo let her hand fall from the curtain and moved to her sister. "That's superstition."

"The picture fell off the wall, then you found Mr. Beau. Don't you see? It's not superstition. You, of all people, should know the power of the *gris-gris*."

She wrapped her arm around her sister's shoulders. "Tara, that picture falling off the wall had nothing to do with Mr. Beau getting shot. Come on, it just isn't logical."

Tara stepped out of her embrace. "You're wrong, CoCo. You can tout Christ all you want, and say how black magic and voodoo are wrong, but the spirits are angry and you can't deny their intervention in life."

How could she explain? *Lord, give me the words.* She took a deep breath. "Tara, I've never said there weren't bad spirits—I can't believe in God and not believe in Satan. Doing any kind of voodoo or spells and such is against God's teachings. It's against His will."

"So this god of yours doesn't want us to defend ourselves? I'm sorry, I don't buy that." Tara shook her head. "You know the teachings—the old ways tie us into the spirit of nature, to allow us to defend ourselves against the bad spirits. If your god is so powerful, why does he allow the spirits to torment us?"

Just what she'd been asking God about earlier. "Tara, God is love. He created nature, so of course, we're in tune to all His creations."

Tara hurried to the door. "I don't want to hear anymore. It's all lies. Voodoo works. It's proven, and I know in my heart it's true."

"Wait," CoCo cried and took a step forward, but Tara rushed from the room and shut the door firmly behind her. It wasn't worth another argument. Besides, she couldn't explain to Tara what she couldn't figure out herself.

She got back in bed, scowling at the clock. The neon numbers blinked 1:41, mocking her inability to sleep. CoCo shoved the clock, knocking it off the nightstand. It thundered to the floor with a loud thump.

Luc sat in his four-wheel drive, staring at his great-uncle's house. No lights blazed, not even a welcoming one burned on the front porch. Maybe he should wait until later to break the news to Uncle Justin. Luc reached for the keys still hanging in the ignition, then stopped himself. The press would be all over the story in the morning. His grandfather had been a respected pillar of the community, having served as a state representative for two terms. No, he couldn't let his uncle hear about this on the morning newscasts.

This evening had been a nightmare, one laced with memories—hard memories, painful memories. He shook his head. No, he couldn't compare the two. He refused. This time was different. Last time, it'd been an accident—this time, it was murder.

Father God, please forgive my human instincts that scream out for revenge. I pray Your justice be served, for Grandfather and all of us.

He opened the door and stepped onto the dirt driveway. His stride slowed, dread weighing down his legs. Before his foot hit the first stair, lights blazed in the windows and the front porch lit up like the bayou during a parish-wide *cochon de lait*. He could almost smell the pig roasting over an open pit.

The front door whipped open with a creak and his burly uncle stood there, shotgun raised. "Who's there?"

"It's Luc, Uncle Justin."

"Luc? What're ya doing here this time of night?" He lowered the gun and squinted in the dark. His thinning hair stuck up at odd angles, its streaks of white sparkling under the harsh porch light.

"I have some bad news. Can I come inside?"

"Of course. Come on in." Justin moved his big bulk out of the doorway, letting Luc pass.

Luc moved into the small living room and dropped to the couch. It always amazed him that his grandfather gave his uncle so much money, yet Justin never seemed to spend a dime of it. At least, not on his house or its furnishings.

Running his hand over his hair, Luc struggled to find the gentlest words available. He must have a limited thesaurus of the brain as nothing came to mind. "Uncle Justin, I don't know how to say this…"

"Just spit it out, boy." His uncle leaned the shotgun against the wall before taking a seat in the recliner across from the couch. The leather popped against his weight.

"Grandfather was found dead in the bayou tonight."

"No!" Justin's face paled under the bright lights.

"I'm sorry." He let out a long sigh. Maybe he should have let Bubba Theriot do the notifying—it was his job, after all. No. This was his family, his responsibility.

"Not again!" His uncle's face turned red as a lobster and his big hands shook when he ran a hand over his haphazard hair. "What happened?"

"Someone shot Grandfather in the back."

"Shot!" His uncle leapt up, no small feat considering the man's large girth. "Who?"

Luc shook his head. "We don't know yet."

"Beau was just here today."

Jerking up his head, Luc stared at his uncle. "When?"

"Today." Justin lifted a shoulder. "'Bout early afternoon, I s'pose."

"What'd he come by for?"

"To tell me about evicting the LeBlancs."

"Oh." Luc lowered his head. Suspicion always circled back to link to CoCo and her family. "Yeah, he told me about that."

"You're still sweet on that oldest gal, aren't ya?"

Luc swallowed. "The sheriff is checking out the LeBlanc family." He rose, the long hours of the day pressing against every muscle in his body. "I'm sure Bubba will be by to talk to you."

"That *cooyon?* He couldn't find his foot in the dark with a flashlight."

"He's the best we have."

His uncle snuffled. "I just can't believe this."

"I know." The emotions filled his throat. He gave a cough and locked stares with his uncle. "I can tell you this, Uncle Justin—whoever did this to Grandfather will be punished."

"Even if it's that gator gal?"

"Even her." Luc opened the front door and strode toward his vehicle, not ready to discuss anything more about the possibility of CoCo's involvement. Yet, the memory of her mixing herbs to make a potion still haunted him. Could she have, *would* she have put a curse on his grandfather? He shook his head. It didn't matter, he didn't believe in all that voodoo stuff anyway. God had always been at his side. Still, Grandfather being murdered…

He steered toward home, his heart already overburdened, and he still had to tell his mother and Felicia. Sometimes being the responsible one in the family just plain wore him out.

Ten minutes and two turns later, Luc parked in the driveway. He sat in the vehicle, in the dark, staring at the house before him. Pristine white columns lined the front of the veranda, much like Twelve Oaks in *Gone With the Wind*.

God, this is harder than I ever imagined. Yes, I was angry with Grandfather, and I confess the anger to You and ask for Your forgiveness. I never wanted him to die. Murdered, at that.

Better to go ahead and get his duty over with so he could go to bed and end this awful day. Luc trod up the front steps, unlocked the door and then stepped quietly over the threshold.

His mother sat at the kitchen table, a glass snifter in her hand. "You're out late, *ma chère.* Everything okay?"

"Not really." He dragged himself to the wood table and pulled out a chair. He sat with all the heaviness of the burdens in his heart. "Grandfather's dead."

His mother's eyes widened and her mouth formed an O, but no sound came out.

"Before you ask, we don't know much. Someone shot him in the back and left his body in the bayou. That's all I know for now. I'm meeting with the sheriff in the morning to learn more."

"What will we do? How will we live? Can we stay in the house?" A hint of liquor steeped from her breath as she gasped in drama.

"I don't know, Mom." He pushed back the chair; it scraped against the tile floor. "I'm going to tell Felicia and then I'm hitting the sack. It's been a really long day."

Luc turned and ambled down the hall, not giving his mother time to voice her panicked concerns. In the past few months, her late-night nip of brandy had become a large glass. He'd have to deal with the drinking issue later, but right now he felt beyond tired.

The hallway walls boasted photographs of him and his sister at varying times in their lives. Birth, christenings, graduations…even his college diploma hung proudly against the white wall. So much of the past stuck here in the present.

Pausing outside Felicia's bedroom, he rapped on her door with the backs of his knuckles.

"Yes?" his sister asked.

He pushed open the door a crack. "Hey, *Boo*. It's me."

"Luc. Come on in." Using her elbows, she pushed herself into a semisitting position. The queen-size bed seemed to swallow her, with the lightweight blue comforter and big fluffy white pillows.

She looked even more frail and fragile in bed. He sat beside her. "Got some bad news."

Her blue eyes blinked in the half-light. "Mom?"

"No, she's fine." He patted her hand. "She's drinking, but that's another story."

"Then what?" His sister's angelic face wrapped in worry.

"It's Grandfather."

"What's he done now?"

"Nothing. They found his body in the bayou tonight."

"Body?" Her eyes filled with tears, reminding Luc of the Caribbean ocean, so clear in comparison to the murky waters around Lagniappe.

"He'd been shot."

"I don't understand." Tears squeezed from her eyes and trickled down her gaunt cheeks.

He gripped her hand tighter, wishing he could erase the pain from her eyes.

"This is awful."

"I know." He planted a kiss on her forehead.

She grabbed his hand as he stood over her. "Luc, I'm mad at him, I mean I was, but I never wanted him dead."

"I know, *Boo*. Me, too."

Felicia wiped away her tears. "Where'd they find him?"

Leave it to his astute sister to ask such a pointed question. He sighed. "Near Grisson Landing." He waited for the reaction.

She made the connection instantly. "Oh, no. Where Daddy died?"

The irony of the situation hadn't been lost on her. The pain tightening her features strengthened his resolve to find the guilty party.

"Yes." His vocal chords strained.

The tears spilled again. "Who found him?"

"CoCo."

· FIVE

Sleep deprived and nervous, CoCo paced the sidewalk outside the Vermilion parish sheriff's office. She glanced at her watch, then peered down the asphalt road. What could be keeping Dwayne Williams? First thing this morning, she'd called his office and left a message. He'd returned her call before eight-thirty, assuring her he would meet her at nine-thirty for her to give her statement. According to Mickey on her wrist, nine minutes had passed since their scheduled meeting time.

Lord, I need a little help down here. I know I'm innocent, but am not so sure about Grandmere and Tara.

Wait! Did she just admit that her grandmother or sister could be involved in a murder? No way, no how. Practicing *gris-gris* and *cunjas* didn't make one guilty of murder, did it? No, course not. Beau had been shot, not poisoned. Voodoo couldn't pull a gun out of thin air, could it? She shook her head. She was being as illogical as Tara about superstitions.

An old Lincoln pulled into the parking lot, its tires crunching the loose gravel. Dwayne slipped from behind the wheel and marched toward her. "Sorry I'm a little late. Had to stop by the office and pick up some papers."

She glanced at her watch. Wonderful, now they were fifteen

minutes behind. What would Bubba Theriot think? She forced a smile. "That's okay."

He clutched a briefcase in his hand, and now that she studied him, he looked like a high-dollar attorney in his fitted suit and tie. Her smile shifted to genuine.

"This is standard and nothing to fret over." He indicated the door with his briefcase. "Come on, *allons*. Might as well get it over with."

Taking in a deep breath, she grasped the handle and jerked the glass door open. The aroma of burnt coffee reeked across the foyer of the police station, mixing with cheap aftershave. It turned her stomach. Good thing she hadn't had breakfast.

Phones rang and people shouted, raising the noise level to a ten on the Richter scale. She fought back the instinct to clap her hands over her ears. Her soul ached for the quiet tranquility of the bayou. However, the memory that it hadn't been so tranquil last night tapped her on the shoulder.

"Keep going, Sheriff Theriot is waving us over," Dwayne said, his deep baritone pervading the noise around her.

She followed her attorney as he wove through the throng of police officers in the tiny station, keeping her attention focused on the floor. The cracked tile needed a good mopping. She studied the ground so intently that she nearly ran smack into Dwayne's back when he stopped. CoCo jerked her head up.

Sheriff Bubba Theriot shook hands with Dwayne, then her. She pulled away from his sweaty, beefy clasp. She forced herself not to shudder. She certainly didn't need to offend the lawman.

"Let's head to the conference room," the sheriff said. Without waiting for a reply, he herded them into a plain room, barren of any furniture save a table with four chairs, two on either side, and a single tape recorder.

She dropped into the chair Dwayne held out for her, then

he sat beside her. Sheriff Theriot took a seat across the table. She glanced around the room, noticing the large mirror on one wall. CoCo gave herself a mental shake. That wasn't an ordinary mirror—there were officers on the other side, watching her. Even though Grandmere didn't own a television set, CoCo had seen enough movies to know.

"This is just a formality, CoCo," the sheriff said as he reached for the tape recorder. "I'll be recording your statement to make sure we get it right."

Yeah, right. He just wanted to trip her up. Nerves bunched in the pit of her stomach. She'd be so embarrassed if she got sick right here in front of the sheriff. Would he automatically assume her guilty if she did?

"Ready?"

CoCo gave her recorded statement, waited for it to be typed and then signed where the sheriff indicated.

"We'll call if we have any more questions," the sheriff said as he showed them out.

"You can contact me directly if you have anything further to ask Ms. LeBlanc." Dwayne passed one of his business cards to Sheriff Theriot.

CoCo and Dwayne escaped the stale air and chaotic noise of the station. Dwayne escorted her to the Jeep. "Would you like to go to the diner over there?" He nodded to the building across the street. "We can discuss what will happen now in regard to the eviction case, and you can ask me any questions you might have about the murder investigation."

Now that her interview and statement were over, hunger pangs gripped her stomach. "That'd be nice. *Merci.*"

"I'll meet you there."

The drive across the street took but a few minutes, yet the time gave her an opportunity to compose herself and get her head on straight. She glanced at herself in the rearview mirror. Using her fingers, she combed her wavy bangs and then pulled at the bags under her eyes. A nap would definitely make it on her *to do* list for this afternoon.

Dwayne waited in the entry of the diner, smiling as she approached. A middle-aged waitress with a sagging mouth sat them in a booth off to the side. While casting them a curious look, she took their orders for coffee, handed them menus, then sashayed back to the counter.

"You did fine, by the way," Dwayne said while perusing the diner's offerings after the waitress had left.

"*Merci.*" She scanned the items listed on the grease-spotted bill of fare. Eggs and bacon with toast sounded mouthwatering right now. She closed the menu and studied her attorney. He had to be close to her age, twenty-nine, or just a few years older. Her gaze slid lower. No wedding band adorned his left hand. How did an African-American lawyer end up in Lagniappe?

"Is something wrong?"

She jerked her gaze to his eyes. "Pardon?"

"You're staring at me. Is something wrong?"

Heat shot up her neck and into her cheeks. "I'm sorry. I was thinking."

"About?"

"Beau Trahan. Who killed him?"

The waitress chose that moment to return. She filled their coffee mugs, took their orders and then hurried to another table of customers.

CoCo caught the stares from some of the people at the other tables, understanding that many wondered why a white woman sat with a black man. Even now, decades upon decades after the Civil War, some of the Cajuns in the area still held racist beliefs. Small-minded thinking drove her insane.

"You know—" Dwayne pulled her attention back to her question "—I've found Beau had a lot of enemies. During his time as a representative, he burned a lot of bridges. And he didn't earn any hero worship during his stint as casino manager."

"True, he never was a really likeable man." She avoided the glare from the man across the way. *Hillbilly redneck in Cajun country, just shoot me now.* She stilled at her uncharitable train of thought. Shoot… "Have you heard what caliber weapon yet?"

He took a sip of his coffee. "While you were reading and signing your statement, I talked to one of the deputies. The autopsy will be later this morning. I'll find out more this afternoon."

"Do they think he was shot in the bayou?"

Setting down his mug, he shrugged. "What're you thinking?"

"If he was killed in the bayou, it would have been farther away from where I found his body. If he'd been shot around Grisson Landing, I'd have heard the blast."

Dwayne leaned over the table and lowered his voice. "Are you saying someone killed him elsewhere and moved him to the bayou, to that particular location? Why?"

She ran her finger along the rim of the cup. "Either to implicate my family or to hurt the Trahans."

"Hurt them? I'm not following."

"Two years ago, Beau Trahan's son died in an accident."

"I just moved here last year. What happened?"

"Caleb, Beau's son, was out in his pirogue and hit a submerged stump. The boat capsized and somehow, Caleb broke his arm."

"How horrible. Did he drown?"

"No." Images of Caleb's body threatened to choke her. *Lord, make them go away.* She gulped coffee, scalding her tongue, but it dulled the horror in her mind. "Best the police can guess is he started swimming toward the bank, but his broken arm slowed him down." Another sip. "An alligator got him."

"That's atrocious. Did they find his body?"

She nodded, closing her eyes briefly against the memory. It didn't block out the visuals in her head. "My grandmother heard his scream and called the police. She called me on my radio. I rushed over, arriving right before the police showed up." She shuddered. "A gator had him in a death roll. I managed to get the gator off him, but it was too late."

They fell silent as the waitress returned with their plates and refilled their coffee before bustling away.

"So, another family member found dead in the bayou would hurt the Trahans?"

"Not just anywhere, but Grisson Landing. Both Caleb and Beau were found there."

Standing outside the sheriff's office, Luc ducked under the cloth awning, gaining relief from the blistering sun. Not even noon, but the heat already danced in the red of the thermometer. Humidity had to be in the high eighty-percent range. Miserable, that's the only way he could think to describe the weather.

He let out a long breath. The sheriff hadn't been in the office, having gone to the coroner's for the autopsy. The thought twisted Luc's stomach. He'd stayed up nearly half the night battling the image of his grandfather being shot. His prayers brought him little peace. Truth be told, guilt had followed his conversation with God. Guilt that he'd accused CoCo and her family of being involved with Beau's murder. No matter what, Luc couldn't picture her, her grandmother or her sister shooting his grandfather. After a long grappling with the Holy Spirit, Luc knew he needed to talk to CoCo.

He should head out to her house, apologize and get back to hear what the sheriff learned from the autopsy. That's what he should do, but his heart screamed at him to say he was sorry for more than accusations. Even if she never accepted his words. He didn't know if he could look into her emotion-riddled eyes and not apologize for leaving her, for ending what could have been their happily ever after. Did that scenario exist?

Staring out across the street, he spied CoCo's Jeep. How ironic. No, that wasn't it. He glanced heavenward. *Guess I'm not gonna get out of this one, huh, God?*

No, the conviction sitting on his shoulders wouldn't let him avoid what needed to be done. He walked across the street, heading toward her vehicle. Maybe he could leave a note and prevent having to see the pain in her eyes.

The door to the local diner swung open and out waltzed CoCo with a tall black man. So much for avoiding. He took a step toward her. "CoCo…"

Her eyes lit on him, not filled with pain or remorse as he'd imagined, but with anger and resentment. The urge to step away nearly strangled him.

"What're you doing here? Following me?"

"Of course not. I just wanted to talk to you for a second." His heart skittered like a young schoolboy's.

She held his gaze for a moment, before turning to the man beside her. "Dwayne Williams, this is Luc Trahan. Beau Trahan's grandson." She jerked her stare back to Luc. "This is Dwayne Williams, my attorney."

Luc shook the man's hand, his mind reeling. Attorney. She'd followed through with her threat to hire one. That shouldn't really surprise him. He turned his attention back to CoCo. "I only need a minute of your time."

"What do you want?" She sounded tired, run down. He'd never really thought about how draining the situation—finding the body—had to be for her.

"I wanted to say I'm sorry."

She tilted her head to the side, her eyes twinkling from the glint of the sun. "For what?"

Oh, she wasn't about to make this any easier for him. "For accusing you and your family of being involved in my grandfather's murder." There, he'd said it, done what he'd been convicted to do. *God, can I leave now?*

"So, you believe me?"

He rolled a rock with the toe of his hiking boot. "Yeah." He chanced looking into her eyes. Big mistake. Distrust flashed with the green. What was he doing? "I never really believed you could be involved."

"Then prove it." Had her tone softened? Was that a crack in the wall behind her eyes?

He straightened and cocked his head to the side. "How so?"

"Help me find the real murderer before my family's name is smeared forever."

Luc swallowed. Hard. "Well, uh…"

"Excuse me, Ms. LeBlanc and I have some documents to go over back at my office," the attorney said.

Luc didn't care for the man's tone, nor the proprietary manner in which he held CoCo's elbow. Then again, Luc had given up the right to voice his concerns over her. A decision, upon reflection, he seriously regretted.

She glanced at her lawyer and nodded, but Luc didn't miss the questions lurking in her eyes. A trip to Mr. Williams's office hadn't been in the plans.

"Uh, right." Yet, she agreed with him. That alone spoke volumes as to who she trusted. And who she didn't. Her eyes clouded over as she stared back at Luc. "Just what I thought—talking out both sides of your mouth."

The attorney tugged on her elbow. "CoCo, we really must get back to the office."

Luc felt his opportunity slipping between his fingers. "I'll call you tonight."

She froze, scrutinizing him in that scathing way of hers, then gave a brief nod. The lawyer escorted her to her Jeep. Luc watched her get inside and drive away. His chest felt hollow and empty.

Turning back toward his vehicle, a question shoved to the forefront of his mind. Why did Dwayne Williams act opposed to Luc and CoCo calling a truce? He wondered if Dwayne could be interested in her, as a man is interested in a woman. Before the green beast could rear its ugly head, Luc's logic shoved his male ego out of the way. He hadn't gotten a sense of romantic interest between CoCo and Dwayne. No, that wasn't it. Maybe this Dwayne was merely protecting his client, not wanting her to speak with the victim's family. That could be it, but a strange sensation roiled in his gut, telling him there was more to the story.

CoCo scrutinized Dwayne from across his conference room table. His head was bowed as he read the document he'd asked her to sign. He glanced up, met her stare, and told her everything was in order. His pause came a moment after she didn't respond. "Is there something else?"

"Your accent…"

He narrowed his eyes for a brief moment. "Pardon me?"

"Your accent, or lack of one. You don't talk with a strong

Southern dialect, yet at the police station, you said *allons* rather than let's go, so you're obviously familiar with the Cajun language."

His smile flashed as he stood. "My mother's family was from this area. They moved after her father died. I was born and raised in California." He nodded toward his law degree. Without the small frame hanging there, the wall would be barren. "I went to school at UCLA."

"What made you come back?"

The smile vanished. "Family issues." He held her elbow and helped her stand. "I'll get back to the sheriff's office and see what I can find out."

CoCo let him lead her to the office door. He gave a quick goodbye before shutting the door. Confused as all get-out, she dragged her feet across the parking lot. The heat slammed against her full force as she made her way to the Jeep. She slipped behind the steering wheel, cringed as the hot leather touched on the bare skin behind her knees. She cranked the engine and flipped the air conditioner to high.

Staring at Dwayne's office, she wondered why he'd acted so odd. And why would someone who'd been established in California move all the way back to Lagniappe, Louisiana? Family issues? As she slammed the gearshift, CoCo wondered if she should check out his family ties to the area.

SIX

Luc needed to talk to her, to assure her that he didn't believe her family guilty. Could he work with her, one-on-one, to figure out who killed his grandfather without falling in love with her all over again? It'd been the hardest thing Luc had to do, calling off their engagement, but he'd had no other options. Not only was she deep into voodoo, something he detested, but then there was the death of his father.

Luc whipped into her driveway, not sure whether to be excited or disappointed to see her Jeep parked in its regular place. The door creaked as he stepped from the vehicle. What, exactly, was he going to say? Some plan he had.

"Luc?"

Her voice carried to him on the breeze off the bayou. And then he saw her. In her airboat, she stood and shielded her eyes with her hand.

Now or never. He picked his steps carefully as he made his way toward her.

"What're you doing here?" Suspicion darkened her eyes. Would she ever look at him with trust again? Probably not.

"I want to finish our conversation." Before the lawyer had all but ordered her to his office.

She sat back in the seat of the boat and crossed her arms over her chest. "I don't see we have anything left to discuss."

"I want to help you." Why did that pop out? He certainly hadn't intended on partnering with her—he'd already convinced himself it was a bad idea.

"Really?" Sarcasm all but dripped from her tongue.

He searched his heart and found he truly did want to solve his grandfather's murder. And he wanted to do it with CoCo. "Yeah. Really."

Her eyes widened for a split second and her lips thinned. "Then hop in."

"What?" Surely she didn't expect him to get on that boat.

"Get in. I've got to do some tracking of a couple of gators, but I thought I'd run by Grisson Landing. Just to see if I notice anything amiss."

"Didn't the police already check everything there?"

She snorted and rested her hand on the throttle. "I think I know the bayou a little better than they do. I'd know if something was out of place."

Luc swallowed against a dry mouth. She had a point. But to get in the bayou? Alone with her?

"Are you coming or not?" Patience never had been her strongest virtue. Her eyes flashed.

Oh, now he understood. This was something like a test— a dare to see if he was serious. He'd never been one to back away from a challenge, and he didn't intend to start now. "Sure." On rubbery legs, he climbed aboard her boat.

She smiled, nearly causing him to stumble as he took his seat. "Hold on."

The big fan that propelled the boat roared to life when she flipped a switch. The sound over his shoulder could compete with a 747. CoCo pulled her hair into a ponytail, flipping it into some kind of knot. When she hit the lever, the boat eased away from the bank. Luc's heart pounded louder than the fan.

Skimming over the water, Luc felt the tension at the base of his neck ease. At one time, he'd gone out on CoCo's runs with her at least every other day. It felt good to be out on the bayou again. With her. He studied her from the corner of his eye. She looked as pretty as ever, but different. Like a glow had been added to her face that hadn't been there before.

The big fan went silent, and CoCo steered the boat to sidle up next to a big cypress tree loaded with Spanish moss. "I need to make sure Moodoo is where he's supposed to be." She grabbed a clipboard, scanned the information with a crease in her brow, then gazed into the clump of trees near the bank. Within seconds, a large alligator bumped against the side of the boat.

Every muscle in Luc's body went rigid. His heartbeat echoed in his head.

CoCo laughed. "Hey, Moodoo. How's my boy today?"

Here he was, about to have a coronary being this close to the beast, and she all but crooned to it. Luc hauled in a deep breath.

She scribbled on her page and attached the clipboard back to its holder. Glancing at Luc, she frowned. "Are you okay?"

"Uh, yeah." He wouldn't dare admit he was more terrified than he'd ever been in his life. Even when he'd gone with her before, they'd never had a gator get this close. It was so big.

"I rescued Moodoo from some poachers. Nursed him back to health myself." She tossed something into the water. The gator swam away from the boat with a swish, and snapped at the object.

Luc didn't want to think about what it might have been.

"Hey, do you think maybe a poacher could have killed

your grandfather? I've seen evidence of them increasing in activity in this area."

She might actually be on to something. "I don't know. It's something we should definitely run by Bubba."

"I think he wants to believe I'm guilty or my family is."

"Bubba may be country, but he's a good guy." He watched her fire up the fan again. "Did you know he's taking an online course in criminal justice?" he yelled over the roar.

CoCo gave a shrug. "Then there might be hope for him yet." She smiled, and it was as warming as the sun sitting high in the sky. He never would have thought they'd be together on the bayou ever again.

Once at Grisson Landing, CoCo activated the trolling motor and maneuvered them around the area. Although they kept their eyes trained, nothing seemed out of place. Luc's hopes crashed. He'd been hoping to find some clue, a piece of evidence or something.

"Guess we should head back. There's nothing here," she said, her voice laced with disappointment.

"Maybe it was a poacher. I'll be sure to tell Bubba."

They made the trip back to her house in silence. Their truce, as it was, seemed as fragile and tangible as the lichen they had to duck under as she banked the boat.

"Thanks for coming with me, Luc." She put her hands on her hips. "We'll figure out who killed your grandfather."

He nodded; no words were needed. Better to savor the peace between them. Luc walked toward his SUV. "I'll talk to Bubba and call you. Fill you in on what he says."

She gave him a shaky smile, then marched across her yard.

Luc headed home. It looked as if the sheriff had beaten him there. Maybe they'd found the murderer already. Luc rushed to the veranda where Sheriff Theriot sat chatting with Luc's mother. Oh happy day, his mother. He could only pray she hadn't been nipping the brandy this early in the day.

He loped up the stairs. "Hey, Bubba."

The sheriff looked at him, a guarded expression in his eyes. His notebook lay open in his lap. "Luc." He nodded toward Hattie. "Your momma here's been telling me about your argument with Beau yesterday."

Luc shot his gaze to his mother. Her eyes were bloodshot and her face drawn. Apparently she'd stayed up much later than he, soaking up the brandy. He'd make it a point to dispose of the whole stinkin' bottle.

"Why'd you fail to mention the big fight you had with your grandfather?" The sheriff held his pen poised over the notebook.

"I really didn't think about it, Bubba. My focus was more on my grandfather's dead body."

"Tell me about this argument of yours."

Sighing, Luc lowered himself to one of the big rockers across from the porch swing. "Not much to tell, really. It's no secret Grandfather wanted me to take over as casino manager once he retired. I finally told him that I had no intention of working for the casino—that I intended to stay an accounting consultant. The news upset him."

"The way I hear it told, he was more than a little upset."

Definitely time to kill his mother's brandy addiction. "He got angry, but you know how Beau was. He'd blow up, simmer down, then cool off."

"Did your grandfather threaten to throw the whole lot of you out in the street, Luc?"

He swallowed, knowing how awful it sounded. "Yes, he did."

The sheriff leaned over the railing to spit tobacco into the oleanders lining the porch. "Sure seems like a strong motive for murder."

Heat shot through Luc's body, and it had nothing to do with the sun beating down. "Are you accusing me of killing my own grandfather?"

Bubba's eyes squinted under the roof of the porch. "I'm not accusing anyone of anything, yet. A threat of that kind is a strong motive for murder. Wouldn't you agree?" He spit over the rail again.

Luc clenched and unclenched his fists. "It sounds bad, sure I can see that. But I had nothing to do with Grandfather's death."

"You were near that part of the bayou yesterday. On the LeBlanc property."

"I already explained that." Could his friend really believe he was guilty—that he'd shoot his own grandfather?

"Do you own a twelve-gauge shotgun?"

The question came out rapid-fire, startling Luc. "I'm not sure. Grandfather was big into hunting, but you already know that. I have no idea what guns he kept here."

"Yet he lived in the casino penthouse."

Luc met Bubba's stare. "In which he couldn't legally have firearms."

"Uh-huh." The sheriff didn't break eye contact. "So, Beau stashed all his shotguns here, at the house you live in?"

"As far as I know." Luc hated grinding out his answers from between clenched teeth, but he couldn't make his jaw relax.

"Can you see if you can find a twelve-gauge?"

"Why?"

"I can get a warrant to search, Luc." The sheriff's eyes hardened.

"Why don't you just ask me what's stuck in your craw?"

The lawman spit again, wiped his mouth with his hand and scrutinized Luc.

"We go way back, you and me. You know I won't lie to you, Bubba."

The sheriff studied him for a moment longer. "The autopsy report shows a shell from a twelve-gauge killed Beau."

"What about the LeBlancs?" his mother interjected.

Luc snorted, but Bubba spoke calmly to her. "I can't see Marie LeBlanc hoisting a shotgun at Beau's back and shooting him." He scratched his red head. "Of course, CoCo or Tara would be strong enough."

"I don't think either of the girls could do that." Luc pushed off the chair and headed to the door. "I talked to CoCo today. She said that poacher activity has increased in the area of Grisson Landing recently. Could a poacher have shot Grandfather?"

"Please, Luc. She's just trying to distract you," his mother chided.

He tossed her a look of warning. She staggered to her feet and went into the house. Luc turned his attention back to his friend. "Is it possible, Bubba?"

"Could be. I'll check it out." The sheriff spit tobacco juice off the porch. "Now, about Beau's guns…"

Obviously, the man wasn't going to let this go. "Let's go see if there's a shotgun in his cabinet."

Bubba followed him down the hall. Luc opened the door to Beau's study—the one room nobody but his grandfather used. "His gun cabinet is in here." He led the way to the closet and yanked open the door.

The sheriff stared at the row of shotguns in the cabinet. "These all Beau's?"

"Far as I know."

"Mind if I take a better look?"

"Be my guest."

With his ruddy hands, Bubba carefully opened the doors. Automatically, a light blinked on inside the top. "Wow, high class."

"Would you expect any less from Beau?" Luc leaned against his grandfather's desk.

Bubba squatted in front of the guns. "No, I guess not. Look at this dust layer."

"We never clean in here. It was Beau's room."

"Check this out." The sheriff pointed at the second row of rifles and shotguns.

Luc's heart sank. Clear in the dust—an outline of the butt of another gun.

Bubba straightened. "Any clue where that gun is or what gauge it happens to be?"

"I don't know. Like I said, we never come in here."

"Uh-huh." The sheriff grabbed the radio from his hip and lifted it to his lips. "Dispatch, I need a crime-scene unit at the Trahan place."

Nerves tangled in Luc's gut. What had happened to that gun? Where could it be? More importantly, who could have moved it?

Bubba completed his request. "I'll be pulling Beau's firearms records. If it comes back that he has a twelve-gauge and the forensics match up the butt outline… Well, I don't have to tell you, Luc, it won't look good for you."

"I did not kill my grandfather, Bubba. You know me better than that." He ran a hand over his stubbly chin, hating the way his hands shook. "We go to church together, for pity's sakes."

"I've been surprised before." The sheriff wouldn't meet his gaze.

Luc chose not to reply. Right now, he couldn't even think straight. He needed to pray. The situation had turned too dire to try to figure out on his own. And then he'd call CoCo.

CoCo walked up the stairs to the old family plantation. She stopped on the porch, taking a minute to notice the condition of the house. The gutter hung lopsided from the eaves. Paint cracked and peeled over the entire home. Nails had worked themselves loose on the railings and the stairs. How long had she neglected to call someone out to do some handiwork? Grandmere usually called Toby, a neighbor's grandchild to help out with the odd jobs, but it'd been weeks upon weeks since anyone had done any upkeep. Now that the threat of losing the plantation sat very real, she realized how much she loved the old house. It'd been her home for thirteen years and she couldn't imagine being anywhere but here.

Not to mention that her grandmother would die if taken from the bayou. While CoCo couldn't condone her traditions any longer, she accepted that it was the way of life for Grandmere. She wouldn't be able to function anywhere else. All her herbs and plants grew wild in the bayou, and some of them weren't available to purchase in stores. At least, not fresh or organic.

She turned to pull open the door, but a flash of light from the blue shed caught her attention. Dropping her hand, she bounded off the stairs toward Grandmere's workshop. The smell of burning plants filtered to her. She jerked the door open, and felt her gut clench at the sight before her.

"Grandmere, what're you doing?"

Her grandmother jumped with her hand at her neck. "Sakes, *ma chère,* you nearly scared the spirits outta me."

Wouldn't that be nice? CoCo took in the herbs lying on the

worktable beside the burner on which a glass beaker simmered. The overbearing stench of burnt roots filled the small and close building. She registered the names of the ingredients present, automatically flipping through her mental recipe book of potions. Her heart stilled, and she turned her glare on her grandmother. "A death *gris-gris,* Grandmere?"

"See, *ma chère,* you are a natural. You were able to instantly pull up the potion recipe."

"Stop! Why are you making a death curse? And who is it aimed at?"

"I'm just cleaning up in here, *ma chère.* Don't be getting yourself all worked up." Grandmere waved her hands toward CoCo. "It's nothing, yes?"

"Tell me the truth, Grandmere. Who are you cursing?" She took a weakened step toward her grandmother. "Or who did you curse? Did you put a death *cunja* on Beau Trahan?"

"That's none of your business, since you turned your back on your heritage."

CoCo gripped her grandmother's shoulders and gave a gentle shake. "It *is* my business. Someone murdered Beau Trahan. I need to know—did you curse him?"

Grandmere's face turned ashen, but her eyes practically shone like neon lights. "Unhand me, child." Her expression looked chiseled in granite, never described as gentle or nonthreatening.

Dropping her hands immediately, CoCo covered her mouth. Had she really just manhandled her grandmother? Horror and guilt pushed the tears into her eyes. "I'm sorry, Grandmere."

Her grandmother turned to her table, her back facing CoCo.

"I said I'm sorry. You have to know how horrible this looks. I just need to know, Grandmere. Did you put a hex on Beau Trahan?"

Grandmere spun around so quickly that CoCo took a step backward. "Yes, I did. What do you care?"

Mortification shoved itself into CoCo's heart. "You really did it, Grandmere? You wanted another human dead so badly you'd conjure spirits to help you?"

Why, God? Why won't You bring her to You now?

"Beau Trahan wasn't about to take our home from us, *ma chère*. Not while there's a breath left in this old body of mine."

"I can't believe you. This is wrong beyond belief. It's— it's despicable, that's what it is." With tears flooding her vision, CoCo turned and fled from the shed into the house, up the stairs and then slammed the door to her bedroom.

She flung herself across her bed, the stinging tears washing down her face. No, it couldn't be. God was more powerful than any *gris-gris* or *cunja* Grandmere or anybody else could cast. Besides, she'd never heard of a spirit getting a gun and blasting someone in the back. Yet the tears wouldn't stop.

CoCo flipped to her back and stared at the ceiling. The fan rotated on medium speed, making a subtle ticking noise. She closed her eyes, blocking out everything but welcome darkness.

God, I don't understand. You said You would never leave me. I'm feeling rather alone right now. Grandmere's attempted to conjure up dark spirits, and You're letting it happen! Why? You called me from it, why aren't You calling her? And Tara, too?

Unlike most times when she prayed, CoCo felt no peace surrounding her—no unconditional love wrapping around her and giving comfort.

A knock on her door interrupted her crying jag. She sat upright, jerked away her tears and called out, "Come in."

Tara stuck her head through a crack. "Luc's on the phone for you." She pushed the door all the way open and stepped inside. "Why've you been crying?"

"No reason." CoCo sniffed. "Look, I really don't feel up to talking to Luc right now. Can you tell him I'll call him later?"

"Are you two talking again? Newsflash to Tara." She crossed her arms over her chest, still studying CoCo.

"No. Yes. Kinda." She ran her fingers through her tangled hair. "I don't know, *Boo.*"

"He sounds like it might be important."

CoCo shook her head. "Not right now. It's not a good time." She locked stares with her baby sister. "Please? For me?"

"Fine. I'll tell him you'll call him later. I'm coming back, and you're going to tell me what 'no yes kinda' means."

CoCo pushed off the bed and meandered into the bathroom. She splashed her face with cold water. It wouldn't do to let Tara know the real reason she'd been crying. Maybe, God willing, she could distract her sister from asking more questions about Luc. Questions CoCo had no intention of answering—especially when she couldn't figure out the answers herself.

SEVEN

Luc's hospitality couldn't muster up to playing nice while his name sat at the top of the suspect list. He waited under the trees for Sheriff Bubba Theriot to finish barking orders at the crime-scene technicians. They'd been in his house for over an hour. His mother made fresh lemonade and passed around tall iced glasses like she was some hostess of a cotillion. He didn't much feel like socializing with the police. He'd called CoCo, but Tara had said she couldn't take the call. What did he expect, a friendship now? Hardly. The urge to talk to her laid heavy in his gut.

Reaching for his cell phone, he then pressed the number to speed dial his Uncle Justin. Might as well keep him in the loop.

"Hel-lo."

"Uncle Justin, it's Luc."

"Any news?" Leave it to his great-uncle to cut right to the chase.

"Actually there is something new. The sheriff has a crime unit over here at the house."

"For why?"

"They determined a twelve-gauge shotgun killed Grand-father. Bubba heard about our argument and came by to question me. I showed him Grandfather's gun cabinet, and wouldn't you know it, a gun's missing. They're doing whatever it is they do to try to pin this on me, I suppose."

"Did they have a warrant?"

Luc watched the sheriff make his way over to his mother on the veranda. "No."

"Mercy, boy, why'd ya let them in Beau's office then?"

"I have nothing to hide, Uncle Justin."

His uncle snorted over the phone. "Listen, I'm on my way. Don't say another word to them, ya hear?"

Before Luc had a chance to reply, the connection died. He let out a sigh and slipped the phone back to its clip, willing CoCo to call him back. Soon.

Sheriff Theriot caught up with him at his SUV. "I don't like this, Luc."

"It's not exactly a day at the carnival for me, either."

"I don't believe you shot Beau, you know, but I have to do my job."

That whole forgiveness thing smacked him upside the head again. "I understand, Bubba. It's just really frustrating for me."

"I get you. Who else has access to the house? Besides you, your mom, your sister and Beau?"

"I don't know. Frank Thibodeaux. He's been dating Felicia and has been over several times. Let me think." Luc wiped the sweat from his brow with his shirt sleeve. "Mom had a couple of friends over a time or two. And Uncle Justin."

Bubba scribbled on his notebook. "We'll release the body this afternoon. Want it to go to Roland's Funeral Home?"

Luc scrubbed his face. He hadn't considered funeral plans. He let out a sigh. Something else he'd have to handle. "Yeah. I'll go by later and make the arrangements."

Breaks squealing on the dirt road captured their attention. Justin's pickup shot down the driveway like a bullet.

"Oh, I called Uncle Justin."

"Good. I need to talk to him anyway."

Justin slammed his truck door and made a beeline for them. Loose rocks crunched under his work boots. Stains covered his denim coveralls, but his expression drew Luc's attention fast.

His pudgy face marked ruddy, Justin jabbed a sausagelike finger in the sheriff's face. "What're ya doing, Sheriff? Bringing out a team when ya didn't have no warrant to begin with."

"Uncle Justin, I let Bubba into the house."

His uncle tossed him a keep-your-mouth-shut look, then went back to glaring at Bubba. "Don't know what game you're playing, but this ain't right and ya know it."

The sheriff took a step back and held up his hands as if to ward off the older man. "Look, Justin, I'm just trying to eliminate suspects."

"By accusing Beau's grandson?"

"No, by eliminating him." Bubba glanced up as the crime-scene technicians made their way to their van. "I didn't know I'd find evidence of a gun missing."

"I watch *CSI*—I know ya can't prove the missing gun is the one that killed my brother."

Luc pressed his lips together as he cut his gaze to Bubba. How many times had his friend lamented over the unrealistic forensics presented in the television series?

Bubba, bless him, kept a straight face. "I'm not at liberty to discuss the forensics of this case with you, Justin." He lifted a pen over his ever-present notebook. "I do, however, have a few questions for you."

"Fire away." Justin leaned against the vehicle and crossed his arms over his chest. The vehicle gave a slight shift.

"Do you remember the last time you were here at the house and saw the gun cabinet?"

"Not that I recall."

"Do you remember the last time you were here, period?"

"Can't recall."

"Uh-huh. How about this one—when was the last time you saw your brother?"

"Yesterday."

Bubba's expression perked up a bit. "What time yesterday?"

Justin shrugged. "Yesterday morning, I believe it was."

Luc opened his mouth, then snapped it shut. Last night, Uncle Justin had told him he'd seen Grandfather late afternoon. Then again, it didn't matter. He was probably confused last night, what with the tragic news.

"Where did you see Beau?"

"He came by my place."

The sheriff stared at Justin, who returned the look with an open expression. Bubba cleared his throat. "And?"

"And what?"

"What did he come by your house for?"

"He's my brother. Families do visit and such, ya know."

Now Bubba's face turned as red as Justin's. "Was there anything in particular he came by to discuss with you?"

Justin lifted a casual shoulder. The strap to his overalls slipped, and he yanked it back in place. "He did mention evicting the LeBlanc family."

"Did he give you any more details about that?"

"Just told me that Marcel LeBlanc signed over the deed years ago to clear a gambling debt."

"Any idea why Beau decided to pursue the matter all of a sudden? As you said, Marcel allegedly signed over the deed years ago. Why did Beau decide to act now?"

"Way I heard it, Beau needed a place to live when he officially resigned at the casino. He couldn't move back here with

Hattie and the kids." He shrugged again. "Guess he thought it best. He never did tell me outright."

"You and Marcel were friends back in the day, weren't you?"

The redness of Justin's face deepened. "We were friends, yeah."

"Did you ever hear about him signing over the deed?"

"Now, I knew Marcel had a gambling problem. By the time he started hanging out at the casino, we'd already parted ways."

Bubba scrawled in his notebook and then looked back up into Justin's face. "Can you think of anybody who'd want to kill your brother?"

Justin let out a whooping laugh. "Beau's a retired politician. The question you should be asking is who *didn't* want to kill him?"

CoCo lifted her binoculars, scanning the banks of the bayou. Where could Moodoo be hiding now? She nudged the trolling control with her knee, moving the airboat about two-hundred feet. Still gazing through the lenses, she realized where she'd drifted—the back side of Grisson Landing. Her heartbeat raced. She lowered the binoculars and glanced about. Sure enough, a piece of yellow police tape hung from the cypress tree, caught in the thick Spanish moss. It looked so much more ominous now than when she'd been here with Luc.

A splash sounded behind her. She turned and caught sight of a big reptile submerging into the murky waters. He surfaced a few feet away. CoCo let out the breath she hadn't even realized she'd been holding. From the orange mark on his tag, she recognized Moodoo.

She noted his location on her sheet. Now if she could just find a couple more of the long-time tracked alligators, she'd be happy. Her report was due to the Wetlands Preservation

Center by the end of the week. If she couldn't prove the re-
production decline, she'd lose her grant. And if she lost the
grant, she'd be out of a job, which meant out of an income.
Grandmere's social security certainly didn't bring in enough
to pay the plantation's expenses. How they'd pay the bills, she
hadn't a clue.

A bump hit against the airboat, sending it into a gentle rocking
motion. Had the young bull returned? She froze, listening for the
growl or the grunt, but only heard the katydids and birds.

Moodoo swam around to the front of the airboat, his tail
tipping at the front. She lifted her binoculars again, following
his quick movements. Only when an alligator had something
in its sights did it move in such a way. Moodoo darted to the
left, toward the place where the yellow tape danced in the hot
breeze stirring the still air. He banked, his short legs making
a flapping noise as he climbed up the mound. He opened his
massive jaws and snapped them shut, capturing a crane.
Keeping his mouth closed, he slipped back into the water.

The wind lifted, moving shadows that had filled the bank.
Something glinted under the newly revealed sun. CoCo
steadied her binoculars, twisting the knob to focus. There, on
the ground beside a fallen tree. The sun played peek-a-boo
behind a cloud. The object blinked in the changing light again.
She zoomed in on it, then gasped as she made it out. A gun.

Oh, God, not again.

Lowering the lenses, CoCo fired up the airboat's main engine
and steered the craft toward the gun. She banked the boat and
turned to locate Moodoo. No sign of the big gator. Surely the
sheriff had searched this area? How could he have missed a gun?
She and Luc had just checked it out as well. Now that she went
over their trip in her mind, had she really looked in this particular area? What if the gun was the one that killed Beau?

She lifted the radio and reported her find. The dispatcher ordered her to stay put until the sheriff could arrive. Déjà vu. While she waited, she made notes on her run. If the tracking kept on schedule as she predicted, she estimated the limit on alligators during hunting season could drop by two per hunter. That's *if* the representative from Wildlife and Fisheries would take her report into consideration. Alligators were a great hunt, but if her research showed the decline of their natural population, then the limits would go down. Not so good for the alligator meat market. But, what did she care about the hunters? She preferred getting more grant money to expand her current tracking system. Very few naturalist environmentalists were willing to work the bayous. She was the sole exception for this parish.

Sirens whirred in the distance. CoCo stood and, shielding her eyes with one hand, watched as the police boat came up beside her. Surprise nearly knocked her into the water as she recognized Luc and Justin Trahan sitting beside Sheriff Theriot.

"Where's the gun?" the sheriff asked before the engine died.

She pointed. "I saw it through my binoculars."

"You didn't go up there and move it or touch it in any way, did you?" The sheriff stepped gingerly onto the bank.

"Of course not." As if. She darted her gaze away and caught Luc's stare. She could tell he wondered the same thing she did—had the gun been here earlier when they checked? Something crept into his face. What was it? Her limbs froze. Did he think she'd come back here and planted the gun? Surely he didn't believe her to be that stupid. Actually, by the look in his eye, maybe he did. She never should have asked him to help clear her name. He didn't trust her, and she sure-as-shootin' didn't trust him. Trying to form a truce of any sort with Luc Trahan was a big waste of time. She turned her attention back to Sheriff Theriot, who hustled toward the weapon but kept jerking his gaze right and left.

With latex gloves, he grabbed the shotgun and then all but ran back to the boat. He held up the gun, inspecting it for a moment before looking at Luc. "This your grandfather's?"

"I don't know. I've never even shot a gun before."

The sheriff nodded at Justin. "You recognize it?"

Luc's uncle squinted as he stared at the weapon. "Looks like it could be, but I couldn't say for sure."

"Uh-huh." The sheriff set the shotgun inside the boat. "Did you notice anybody in this area before you saw the gun?"

"No. And when Luc and I came by here earlier, we didn't notice the gun, either."

"Luc?" The sheriff pivoted, sending gentle waves into the bayou.

"Right. We were here. And no, we didn't see anything." He lowered his eyes, not meeting her stare. "I don't know for sure if either of us really looked up there."

The sheriff sighed. "We'll run a check on it to see if it's registered."

The desire to slap Luc made her fingers itch. He wouldn't even look at her. Guilt? Had he agreed to help her, only to set her up? Maybe he was the one who came back and planted the gun.

She chanced looking at Luc again. His eyes bored into her, but she couldn't read the emotions behind them. Was he guilty— or accusing? Her emotions were a mess when it came to him, and she'd thought she knew him. Obviously not well enough.

Justin, however, didn't hide his thoughts. "Funny how things always come back to *you,* Ms. LeBlanc."

CoCo willed her temper back in check. "Maybe because I'm the one out on the bayou more than others, Mr. Trahan."

"Odd, ain't it? That dead bodies seem to land here, at Grisson Landing—right by you."

"That's enough, Uncle Justin!" Luc's words were sharp, but his gaze soft as it lit on her face.

"I don't enjoy it any more than you do, sir." Despite her irritation, her southern manners wouldn't allow her to show disrespect. No matter that what she really wanted to do involved pushing him into the murky water.

"We're all a little upset, I s'pose. I didn't mean no insult." Justin actually appeared contrite. What a revelation.

"No worries." She shifted her attention back to the sheriff, who'd been standing silent, observing the exchange. "Is there anything else?"

"No." Sheriff Theriot turned over the boat engine.

She watched until the boat disappeared on the horizon. With a deep sigh, CoCo shrugged off her uncertainty and fired up the airboat to complete her run. Too bad her heart wasn't in her actions. On the north bank, she found the last reptile she sought, one of the missing four alligators. She logged the location on her tracking sheet, and turned the boat homeward.

Her thoughts meandered as she tied off the airboat. Why hadn't the police found that gun last night? Why hadn't she or Luc seen it earlier? Maybe because it wasn't there then. The killer had to have come back and left the gun. Why? Just the thought of being out in the bayou alone with a killer made her flesh crawl. She shook her head and trekked up the yard.

The big live oaks and magnolia trees offered a canopy against the backdrop of the setting sun. CoCo paused and stared, her soul stirring with the gentle swaying of the wind. The hydrangeas lining the front porch boasted full blooms of pink, white and blue. How did the flowering plants flourish, while the house decayed before her eyes? Or maybe she only now truly looked.

Wanting to observe the plantation home from all angles, CoCo walked around the side. The breeze kicked up, lifting the sweet hint of the Confederate rosebush. She stooped to touch one of the blooms, rubbing the satiny petal between her thumb and forefinger. Smiling, she shifted to stand. Something shiny under the lower branches caught her attention. She bent again and reached for the object. Staring at it lying in her hand, CoCo ran a finger over the coin.

"CoCo!"

She jerked her head at her grandmother's call. Pocketing the coin, she headed around to the front of the house. "Yes, ma'am?"

Grandmere stood on the porch, her hand over her eyes. "Alyssa's on the phone. Wants to talk to you."

CoCo climbed the stairs, her stomach already bunching in a tight wad of nerves. She derailed her train of thought— maybe Alyssa called just to say hello. Yeah and hippos flew on purple broomsticks, too.

Tara stood at the kitchen stove stirring a mouthwatering pot of gumbo, the cordless wedged between her chin and shoulder. She looked up as CoCo entered, and smiled. With her hands, she made a she's-jabbering-on-and-on-and-on gesture. CoCo bit back an answering grin when Tara said, "Oh, CoCo just walked in. Hang on a sec," then held out the phone.

CoCo narrowed her eyes at her baby sister, gulped in a deep breath and then greeted their middle sister. "Hello, Alyssa."

"What's this about you finding Beau Trahan's body in the bayou and all of you being suspects? I declare, CoCo, you need to keep a closer watch on things. You're supposed to be taking care of Grandmere and Tara. I'd come down there and straighten it all out myself, but work's got me so busy. Tara said you'd hired a lawyer because of some eviction notice? I can't bel—"

With a glare at Tara, CoCo sank onto a kitchen chair and waited for her sister to finish her tirade or run out of breath, whichever came first. Either way, Alyssa wouldn't shut up until CoCo assured her all was under control. Unfortunately, nothing was under control. Not one single thing.

EIGHT

Swaying his body with the Zydeco beat, Luc held the last note of the song on his sax. As the drummer hit the cymbal a final time, silence filled the small jazz club. A pause, then a burst of applause sounded. He nodded a bow before striding off the stage.

"Good set, boys," Ralph the stage manager said as the four musicians hit the backstage area.

"Thanks. It felt good." Luc packed his saxophone in its velvet-lined case. "I've missed playing." He'd dearly needed the emotional release tonight. He and Justin had spent all afternoon at the funeral home, planning his grandfather's funeral. At least they'd managed to keep his mother away— she'd have turned the somber event into a social setting.

And CoCo hadn't called him back, despite his having left her three messages.

"You're too good to let so much time pass." Ralph turned to include the other three men. "Drinks are on the house."

Lifting his case, Luc smiled at the club owner. "A cola sounds perfect right about now, *merci*."

The four band members followed Ralph around side stage to the club itself. People offered their appreciation as they wove through the throng in the hazy room toward the bar. The other three men nodded at Luc, indicating they'd catch him later, before walking over to sit with a group of women at a nearby table. Luc grabbed a stool, handing his case over the bar to Mike. "Keep this back there safe for me, will you?"

The bartender took the case. "Sure. What can I get ya?"

"A cola. With lots of ice." Luc let his gaze roam over the crowded club.

A cloud of smoke hovered in the air, giving the appearance of mystery and intrigue. The jukebox kicked on now that the band had finished its last set. A modern, jazzy tune blasted from the speakers. Laughter periodically burst over the music.

"Here ya go."

Luc swiveled around and grabbed the glass. *"Merci."* The cold carbonated drink slid down, quenching his parched throat.

A buxom blonde in a red dress cut up to here and down to there sashayed to the bar and sidled beside him. "You blow that sax very well." Her voice came out thick and hoarse, indicative of years spent smoking.

"Merci." Luc took another gulp of the drink. Ice clanked against his front teeth.

"It's been some time since I've seen you here." She ran a bloodred fingernail down his plain T-shirt. "Where've you been hiding?"

That parched feeling returned, despite the empty glass he held in his hand. His biceps jumped as if they had a mind of their own. "Just been busy, Sadie."

"Too busy for me?" Suggestiveness oozed from her every pore as she leaned closer, her bare shoulder grazing the side of his arm.

He jerked back as Mike tapped the bar. "Need another cola, Luc?"

He slid the glass to the bartender. "Please."

"So, how've you been?" Sadie never did know when she fought a losing battle.

"Fine. You?" Luc took the glass from Mike and nodded his thanks before taking a sip. He made sure he rested his elbow closest to her on the bar. *Lord, make my actions honor You.*

"Missing you."

"You know, Sadie," a distinctly familiar voice said from over his shoulder, "most cats don't stay in heat permanently."

Luc spun around to face Tara LeBlanc. Hardly an angel sent to save him, but save him she had. Disdain dug deep into her delicate features. He swallowed. She looked so much like CoCo, his heart ached. Same dark eyes, although CoCo's tilted up more in the corners, like a cat's. The hair was the same dark color. While Tara's was board straight, CoCo's curled in long ringlets down her back. The memory of their silky feel caused Luc to clench his fists.

"Little Tara LeBlanc. Don't you have to be of age to get in here?" Sadie's throaty purr now came out like a growl.

"Don't play with me, Sadie. I haven't the time or the inclination to go slumming tonight, but I will if you insist." Tara cut her eyes to Luc's face. "Glad to see you're at home, waiting for my sister to call you back."

He swallowed again. "Just played a little music, Tara." How did this much younger girl make him feel like a scolded boy?

She arched a single brow. "Oh, I can plainly see you're playing, Luc."

CoCo had taught her well. Her claws were out and they were sharp.

"Isn't it past your bedtime?" Sadie asked.

Tara's icy stare froze the other woman's fingertips on his

shoulder. "If you know what's good for you, Sadie, you'll just push off."

Now it was Sadie's turn to swallow hard. Hard enough that Luc heard it over the drone of the music. Finally she let out an exaggerated sigh and tapped his shoulder again. "I guess you need to babysit, Luc. Some other time, maybe?" Without waiting for a reply, Sadie popped on her tiptoes, planted a wet kiss against his lips, then turned and hustled away.

Luc wiped his mouth with the back of his hand and focused his full attention on Tara. While grateful for her intervention, he knew that expression. "What's bugging you, Tara?"

She popped her hands on her hips, once again reminding him of CoCo. "I just find it amusing that you try to weasel your way back into my sister's life, and then I find you out in a bar, hanging with sleaze."

"I'd just finished playing and came for a soda. Sadie stopped by to say hello." He downed his drink and set the glass on the bar.

"Yeah, I know how Sadie says hello." Tara flipped her hair over her shoulder. "The whole town knows how Sadie greets men."

"That's not fair."

"Isn't it?" She raised one eyebrow again. "Shocking, really, to find Mr. Religion hanging out in a bar with a woman of, oh, let's just say, loose morals." She made a *tsk* with her tongue. "I wonder what CoCo will think."

Heat infused his chest. "Just because I know God intimately, Tara, doesn't mean I condemn others who don't."

"Like you did with CoCo?"

Touché. Yes, her sister had definitely taught her well.

"Need another cola?" Mike interjected.

Luc shook his head. "No, *merci.* I'm about to head home. Just need my sax."

The bartender passed his case over the bar to him. "See you next week?"

"Maybe." Luc faced Tara. "Always a pleasure to see you, Tara."

She threw back her head and chuckled. "I'm sure it is." She stopped laughing and leaned next to him—close enough he could feel her words on his cheek. "Just remember this, Luc Trahan, if you hurt my sister again, you'll have to deal with me."

He smiled down at her. "Is that so?"

"That's so." She gave a grin that hinted at something in the corners. Something he couldn't quite make out. "And trust me, there's no place you can hide that the spirits I send after you can't find."

Her sister had taught her well, indeed.

CoCo tossed her shorts at the laundry hamper and missed. A *clank* echoed on the bathroom's tile floor. For a moment, she was confused. Then she reached for what had fallen from her pocket.

Talking with Alyssa, or should she say, getting an earful from her sister had caused her to totally forget about the coin she'd found. Now she studied the metal doubloon. It looked like a genuine Confederate coin, but she couldn't be sure. She'd have to take it to be inspected. What if it was the real deal? How'd it end up under her rosebush?

She combed her wet-from-the-shower hair free of tangles and then brushed her teeth, all the while staring at the coin. What did it mean? How did it get in her yard? She tightened the sash of her tattered terrycloth robe, admonishing her runaway imagination. It was probably just a replica, something left over from Mardi Gras.

With a sigh, CoCo shoved it in her pocket, flipped off the bathroom light and marched into the hallway.

And ran smack into her sister.

"Tara!" She jumped back against the wall, her hand to her chest. "You scared me silly."

Her sister laughed.

CoCo leaned forward and took a whiff of Tara. The stench of cigarette smoke clung to her sister like lichen to the cypress trees. "Have you been smoking?"

"No, of course not." Tara narrowed her eyes. "If I had, it wouldn't be any concern of yours."

The rebellious imp had taken over her sister's body again. "I just noticed you smelled like an ashtray, that's all."

"I was down at the jazz club."

CoCo moved past her sister toward the kitchen. She opened the icebox, in search of a cold canned drink. "Oh." The liquid did nothing to put out the fire burning in her chest.

Tara followed on her heels. "No comment?"

If CoCo made a big deal about Tara's outing to a bar, her sister would turn on her. As much as it hurt, CoCo shrugged and acted as if it didn't matter, then took another long sip of soda. "None of my business, right?"

"Then I guess you don't care who I saw sitting at the bar with Sadie Thompson hanging all over him..." Tara dug her hip into the counter.

No. Not Luc. Not Sadie. Tara had to be teasing, or mistaken. *Don't say it, don't say it...*

"I don't know, who?" She finished the drink, giving her an excuse to avoid eye contact.

"Luc Trahan."

She crushed the aluminum can in her hand. After everything she'd suffered, she thought the pain couldn't hurt anymore. It did. Her heart still broke over Tara's words.

"Good for him." CoCo tossed the can into the trash and headed down the hall.

Once again, Tara dogged her. "That doesn't bother you?"

Spinning around in her bedroom doorway, she faced her sister. "It's none of my business."

"Funny, your expression doesn't match your tough words."

Tears stung the back of her eyes. She couldn't take much more; she already felt like a big, fat failure, thanks to Alyssa pointing out all her shortcomings. On top of everything else, she didn't need to be reminded she'd given her heart to the wrong man. A man who didn't want her—a man she couldn't trust.

"Hey," Tara reached out and gripped her elbow. "I'm sorry. That was mean of me."

"It's okay. Seriously." Maybe if she blinked hard enough, the tears wouldn't fall.

"No, I'm sorry." Her sister shifted to put her arm around CoCo's shoulders. "And he wasn't really with Sadie. You know how that vixen is, she just draped herself over him. He was probably just sitting there, minding his own business. He'd been playing his sax."

The memory of the song he'd written for her—and played so many times to an audience of her and her alone—assaulted her mind. Blinking didn't work. Tears pushed through and down her cheeks.

Tara hugged her tighter and moved her into the bedroom. "Oh, CoCo, I'm so sorry."

"No." She swiped away the moisture. "I'm just tired and overwhelmed. Really. I shouldn't even care what he does anymore."

"*Shouldn't* being the operative word, right?" Tara eased her to the edge of the bed and gently pushed her to sit.

CoCo smiled at her sister. "Right." She shook her head. "I don't know what's wrong with me. You'd think after all this time just the thought of him wouldn't twist my insides into knots."

"It still does, doesn't it?"

"Yeah, as much as I hate to admit it." As much as she hated part of herself for still loving him.

Tara sat on the edge of the bed and took CoCo's hands in her own and squeezed. "I told you, I think there's still a chance for you two."

CoCo opened her mouth, but Tara shushed her. "No, after seeing your reaction, which you normally hide, I know you're still in love with him."

"Doesn't matter."

"I think he's still in love with you, too." Her sister's tone was soft, as gentle as the breeze rustling through the magnolia leaves outside the window.

"He isn't. He left me, remember?"

Tara flicked her wrists and made a *pfft* sound. "He was emotional then. He'd just lost his father. Surely you can understand that."

"He blamed me, Tara. Me!"

"And he's had time to realize he was wrong."

"Apparently not. He immediately accused me of murdering Beau. Yeah, that's showing he doesn't blame me." CoCo lowered her head and picked at loose threads in her robe. "I realize he's hurting now, too, over the death of his grandfather, but it's becoming his pattern—someone in his family dies and I'm somehow to blame."

Tara stood and held CoCo's chin in her hand, tipping it to

look into her sister's eyes. "I see a man in agony because he's not with the woman he loves—you. And you're both too stubborn to recognize y'all belong together."

CoCo jerked her chin free. "Now, with Beau being murdered, the eviction notice..." She flung herself back on the bed and laid her forearm over her eyes. "I feel like I'm caught in some stupid Shakespearean play."

Tara chuckled. "Juliet you aren't, *cher.*"

"Thanks." She flopped her arm onto the mattress beside her. "I feel like the Montagues and the Capulets, trapped in some stupid family argument."

"True love can prevail, CoCo."

She sat up straight and met her sister's stern expression. A laugh bubbled from her chest and escaped. "Uh, Tara, Romeo and Juliet died in that play, remember?"

Tara's brows knitted, then she laughed. "Oh, yeah. Right."

CoCo stood and hugged her sister, still laughing. "Thanks for trying to cheer me up, though, *Boo.*"

"I didn't mean to upset you. Seriously, you can't keep running from this, you know?"

She sighed. "I know. I'll deal with my feelings after we get all this..." she flipped her hands through the air "...*stuff* handled." Maybe once Luc Trahan proved himself not worthy of her trust again her heart could let him go.

"Don't wait forever. It's simmered for a long time as it is." Tara moved toward the door. "You know, I can always mix up a little potion. Love or truth. Either way, you'd know how he felt about you."

And here she was, thinking she'd made some headway with her little sister. "Tara, how many times do I have to tell you? I don't want anything to do with voodoo, period."

Her sister shrugged. "Suit yourself. Don't linger too long,

CoCo, because if you do, someone like Sadie Thompson *will* make a move on him, and then it'll be too late for your happiness."

CoCo watched Tara slip outside the bedroom, pulling the door behind her.

CoCo opened her word processor and added another paragraph to her grant proposal. She had to get funding, or she'd be out of a job. What would happen to Grandmere and Tara then? Herself? After adding the finishing touches to her document, she stood, stretched, flipped off the light and threw herself across the bed.

Alone in the dark, tears sprang until she'd cried enough to fill a bayou offshoot. When her eyes finally ran dry, she moved to the window and pushed aside the curtain.

This is so hard, God. Surround me with Your love, the only love I need.

The wind kicked up, blowing the leaves to make a whirring in the night air. No tree frogs croaked. A flash of lightning crawled across the sky.

She pressed her lips together. A storm headed to Lagniappe. She could only hope it wouldn't be as turbulent as the emotions shattering her heart tonight.

NINE

Within the casino walls, the sounds of chips clanking, slot machines spinning and the *cha-ching* of coins falling into metal, not to mention the roar of voices, muffled the rumble of thunder. Luc, Justin and the sheriff waited for Sammy Moran, the casino's assistant manager, to unlock the penthouse suite. Raindrops from their shoulders plopped to the plush carpet. The storm, which had started last night, still raged outside this early morning.

Sheriff Theriot shoved his glasses back to the bridge of his nose and sniffled. "No one's been inside since Beau died, right?"

Sammy pushed the door open and shook his head. "Not that I'm aware of. *I* certainly haven't given anyone access."

"Good, good." The sheriff strode into the foyer of Beau's residence. "We'll lock up when we're done." He glanced over his shoulder.

"Oh. Very well." Sammy faced Luc and Justin, his eyes half-lidded. "I'm sorry for your loss. However, I wondered when Beau's things would be removed. This is a corporate suite."

Justin's face turned red. "Don't worry, you can move in here before we even hold the funeral, which will be Saturday. Even though ya didn't bother to ask."

Sammy's face flushed all the way to the tips of his exposed

ears. "Of course I'm interested in the funeral. All of management will attend."

"Why bother? You didn't much like him in life, why show up to pay last respects?" Justin shifted his large build into the room, glaring at Sammy.

The assistant manager twirled the key ring on his index finger. "Th-th-that's not accurate. And it's unfair."

Sheriff Theriot scratched his pen on his notebook. "Did you like Mr. Trahan?" He directed his question to Sammy.

"We weren't friends, but I respected him as my boss." Sammy pocketed the key ring.

Justin gave a loud snort. "That's a lie. You couldn't wait for him to retire, and ya kept pushing Luc here, to decline taking over. You want the manager position and ya know it. No sense in denying the facts."

"I only told Luc to follow his heart. I knew he didn't want the managerial position." Sammy shoved his hands in the pockets of his khaki slacks.

"Is that a fact?" Bubba looked to Luc.

"In Sammy's defense, I did mention to him that I had no interest in working for the casino." All the past conversations they'd had rang in his ears. How many snide comments had Sammy made about Grandfather that Luc had ignored? Luc raked his gaze over Sammy. "He didn't hide the fact he had his eye on becoming casino manager."

Sammy gasped. "Luc! You make it sound like I would do anything to get Beau's job, and that isn't true."

"You know good and well Beau wasn't going to recommend ya take over, even if Luc didn't take the job." Justin clasped his beefy paws in front of him.

"Is that true, Mr. Moran?" The sheriff scribbled on his notebook as he kept up with the conversation. "If Mr. Trahan recommended someone else take his place instead of you, would you get the job?"

Still red-faced and now visibly shaken, Sammy shrugged. "I don't know. You'd have to ask the owner that question."

"What's your position now, since Mr. Trahan's death?" Bubba stared at the assistant manager.

"Well, uh."

"You're acting manager, aren't ya, boy?" Justin's voice boomed off the marble walls of the penthouse foyer.

"Until the owners make a decision, yes, I'm acting manager." He inched toward the door. "As such, I need to get back downstairs and check on things. Am I done here?"

Sheriff Theriot gave a curt nod. "For now. I'll find you later to ask you a few more questions and let you know when an officer will come by to help with the clearing out of Mr. Trahan's things."

Sammy nodded and rushed from the suite.

"There's another suspect for ya, Sheriff." Justin shut the door with the toe of his boot. "And why can't we, Beau's family, pack up his stuff?"

"Because we need to log everything." Bubba stared at Luc's uncle. "Just in case there's something important found. Or something important that's missing."

Justin snorted. "Right. So, whatcha looking for here?"

"I'd just like to glance over your brother's belongings in their place." Bubba moved toward the living area. He jerked his head around. "Nice digs."

"Beau always did have champagne taste." Justin chuckled as he followed the sheriff. "Good thing he could afford to support his indulgences."

"Is there anything in particular we should be looking for?" Luc asked. A sense of inferiority always washed over him in this place. Like he didn't measure up to his grandfather's expectations.

Bubba headed toward the bedroom. "Just see if you notice anything out of place." He paused in the doorway and hollered back to them. "Don't touch anything, though."

Still chuckling, Justin wandered into the kitchen. "Wonder if Beau has a cold drink in the icebox." He pulled open the door and bent. "Hey, Luc, look at this."

Luc moved into the kitchen and peered over his uncle's shoulder into the icebox. "What am I looking at?"

Justin pointed at the clear top of the crisper bin. "Funny place to keep a checkbook, wouldn't you say?"

"Don't touch the drawer." Over his shoulder, Luc hollered for Bubba.

The sheriff strode into the kitchen. "What'd you find?"

With a jerk of his chin, Justin indicated the bin. "Never knew my brother to keep his banking stuff in the icebox."

Bubba waved Justin and Luc back. "Let me take a look." Hunched over, he used the tip of his pen to slide the drawer out. A leather bankbook lay at the bottom of the bin. He popped on a set of latex gloves from his pocket to grab the checkbook.

Luc and Justin followed the sheriff as he laid it on the counter and flipped the top open. He let out a low whistle.

"What?" Luc and Justin asked in unison.

"There's an entry dated this past Tuesday. A check written in the amount of fifty-thousand dollars."

"To who?" Luc rested his shoulder against the kitchen doorway. He'd never known his grandfather to be that generous with anyone. Not anyone in his family at any rate.

Bubba lifted his gaze to peer at them. "To Frank Thibodeaux."

Luc's gut tightened. "Frank Thibodeaux?"

"Who is that?" Justin wanted to know.

"He's Felicia's boyfriend." As soon as the words were out of his mouth, Luc caught the interest in Bubba's eyes.

"The way your momma tells it, Beau didn't much care for Frank."

"He didn't. I can't imagine why Grandfather would loan him such an amount of money. It must be a mistake of some sort." Luc pressed his lips together, wondering what Felicia hadn't told him.

Justin snorted. "Beau didn't loan nobody money."

"Then how do you explain this check entry?" Bubba held his pen over his notebook, a questioning look glimmering in his eyes.

"I can't." Luc glanced at his uncle.

"Beau didn't mention Felicia's boyfriend to me." Justin jerked on his earlobe.

"Could he have been blackmailing Beau?" The sheriff spoke in a low tone.

"Blackmail? Why would ya think that?" Justin's roar ricocheted off the pristine white kitchen cabinets.

Bubba tapped the top of the pen against his chin. "When a large amount of money is paid to someone in a lump sum, it's normally either to pay off a debt, a loan or a blackmail payment." He shoved his glasses back against the bridge of his nose. "Since we can assume Beau wasn't repaying a debt to this Frank, and y'all claim Beau wouldn't have loaned the man money, that's the only other thing that comes to mind."

"I can't think of anything Frank would even know to blackmail Grandfather about." Luc's discomfort grew the longer the conversation wore on. What did this mean for Felicia?

"I'll talk to him today, that's for sure." Bubba's glasses slipped down his nose again. "Luc, you said Frank had been to the house. No telling what he had access to."

"Grandfather wouldn't tolerate blackmail." He studied his friend's face and let out a sigh. "Come on, Bubba, you know how he was. He wouldn't put up with anybody having something on him." He gave a shrug. "Besides, according to Felicia, Grandfather had threatened Frank with financial ruin if he didn't end the relationship with her. Why would he pay Frank a dime?"

Recognizing the excitement in Bubba's eyes, Luc shook his head. He'd done it again—unwittingly placed his sister's boyfriend at the top of the suspect list. Then again, he couldn't help feeling bewildered about the check. He nodded toward the checkbook. "Any chance it's a mistake?"

The sheriff lifted the checkbook and held it up where both Luc and his uncle could read the register. "Would you say this is Beau's handwriting?"

"Yep, that's my brother's neat penmanship."

"Then what other explanation can you offer, Luc?" Bubba stared at him.

He couldn't come up with a single reason. What he did know, however, was the pain this would bring his sister. God help them all.

CoCo stared out the living room window, watching the lightning dance across the sky. She itched to be on the bayou, but knew the weather wouldn't permit her morning run. She'd finish her report and get it in the mail, the sooner the better. If she beat some of the other grant petitioners, maybe she'd get approval. She desperately needed that grant—without the money, she didn't know how she'd help support Grandmere and Tara.

"Watching the storm won't make it dissipate, *ma chère*."

She turned to smile at her grandmother. "I know, but I feel like my whole morning is wasted."

Grandmere laughed and lowered the dream catcher she was working on to her lap. "You always were happiest when out in the bayou."

Moving to sit on the couch beside her grandmother, CoCo studied the older woman. "Grandmere, tell me the truth—do you believe Grandpere signed over the deed to this house?"

"I really couldn't say, *ma chère.* He never said as much to me."

CoCo licked her lips, dreading the territory she inched into. "Would he have told you?" She held her breath, waiting for the explosion that was sure to follow.

Her grandmother didn't blow. Instead, she let out a long breath. "I'd like to think he would have, but he might not." Her fingers reached for the round beads in the bowl on the coffee table.

So, it *was* possible. Just as she'd feared.

"Grandmere, if it's true, why would Beau Trahan have waited all this time to act on it?"

"*Ma chère,* I can only surmise his grandson stopped him, out of deference to you." Her grandmother's eyes probed deep into CoCo, exploring a place she didn't want tapped into.

Doubtful. CoCo recalled her conversations with Luc. "No, that can't be it. When I told Luc, he was as surprised as we were to hear about the eviction." She let out a soft sigh. "Besides, Luc never did have the backbone to stand up to his grandfather." Or even to his own feelings.

"Hmm." Grandmere threaded a bead onto the twine and tied it off. "I suppose Justin could have stopped him."

"Justin Trahan?" After the way he'd acted yesterday, CoCo couldn't see him asking his brother to stop taking over their home. He'd seethed animosity toward her family.

"Of course, Justin Trahan. He and your grandfather were best friends for the longest time, you know."

News to her. CoCo lifted a bead from the bowl and passed it to her grandmother. "When was this?"

"Oh, my, *ma chère*. Going back before I had Robert, I suppose."

Hearing her father's name spoken aloud, CoCo's memories of her parents and the pain of her loss slammed against her heart. In thirteen years, not a day had passed when she didn't long for her mother or father. The yearning hit her full force. She swallowed hard. "I didn't know."

"Oh, yes. Marcel and Justin went hunting 'bout every weekend." Grandmere looped twine around the hoop, stretching it taut. "Those two were thick as thieves."

"What happened? I never remember Grandpere and Justin being together after we moved here."

Her grandmother smiled, but kept weaving on the dream catcher. "I suppose they outgrew each other. Marcel and I became wrapped up with Robert. Justin never married, so he couldn't understand the family life Marcel chose."

"After all the time that passed, why would Justin stop his brother from taking over this house years ago?"

Grandmere lifted her gaze. A sly smile tugged at the corners of her mouth. "I don't know for certain, *ma chère,* but I've always suspected Justin had a bit of a crush on me."

"Really?" CoCo tried to imagine her grandparents in their younger years. She could see her grandmother's strong features. In her youth, she must have been quite attractive.

"Don't sound so surprised, *ma chère.* I turned a few heads in my time." Grandmere laughed.

CoCo had never considered another man might have been interested in her grandmother. Just the thought…eww, CoCo didn't want to give herself a mental image to carry around. "I didn't mean any insult, Grandmere. I just never knew."

"No reason for you to. I never batted so much as an eyelash at Justin Trahan." She reached into the bowl of beads again. "Even if I hadn't been so in love with Marcel, I would never have gotten involved with Justin. Even then, Beau had his family under his thumb."

Thinking back to the reaction Justin had given her yesterday, CoCo couldn't imagine such. "Justin seems to have outgrown that."

"Oh, no, *ma chère*. Make no mistake, Beau Trahan kept a stronghold over his family. Why, I remember a time when he threatened Justin. Told him that if he and Marcel didn't stop hunting together, he'd tighten all the Trahan purse strings."

"Really?"

"I don't know why he didn't like his brother being friends with my Marcel." Grandmere slipped a gold bead onto the twine. "I think he realized the LeBlancs were a threat to him and his popularity. Back then, his political aspirations were just forming. The LeBlancs weren't as affluent and well-to-do as the Trahans." She paused, running a gnarled finger over her bottom lip. "Now that I think about it, that could be the reason why Justin and Marcel went their separate ways."

How had she never known any of this? CoCo passed another gold-plated bead to her grandmother. The shine caught her attention. And reminded her of…what?

Grandmere tied off the bead. "You know, *ma chère,* I've noticed you've got that sappy look again."

She jerked her attention back to her grandmother. "What?"

"That look in your eyes. Same one from when you were wrapped up in Luc Trahan." Grandmere made another loop on the dream catcher. "You've been spending quite a bit of time with him." She clucked her tongue. "I'd hate to see you hurt again. Once a man breaks your trust, you can never fully recover it."

CoCo dropped her gaze to the dream catcher. "I'd rather not discuss it." As if she'd talk about her love life with her grandmother…. That was just wrong.

The bead drew her gaze again. Round and shiny. The Confederate coin—that's what it reminded her of.

"I'm here if you decide you want to talk, *ma chère.*"

"*Merci.* I'll keep that in mind." CoCo jumped up. "I have an errand to run, Grandmere. Do you need anything from town?"

"You sure you should be going out in this weather?" Her grandmother glanced to the window. "Looks pretty nasty out there. Some of the spirits are angry."

"I'll be fine." CoCo yanked her keys off the peg by the door, refusing to get into the constant debate. "I'll be back in a few hours. Tell Tara to call me on my cell if you think of anything you need." Without waiting for a reply, she rushed to her bedroom and grabbed the coin. She flashed her grandmother a quick smile as she darted out the door.

Rain smacked against her bent head and shoulders as she ran to the Jeep. She glanced up to the sky as she started the ignition. Dark clouds hovered over the bayou. Maybe Grandmere was right—maybe she should wait until the storm passed.

The small treasure felt cold in her palm. No, she'd go ahead. When the storm passed, she could be out on the bayou again. She cranked the Jeep, then set the coin in the console.

She'd no more gotten out of the driveway when her phone rang. Jerking it up, she flipped it open. "Hello."

"CoCo." Luc always did say her name with a caress.

The memory of what Tara had told her last night banished her fantasy. Do. Not. Trust. Luc. Trahan.

"What do you want, Luc?" She hoped he picked up on her snarkiness.

"I just left Grandfather's penthouse with the sheriff. Found out something interesting. Since we're working together, I thought you'd want to know."

"Are we?" She braked at the end of the road, staring through the rain coming down in sheets.

"Are we what?"

"Working together. You know, since I found the gun, you've acted like you suspected me of putting it back in the bayou."

He let out a slow sigh. "No, I don't suspect you." A pregnant paused filled the connection before he spoke again. "Look, I'd like to share this information with you. Your grandmother said you'd left to run errands. Can I meet you somewhere?"

For just a split second, she considered telling him about the coin. Then logic swooped in. She couldn't trust him, but she did want to know what he'd discovered. "I should be done in less than an hour."

"Would you like to meet at the diner or something?"

"That sounds fine." Although she'd probably regret it, she needed to see him. She'd blame it on curiosity as to what they found at Beau's place, but her heart had other ideas.

"Be careful in the rain."

He didn't have the right to care about her anymore. Or make her think he cared. She shut the phone and dropped it back into the console. It clanked against the coin. The whole trip to the appraiser was probably just a wild-goose chase.

But what if it wasn't?

TEN

CoCo watched the appraiser, Billy Monahan, run a series of tests. The longer he inspected, the more she wished she hadn't bothered. The coin couldn't be authentic.

She rubbed her bare arms. The air conditioner sure worked great in this business. If this took much longer, she'd have to grab her jacket from the Jeep.

"Where'd you say you found this?" Billy laid the coin on a velvet pad sitting on the counter.

"In my yard." She touched the edge of the metal. It felt cold. Or maybe it was just the blast of air coming from the vent above.

"Hmm." He adjusted the light to shine more directly. "This is the second one of these I've seen this month."

Her hopes crashed to her feet. "Really?"

"I'm going to tell you the same thing I told the gentleman." He lifted his gaze from the coin to stare into her face. "Let me give you a little history, if you'll bear with me." He took off his bifocal glasses and set them on the counter. His bald head shone under the fluorescent lights. "At the New Orleans Mint, they made half-dollar coins with a Union obverse and a Confederate reverse. These are very rare, and worth quite a bit of money."

"Why would the Confederacy use a Union obverse on their coins?"

Billy shrugged. "According to history, in early 1861, Jefferson Davis, then President of the Confederacy, authorized production of a Confederate Half Dollar. They took an ordinary half dollar with the Liberty on the obverse, removed the reverse motif and added a shield with seven stars representing the only seven states that had joined by that time and adding Confederate States of America—Half Dollar. Only four were made."

"But if only four were made…"

"Let me continue. In 1879, a man named Scott came into possession of the original reverse die. He obtained several 1861 USA half dollars and removed the reverses, then stamped them with the Confederate die. These are known as restrikes or Scott restrikes, and while not as valuable as the originals, they're still worth a considerable amount of money."

"O-kay." Bless his heart, he was trying to break it to her gently that hers was nothing more than a dollar-store replica.

"I'm talking quite a bit of money, even for one coin." He peered at her and perched his glasses back on his hawk nose.

"How much?" It couldn't hurt to know, at least.

Billy hedged a moment, flipping through pages in a magazine. "According to the listings in my catalog, and the sources are based on supply and demand and what current offers have been, these restrikes are valued at $5,000 in uncirculated condition."

Wow, she'd no idea. No wonder Billy ran all those tests. He had to tell her he knew beyond a shadow of a doubt that it wasn't real. She felt sorry for him—he said he'd had to do it recently for someone else, too.

"And all metal currency made from dies 1861 and later are genuine Confederate coins."

She glanced down at her coin—1862. Her heartbeat kicked up a notch as she glanced back at Billy. *It couldn't be.*

"The restrike coin can be identified by an imperfection in America between the letters *E* and *R*."

Once more her eyes dropped to the velvet pad. She squinted, but couldn't see any irregularities. Billy pushed the velvet pad to an angle where the light hit it just right.

Just enough to see the imperfection.

Her heart pounded as she lifted her stare, not trusting herself to speak.

Billy laughed. "That's right, Ms. LeBlanc. You own a genuine restrike coin of the Confederacy."

Words trapped in her throat.

"As I told the other client, I would highly recommend you put this in a safety deposit box or in another very safe and secure place."

She nodded and chewed her bottom lip. Finally, her vocal chords unwound themselves from around the lump. "How much do you think this particular one's worth?"

He studied the coin again. "It appears to be uncirculated." He paused for a moment. "I'd say you'd get about five grand, give or take a hundred or so."

"Oh, my."

"Let me get you something to put it in." Billy reached under the counter. "You say you found this in your yard?" He passed her a small acrylic case.

"Yeah, under a rosebush."

He nestled the coin in the plush velvet. "Is your house old?"

She nodded. "I really couldn't say how old it is."

"The reason I ask is that lots of people during the Civil War buried their money and silver, or hid it within their houses to keep the invading Yankees from getting their hands on it." He closed the lid to the case. "And that gentleman I told you about said he found his around a pre-Civil War home as well."

She took the case, holding it tight. "So, you think there could be more?"

"If your house dates back to pre-Civil War and you uncovered this coin due to erosion and such, I'd say start combing your property."

"Wow."

"Now, would you like to hear a local legend?"

"Sure."

"We know the Klan was created after the end of the Civil war, originally to protect women from carpetbaggers, yes?"

CoCo nodded.

"Well, local legend says that when the Klan formed in the bayou area, they stockpiled these particular restrike coins."

"Whatever for?"

"Rumor has it that they believed the South would rise again and these coins would become quite valuable when that happened."

"Very interesting."

"Just think, you could have found part of a stockpile of the Klan's coins."

She didn't believe that possible.

Billy laughed and took off his glasses again. He nodded toward the door. "Too bad it's coming down like cats and dogs. I imagine you'll want to have a treasure hunt in your yard."

"*Merci.*" She laughed. "What do I owe you for the appraisal?"

"Twenty-five."

After paying Billy and offering her sincere thanks, CoCo rushed to the Jeep. She felt like a drowned river rat. A quick glance in her rearview mirror confirmed she looked as bad as imagined. She cranked the engine and let it idle. The news hadn't sunk in yet. A real Confederate coin. But linked to the Klan? Not in *her* yard.

She tapped her front tooth with her nail. What to do now? Reaching into her pocket, she grabbed the case and pulled it out to sit in her lap. Such a little thing, but worth so much money. Worth so much, and she needed any money she could get until she knew whether or not she'd get her grant. Billy was right—she must get it to a safe place.

CoCo steered toward the closest bank. She'd get a safety deposit box as Billy had suggested. As she dodged fat raindrops on her trek into the bank, she nearly slipped on the muddy concrete. She'd conclude her business as soon as possible, then go meet Luc. Her pulse hiccupped. She couldn't trust Luc with this information. Besides, they'd only agreed to work together to find his grandfather's murderer. She didn't owe him anything more. This coin had nothing to do with Beau Trahan being shot.

If anything, the past few years had enhanced CoCo's natural beauty. There was something different, something almost pure about her. Luc couldn't help but stare as she waltzed into the diner. He shoved to his feet as she approached the table.

"Sorry I'm a little late," she gushed as she slid across the table from him, shaking off raindrops.

She was worth the wait. "That's okay." He sat and smiled. "Are you hungry?"

"No, but I'd kill for a cup of coffee."

Bad choice of words. He lifted his cup at the waitress, and shot CoCo a look. "Did you get your errand run?"

She pressed her lips together. "Um-muh."

He waited, but she didn't elaborate. What errand was so important that she'd gone out in this horrid weather?

The waitress filled their cups with steaming coffee, asked if they wanted to order, then rushed away.

"You said you found something new?" she prompted him.

"This morning, Uncle Justin and I went with Bubba to Grandfather's penthouse."

"And?"

Luc considered stalling for a few more moments, just so she'd keep staring at him with such intrigue. As much as he hated to admit it, he knew her well, and knew she sorely lacked in the patience department. "We found his checkbook."

She cocked her head.

He took a swig of the hot coffee. "The register reflected a check made out for fifty-thousand dollars to Felicia's boyfriend."

"Oh." CoCo took a sip of coffee. "What does this mean?"

"It means that the sheriff is going to question Frank."

"What's your take?"

He rubbed his thumb over the cup's handle. "Bubba's thinking it might be blackmail."

"What do you think?"

"I can't imagine Felicia being involved with someone who'd dare to try and blackmail Grandfather."

"Mmm."

"What?"

Darkness held her eyes as close as the night. "People can surprise you." The icy look she tossed hit him square in the chest.

Touché. "Maybe so." He felt as low as the scum growing on the pond. "CoCo."

She took a long pull on her coffee, then stood. "Don't, Luc. Just don't."

He rose to his feet. "But…"

"Let it go. It's over and done with." She tugged her purse strap over her shoulder. "Maybe joining forces wasn't the smartest idea."

Before he could argue, she was out the door to the diner.

Over and done with? He wished someone would send that memo to his heart.

Luc hung up his slicker and headed toward the kitchen, following the enticing aroma of crawfish bisque carried on the waves of laughter. He turned into the room and paused, drinking in the sight of his family laughing. His mother—looking sober, thank goodness—ladled bisque into bowls at the table, while Felicia giggled as she passed a glass of iced tea to Frank.

Home. How long had it been since they'd all joked and ate together? Had Grandfather really kept them so tightly wound that they couldn't relax, even amongst themselves? He dropped into a chair. "Got some for me, Mom?"

"Of course, Luc." She reached to the counter and grabbed another bowl. "It's nice to have you with us for lunch."

Just pack his bags for the guilt trip. Yet, she had a point. He'd deliberately had working lunches to save himself the drive home. Now, seeing his sister's face lit up like the stars over the bayou, he regretted his decision. *Lord, forgive me for being so selfish.*

"Here you go." His mother handed him a bowl.

His stomach rumbled. "Smells wonderful, *merci.*"

"It tastes perfect, Mom." Felicia slipped another spoonful into her mouth.

Frank nodded and swallowed. "It's wonderful, Mrs. LeBlanc."

"How you do go on," Luc's mother said.

An abrupt knock on the door brought up their heads. Luc shoved back his chair and stood. "I'll get it."

He opened the door to stare into the face of Sheriff Bubba Theriot. "Bubba, what brings you by in this nasty weather?"

"I told Sammy a deputy would help box up Beau's things and send them here."

"That's fine. Surely you didn't drive over here in this mess to tell me that?"

"I went by to talk to Frank Thibodeaux, but his roommate said he was out. Thought he might be here." Bubba dusted raindrops off his shoulders.

"Can this wait until later? I'd rather not do this in front of Felicia."

"I don't think there's much point in drawing this out any longer." Bubba wiped his boots on the welcome rug. "The sooner I get some answers, the quicker I can solve this case."

Luc sighed, but opened the door wide to let the sheriff enter. "Let me go get Frank." His steps were heavy as he trudged to the kitchen. The laughter continued.

His mother smiled. "Who is it, Luc?"

"Frank, can I see you in the living room for a minute, please?" He fought to keep his expression neutral.

"What?" Felicia pushed her wheelchair from the table. "Luc?" Her eyes repeated the question.

"Bubba's here and wants to ask Frank a couple of questions."

"What about?" Felicia grabbed her boyfriend's hand, her gaze never leaving Luc's face.

He struggled with how much information to share with his sister. He let out a long sigh. "I think Bubba would be the best person to answer that."

"Well, *allons* then." She shifted her gaze to Frank's face. "Frank?"

"I can't imagine."

"Why don't we all go into the living room? I'll make some coffee." His mother moved to clear the table. "Y'all go on ahead, and I'll be right along."

Luc led the way to where Bubba sat on the couch. The sheriff jumped to his feet as they entered. "Frank Thibodeaux?"

"Yes, sir?" He didn't let loose of Felicia's hand.

"I have a couple of questions for you."

"In regards to what?" A sheen of perspiration glistened on Frank's forehead.

Bubba pulled out his notebook and pen. "We found a checkbook register at Beau Trahan's that reflects a check written to you on this past Tuesday."

"A check to me?" Frank's eyes went wide.

"A check in the amount of fifty-thousand dollars."

Luc couldn't tell who gasped louder, Frank or Felicia. Then silence fell over the room.

"Can you explain, Mr. Thibodeaux?" Bubba held the pen over the notebook.

Frank glanced at Felicia and dropped into the chair. Felicia rolled her wheelchair beside him. "Frank?"

"Aw, 'Licia, I never wanted you to find out. Especially not like this."

Luc sank onto the couch. Was he about to witness a confession? He noticed Bubba stared at the couple. The lawman knew when to keep his mouth shut and merely observe.

"Frank?" Felicia's voice cracked.

He raked a hand over his face. "Remember I told you that your grandfather had come to see me?"

She nodded, but tears shone in her eyes.

"The threats came after I tore up the check he offered me. The payoff to break things off with you."

Felicia sniffed, pressing a hand to her mouth. Luc's heart ripped at the pain in her expression. He fought against every fiber in his being screaming at him to go to her. This was one time big brother couldn't make it all go away. Grandfather's underhandedness knew no boundaries.

"You tore it up, right? You didn't cash it." Her eyes held such hope.

"Of course not! I would never take a payoff to leave you." He took her hand in his. "I love you, 'Licia."

"Oh, Frank." Tears streamed from her eyes.

Bubba cleared his throat. "Why don't you walk me through yours and Mr. Trahan's conversations?"

Frank turned back to the sheriff. "Felicia's grandfather came to see me Monday or Tuesday. At work. Said he had a business proposition for me."

"And?" Bubba wrote in his notebook.

Luc sat on the edge of his seat.

"He said he didn't want me breaking his granddaughter's heart. Accused me of pretending to be interested in Felicia only to get some money out of him." Frank jerked his stare to her. "Which wasn't ever a factor in my attraction to you. You're the sweetest, most gentle woman I've ever met. From the first moment I laid eyes on you, I—"

"What did you tell Mr. Trahan?" Bubba interrupted.

"I told him I loved her." He cut his eyes to Felicia. "Which I do." Frank nodded at Bubba. "He offered me that check. Told me to think it over and tucked it in my pocket."

"Uh-huh." Bubba hiked his brows. "Then what?"

"I tried to give the check back right then and there, but he wouldn't take it." Frank turned pleading eyes to Felicia. "He drove off in that Cadillac of his. Just left me standing in the dirt."

Felicia's expression softened.

"What'd you do?" Bubba brought the conversation back to the subject at hand.

"The next day, I went to see Mr. Trahan. I told him I wasn't interested in any of his money." His voice dropped a decibel. "I was only interested in his granddaughter." His eyes met Felicia's. "Still am."

"Mr. Thibodeaux, what happened then?"

"Mr. Trahan's the hardest-hearted man I've ever met. He wouldn't listen when I told him I wanted to spend my life with her." He shook his head. "He kept calling me a gold digger." His hands trembled.

"What'd you do?" Bubba stopped writing and studied Frank.

Frank ran a hand over his slicked-back hair. "I got so mad. I yelled and hollered at him. Raised my fist to him. Said things I shouldn't have."

"Such as?" The words slipped out before Luc could swallow them back.

Bubba tossed him a glare.

"I told him I didn't want his money and neither would 'Licia." He spun to face Felicia. "I'm sorry I put words in your mouth, baby. I just couldn't take his accusations anymore. It just popped out of my mouth."

Luc could relate.

"What did you do?" Bubba's expression reflected he was clearly tired of the side trips in the conversation.

"I ripped the check up and dropped it on the floor at his feet. That's when he told me he'd ruin me financially." Anger etched deep into his face. "Told me I wouldn't be able to find a job to support 'Licia."

Luc shifted on the couch. Frank's story hit a little too close to home.

"What did you do?" The sheriff spoke between clenched teeth. Clearly, his patience had worn out.

"I told him that I'd take 'Licia and he'd never see her

again." His voice grew thick and he turned to Felicia. "I'm so sorry, baby. I spoke in anger. Please forgive me."

Felicia laid a hand against his cheek. "There's nothing to forgive. You love me that much?"

Even Luc's hardened heart couldn't deny the love on their faces. He glanced at Bubba. The scrawny redhead pushed his glasses to the bridge of his nose and cleared his throat. "Then what happened?"

Frank stared at the sheriff, glassy-eyed. "I think I shocked him. I didn't give him a chance to think about it—I just left. Never heard from him after that."

Southerners loved their history.

CoCo sat in the library, staring at the umpteenth book portraying the Confederate side of the Civil War. While she now had all the historical facts on the war, she had found very little about coins of the Confederacy. Only two books out of the twelve she'd pulled reflected specific information on the mints of the Confederacy. She slammed the last book shut and pushed it to the center of the table.

This was getting her nowhere. Nothing in any of the books would tell her how those coins wound up in her yard. But she did know someone who might be able to shed some light on the situation.

CoCo grabbed the printout of her grant proposal, which she'd finished before she'd started her research. She carefully folded it and put it inside a large envelope, whispering up a prayer. She simply had to get the funding. Had to.

ELEVEN

When it rained, it poured. And in South Louisiana, all the dirt turned to mud.

Luc pulled up to the mailbox after seeing Frank safely back to his house. The family had spent the afternoon assuring Frank they held no animosity toward him for his harsh words against Beau. Who could blame him? Dusk had crept up on them, so Luc had followed Frank home to ensure his little car didn't get stuck on the dirt roads. Good thing he'd bought the four-wheel drive last year.

The torrential rains continued to beat down, soaking Luc to the skin as he retrieved the mail through the window. He parked the vehicle, then ran to the porch, gripping the mail. Luc stomped his feet and shook the rain from his shoulders before entering the house. If he tracked mud on the entry rug, his mother would have a conniption. She'd complain about the water anyway.

"Luc, is that you? I hope you wiped your feet," his mother yelled from the kitchen.

Smiling, he shook his head and dropped the mail on the sideboard. Some things were simply a foregone conclusion. His mother's dramatics being one. "I did."

"Good. Supper's almost ready." She hummed an old tune.

He sniffed—cayenne pepper and okra permeated the air in an enticing aroma. Gumbo, one of his favorite meals. His stomach rumbled, so he headed to the kitchen to see if he could swipe a quick taste.

His mother wore an old apron over a housedress. Lipstick tinted her lips, and a little smudge of flour decorated the tip of her nose. He narrowed his eyes and went over for a quick hug. He couldn't detect any telltale stench of liquor.

Pulling back, she looked into his eyes. "What was that for?"

"It's just nice to see you so content." He shifted his weight, guilt pressing against his chest as he swallowed back his suspicion of her being tipsy. He planted a peck on her cheek. "Besides, when did it become against the law to appreciate one's mother?"

She smiled, lighting up the whole room, despite the approaching night outside. "You're a sweet boy, Luc Trahan." She laid a hand against his cheek for a brief moment before turning back to the stove. "That nice man from the casino called."

"Oh?"

"He said he'd have your grandfather's personal belongings sent over sometime tomorrow."

"Yeah, I forgot about that." He reached into the drawer and pulled out a spoon. "This smells divine."

"Ah, so that's it. You buttered me up so you'd get a taste." She shook her head.

He dipped the spoon into the creamy sauce, blowing on it before sliding it into his mouth. His tastebuds exploded, and he sighed his appreciation. "Nobody cooks as good as you do, Mom. This is amazing."

"Beau's lawyer called while you were out."

That stopped his enjoyment. "And?"

"He said he's been in touch with Justin and that he'll need all the family to meet after the funeral—for the reading of Beau's will."

"Oh. I hadn't really thought about that." Truthfully, his mother would need some income since she'd never worked a day in her life. Maybe they could sell the house and split the profit. He shook his head, clearing his mind of the questions and uncertainty. He reached toward the pot again.

His mother swatted his hand, but the blush spread across her face. "Flatterer. Now get, so I can finish."

Luc chuckled as he dropped the spoon into the sink and headed back to the living room. Now his stomach really growled. Had lunch only been four hours ago? He grabbed the mail off the sideboard, then plopped onto the recliner. The old leather groaned when he lifted the footrest. He flipped through the envelopes.

Sales flyers, grocery ads…all addressed to the occupant. He tossed them into the trash can beside the chair. Four envelopes with the return address of medical facilities. Bills for Felicia's treatments. How would he be able to continue paying for her medical attention? He set the bills in another stack on the table before continuing to go through the stack.

A handwritten envelope addressed to Beau Trahan from Dwayne Williams.

He ran his finger over the return address. A raindrop had smudged the ink, but the writing was still legible. His heart quickened. Why would CoCo's lawyer be writing his grandfather? He took in a gulp of air and slipped his finger under the envelope's flap. The ripping sound echoed.

Luc withdrew the single piece of paper from the envelope and unfolded it. He took a deep breath, then let his gaze scan the single paragraph.

Mr. Trahan, it is my belief you played a mitigating role
in the death of my sister, Beulah Williams. It is my
intent to uncover the truth and see that those who are
responsible are brought to justice.

Finding it hard to breathe, Luc blinked furiously. He stuffed
the letter back into the envelope and shoved it in his jeans
pocket, then pushed to his feet, lowering the footrest with a
loud pop. He snatched his keys off the buffet and hollered,
"Mom, I've got to run a quick errand. I'll be back later."

His mother peeked around the open doorway. She stared
at him for a moment, her eyes widening. "Is everything okay?"

"I don't know. I need to find Bubba."

The concern blinked in her eyes. He planted a kiss to her
forehead. "Don't worry, it's probably nothing. I'll be back as
soon as I can." Not giving her a chance to ask for further explanation, Luc turned and rushed out the door.

Rain pelted down, causing visibility to be nil in the early
evening. He should have grabbed a baseball cap. He turned
to the door and heard Felicia's voice blending with his
mother's. If he went back inside, he'd just have to answer
more questions. Ones he didn't feel up to answering right now.
He sprinted for his vehicle.

Luc headed toward the sheriff's office, taking a quick
glance at the digital clock—5:46. He hoped Bubba would be
working a little later than usual. He didn't relish the thought
of having to drive clean out to the other side of the bayou if
the sheriff had already gone for the day. He touched his jeans
pocket—the folded envelope rustled. Why did he feel the
need to reassure himself?

The pounding rain made the drive longer than normal, but
Luc managed to make it to the station inside of thirty minutes.

Sure enough, Bubba's cruiser sat parked out front. Luc rushed under the awning. He took a moment to catch his breath before jerking open the door.

"Why, Luc Trahan, what brings you by this time of the evening and in such nasty weather?" asked Missy, the town's dispatcher. She fluffed her platinum curls and batted her eyelashes. She actually batted them.

"Is Bubba still around?" Dumb question since his car was parked outside. Women coming on so strong always made him uncomfortable. Unfortunately, since he and CoCo had broken up, half the women in town seemed determined to change his single status. Now, with Beau dead...the Trahan fortune had to be willed to somebody.

"Sure, I'll tell him you're here." She flashed him a big smile and lifted the intercom receiver. "Sheriff, Luc Trahan is here to see you." She nodded and hung up the phone. "He'll be right out." She popped her gum as she continued to stare and smile.

The popping grated on his nerves.

"How's your momma and Felicia?"

"Fine. Good, considering." Maybe if he didn't look at her she'd go back to doing whatever it was she'd been doing when he'd entered.

"I'm so sorry for your loss." No such luck. She would continue talking to him until she turned blue in the face.

Fate smiled upon him. Bubba ambled up behind Missy. "Luc. What're you doing here?"

Luc sprung to his feet. "I have something to show you." He glanced into Missy's interested eyes, then back to Bubba. "Can we go in your office?"

"Sure." Bubba pushed the swinging door to let him behind the counter.

Following the sheriff, Luc felt Missy's eyes burning into his back. Now she would be more than interested, she'd be downright curious about what he had to show Bubba. Someone else speculating—just what he didn't need.

"Have a seat." Bubba waved toward a wooden chair in front of his desk and then plopped down in his own. "What's so important you got out in this weather to show me?"

Luc took a deep breath before pulling out the crumpled envelope. He pushed it across the desk. "This came in the mail today."

Bubba's eyes widened, and he lifted the envelope. "You opened this?"

"Yeah. I was curious why CoCo's lawyer would be sending Grandfather anything." He inched to the edge of the chair. "The return address isn't his law firm's, it's his personal one."

"I see." Bubba pulled out the letter. His eyes darted back and forth as he read. He set the letter down and peered at Luc. "This definitely throws another twist into an already messy case."

Luc swallowed. "I know. It does bear looking into, right?"

"Most definitely." He leaned back in the chair. "I'll pay Mr. Williams a visit first thing in the morning."

"Can I go?" Excitement pushed Luc's leg to bounce.

"It's official police business, Luc. You can't go. You're the grandson of the victim."

"I rea—"

Bubba held up his hand. "I know. I promise if I find anything, I'll call you." His gaze raked over Luc. "That's the best I can do."

"Okay." He pushed to his feet, the excitement drained from his limbs. It'd been another long day. "I'll wait to hear from you."

"I'll let you know what I can, as soon as I can." Bubba moved around the desk and clapped Luc's back. "Hang in there, buddy. We'll find who killed Beau and see that justice is served."

The intensity of the rain had decreased. Luc strode to his vehicle, then sat behind the wheel, trying to organize his thoughts. The security lights outside the police station blinked. Through the rain, they cast prisms of light across the windshield. Like a spell. Luc swallowed. Would everything remind him of CoCo?

He started the ignition and pointed the SUV toward the LeBlanc's place. No matter what Bubba found out tomorrow, CoCo had a right to know her lawyer could be involved in his grandfather's murder. Luc didn't want to wait to tell her.

As he headed down her street, he couldn't help but question his own motives. Wasn't he going to tell her for a more personal, selfish reason?

So he could see her again.

CoCo waited until Tara had retired to her room to speak to Grandmere. Her grandmother sat on the couch, flipping through one of her handwritten journals. She glanced up as CoCo plopped beside her.

"What is it, *ma chère?* You look like you have something on your mind."

"I do. Can you tell me anything about the history of this house?"

Grandmere closed her leather book. "Anything in particular you want to know?"

How could she extract the information without setting off alarm bells in Grandmere? She licked her lips. "I know it's pre-Civil War. Has it always been in our family? Like during the war?"

Her grandmother smiled. "My grandpere built this house himself, *ma chère,* well before the war. My father was born and raised here." Her eyes became unfocused. "Did you know several families holed up in this here house when the Yankees came?"

"Really?"

"Oh, yes. Many local families had already lost their homes and took refuge here." She smiled that distant, I'm-not-in-the-present smile. "They brought their silver to bury alongside my family's in the backyard."

CoCo fought to not jump with all the adrenaline coursing through her veins. She forced herself to speak calmly. "Silver? Buried here?"

Grandmere broke out of her memories and stared at CoCo. "The Yankees found most of it anyway." She looked to the floor, the wistfulness covering her expression again. "Some say that money is hidden in these walls, but I've never seen proof of such."

"Money?" CoCo's heart sped into overdrive. The coin. The coin!

"Oh, *ma chère,* I think that's just a story. Legend. Something to tell the little ones." Grandmere smiled, years taken off her appearance by the gesture.

"You never told us that tale."

Her grandmother shrugged. "There were other things to occupy your minds." Her voice held a hint of grief.

The sentiment was contagious. CoCo's own heart twisted at the thought of the loss of her parents. She shoved the memories and pain from her mind. "People really believe there might be money hidden in this house?"

Grandmere laughed. "Most folk like to believe in treasures, pirates and hidden riches, *ma chère*." She lowered her brows. "Why all the questions?"

"Just wondering. Never heard the story before."

"Wasn't important." Her grandmother grabbed her book and struggled to her feet. "I think I'm going to retire."

CoCo pressed a kiss to her grandmother's parchment-paper skin. "Good night, Grandmere."

Her grandmother shuffled down the hall, her steps weighted with age. CoCo closed her eyes and offered up yet another prayer for the woman she dearly loved. Why couldn't Grandmere understand salvation was hers for the asking? Stubbornness, that's what stopped her.

A knock rapped on the door, causing CoCo to spin around. Who'd come calling this time of the evening? She cracked the door, her heart tripping as she peered at Luc Trahan's large form on her porch.

"CoCo, I need to talk to you." His voice still sent spirals of joy through her.

She toughened her tone. "I don't think that's such a good idea."

His eyes, the ones that always spoke directly to her heart, blinked. "Please, just hear me out. There's new information."

Curiosity always had been a weakness of hers. She pulled the door open. "Come on in, I guess."

He hovered at the threshold, his broad shoulders nearly touching both sides of the doorjamb. "Actually, I'd rather talk to you alone. Can we sit on the porch?"

She glanced over her shoulder. No sign that the knock had disrupted her grandmother or sister. "I guess so." CoCo flipped on the porch light before following him to the porch and taking a seat in one of the big rockers.

The rain had softened to a gentle mist, but had cooled the air. A breeze swept off the bayou, filling the wind with the smell of fresh soil. CoCo breathed in the scent, drawing strength from its familiarity.

Luc hunkered down in the rocker next to her. "I found a letter today. A letter to Beau."

She cocked her head. "I'm listening."

He paused, as if to garner fortitude. "From your lawyer."

Now *that* could be interesting. "About the eviction?"

"No. It was a personal letter to Beau, not even on Williams's law firm letterhead." He shifted in the rocker, the wood creaking under him. "It basically accused Beau of being involved with the death of his sister."

She couldn't stop the gasp from escaping. "What?"

"I know. The letter also said Dwayne Williams would prove it." He ran a hand over his dark hair.

"Oh, my." Things seemed to fall into place. The quick initial appointment...Dwayne's fast acceptance of the case...his comment about already having an investigation going on Beau. CoCo's hands shook when she lifted them to cover her mouth. "This puts a new spin on things, doesn't it?"

His eyes were soft as he studied her. "I took the letter to the sheriff tonight. He's going to talk to Williams in the morning."

Words failed her. The enormity of the situation hit her. "Could I have unwittingly been a party to Beau's murder?"

He grabbed her hand and squeezed it. "Of course not. No one is responsible for the actions of others."

She grazed her teeth over her bottom lip and met his stare. Hadn't he blamed her for his father's death, making her feel responsible for the actions of an animal? She jerked her hand from his and shot to her feet. "I need to call Dwayne—find out what's going on."

"No." He stood and laid a gentle hand on her shoulder. "You can't. You aren't supposed to know about the letter."

"He's my lawyer. I deserve to know what ulterior motives he had for taking my case." Another thought marched across her mind, filling her with trepidation. "Luc, he's my representation in the investigation of Beau's murder."

Luc pulled her to him, drawing her into a hug. She laid her head against his chest. Just for a moment, she'd let his strength feed her. She needed the support right now. Her world had just tilted on its axis, and she couldn't think straight.

"Bubba will find out more tomorrow." The words came not only from his mouth, but she could feel the rumble from his chest.

Along with the thudding of his heart. Hers matched his, beat for beat. What was she doing? This was Luc, the man who'd deserted her, blamed her for his father's death, walked away when she needed him most.

CoCo pushed herself free from his embrace and met his stare. His eyes held questions, but something else glimmered there. Something familiar…something recognizable…oh, she knew that look. Attraction. She swallowed and broke eye contact. One thing she didn't need was to get tangled up in an emotional tornado with Luc Trahan. Not again.

"Are you okay?" He moved toward her.

She backed up a step. "I'm just wondering what's going on." She pressed her lips together.

"I meant what I said before. I don't believe you or your family had anything to do with Grandfather's death. And about the diner—I'm sorry. I was way out of line." He let out a long sigh, as if it'd been pent-up too long. "I realize how innocent words and events can sometimes make you look guilty."

Could that be the voice of experience talking? "What do you mean?"

He stared out into the darkness. "I need to be honest with you, CoCo. I'm a suspect in my grandfather's murder."

TWELVE

Surprise stole her voice.

Luc turned to meet her gaze. "It's true. Bubba's running tests on that gun you found because one of Beau's shotguns is missing from the house. If it comes back registered to Grandfather…" He held her look.

Who in their right mind would think Luc could have anything to do with the murder of his own grandfather?

"Just because a gun is missing, doesn't mean you killed your grandfather, Luc."

"He and I argued the day he died. Seems that gives me motive." His voice cracked and his eyes glistened.

Her heart ached. She'd seen that same expression when his father had died. Now he looked broken in spirit. CoCo moved to him, taking both his hands in hers. "No one would believe you had anything to do with his death." She stared straight into the depths of his eyes. "No one."

He smiled crookedly. "*Merci* for the vote of confidence." He squeezed her hands. "See, we're both suspects because of appearances, not because of guilt."

She let him go and crossed her arms over her chest. "So, what do we do now?"

* * *

It took every ounce of self-control not to pull CoCo back
into his arms and hold her. Comfort for him, or her? He
couldn't tell, didn't really want to analyze it right now. All he
wanted was to feel the close connection with her again.

Lord, help me to open myself up to her.

"Luc?" Her tone matched the questioning look in her eyes.

Time to bite the bullet. "I really am sorry for stepping over
the line in the diner." He ran a hand over his wet hair. Why
was it so hard to speak his heart? "I want to keep working
together to find out who killed my grandfather."

Her almond-shaped eyes widened. The green flecks practically blazed.

Better think fast. Luc touched her hand but didn't hold it.
"We're both suspects, but we're both innocent. You know
how things can get twisted. I think we stand a better chance
of clearing our names if we keep working together."

He could almost see her mind whirring behind her eyes.
A wide range of emotions stomped across her face—shock,
disbelief and hesitation. He could understand each one of
them. Two years ago, he'd caused all those feelings to surface in her. Remorse nearly strangled him. *Lord, forgive me
for the pain I caused her. Forgive me for not staying to witness to her, to bring her into Your fold. Help me to do Your
will this time.*

"I don't know, Luc... I'm not sure this, uh, partnership is
working." Confusion clouded her words.

This time, he did take hold of her hand. "Just think about
it. We know this area and the people here as well as Bubba.
We've lived here all our lives." He gripped her hand tighter,
but she made no move to pull away. That was a good sign,
right? "You know most people don't want to get involved in

things, especially a murder. Between you and me, we have enough of a relationship with them to get them to open up."

She didn't respond. At least not verbally. But her eyes danced. He might have a chance to apologize for the past and maybe get a chance at a future. His pulse did a little tap-dance. Until the main hurdle between them slammed against his heart—her not being a Christian. He hardened his dream. No, they could work together to prove their innocence, but that was the extent of what their relationship could be. Still, he did owe her an apology for his past behavior.

God, in Your time, show me the way to apologize. Lord, please strengthen my resolve. I've always loved her, but I can't let myself be unequally yoked. You can help me lead her to You this time. Please, Lord, I want her to belong to You, even if she never loves me again.

"I suppose we could keep working together, just until the killer is found." Her voice lacked hope and enthusiasm. "That's it, Luc."

He'd take what he could get. Small steps. "Great." He released her hand. "Bubba said he'd let me know what Williams said, after he'd had a chance to speak with him tomorrow. I'll be sure and let you know."

"I'm going to call Dwayne myself tomorrow. See if he tells me something different than what he tells the sheriff."

"Good idea. We can compare notes." And maybe find the truth.

"Should I call you after I talk to Dwayne?"

And miss seeing her, even if she was off-limits to him? Then again, maybe he could reach her this time. God was, after all, still on the throne. "How about we meet at my place? We can go over everything we both know and see what we can come up with, and Felicia would love to see you."

"Okay." Her voice held a lilt of uncertainty.

He smiled, then planted a quick kiss against the crown of her head. Too bad he remembered all the times he'd done the same thing and she'd snaked an arm around his waist. Luc pulled back and rushed to the stairs. "I'll see you at the house around noon, yes?"

She nodded.

His heart thudded as he headed home. He spared a glance in his rearview mirror—CoCo stood on the porch, her stare following the taillights. An empty feeling filled him.

CoCo blew her bangs off her forehead and hauled in a deep breath before she climbed out of the Jeep. The morning sun blistered above, turning the previous day's moisture to steam. Heat hung in the air as thick as the fog over the bayou. She quickened her steps toward Dwayne Williams's office.

The flash of cool air hit her as soon as she entered the plush office, and she breathed a thankful sigh. The receptionist glanced up, her plastic smile already in place. "Good morning, Ms. LeBlanc. Did you have an appointment with Mr. Williams?"

"No, I was hoping he could fit me in."

"Have a seat, and I'll buzz him. He's already behind schedule this morning." She motioned CoCo toward the leather settee with one hand and lifted the phone receiver with the other.

CoCo studied the two pieces of art hanging on the walls. One, a photograph of New Orleans at night. Her stomach knotted. New Orleans, the city of her birth, where she'd lived happily with her parents until they'd died in a car accident. CoCo blinked and swallowed back her grief.

"He'll be with you shortly, Ms. LeBlanc."

CoCo nodded as she moved closer to the picture. She didn't miss the city as much as she missed her parents.

"CoCo, good morning."

She turned and accepted Dwayne's handshake. "I was wondering if I could have a few minutes."

"Certainly." He waved toward the hall. His steps thudded behind her as she made her way to the conference room.

"Please, sit down." He shut the door and half sat/half leaned against the table. "What can I do for you?"

She dropped into a chair and studied him. His tie sat neatly against his throat, his hair laid smooth against his head—no sign of distress. Maybe the sheriff hadn't spoken to him yet. This could be awkward. She cleared her throat. "I heard you had a personal vendetta against Beau Trahan."

The smile slid from his face, and he lowered himself into the chair catty-corner to hers. "The sheriff sure is one busy man. So, he called you, did he?"

"No, I haven't talked to him, but that doesn't matter. I just need to know if I've made a mistake in hiring you."

"Of course not!" Dwayne straightened his shoulders. "Let's just say I had some strong suspicions and wanted the truth."

Me, too. "The truth about what?"

He leaned back in the chair. "Remember I told you I came home for family issues?"

She nodded.

"My sister died of a drug overdose."

Sympathy welled inside her. "I'm so sorry." She laid a hand over his steepled ones. "What happened?"

He swallowed. "She quit her job at the casino, without a good reason. Went to work as a waitress at a local bar." Humiliation cloaked his features. "She began using drugs."

"I'm so sorry." *Lord, I don't know what to say.*

His gaze rested on her.

"Then…why would you think Beau was linked to her death? I mean, if she died of a drug overdose…"

"I have reason to believe Beau was the reason she quit."

"Oh." What could she say to that? Her heart raced. All sensible words escaped her. The tragedy of it all sat heavily in her chest. "Did you talk to Beau about your sister?"

He let out a snort. "I tried. Of course he denied the truth, but I knew better." His eyes hardened. "I could see it."

"You wrote him threatening letters?"

Shame popped into his eyes. "I'm not proud of my actions, but I was so upset, so outraged that he could get away with…well, I didn't use the best judgment."

"Did he reply?"

"At first, he didn't bother. Then, as I kept calling and writing, he threatened to have me arrested."

"For what?"

"Harassment. He said if I told anyone my theory, he'd sue me for slander, too." Dwayne shook his head. "His tone said he feared the truth being exposed."

CoCo considered his statement. From what she knew of Beau Trahan, how others saw him meant everything to him. Two of the reasons he'd been against her and Luc being together proved that. She, of course, was from the wrong side of the tracks, and her grandmother was the voodoo priestess of the parish.

"Dwayne, why would Beau get her to quit? That doesn't sound like him at all."

He leaned forward, as if to share a secret. "You know, at first I couldn't understand it myself. After we managed to get her belongings, I found her diary."

Now this was getting juicy.

"She wrote about being romantically involved with a man. She never wrote his name, always used a name in all caps like a code—SAM—but wrote his family would be mortified if they ever found out. That's why the relationship had to be kept secret. She met him through the casino."

CoCo sat back. "Are you implying the man, this SAM was Beau Trahan?"

He shrugged. "I don't know, but it sure looks funny."

Nothing made sense.

"She was only twenty-one years old. What if someone found out about them? He'd do anything to protect his *up-standing* name, right?"

He had a point. She mulled the scenario over. "So, he would encourage her to quit to protect his reputation?"

"Exactly."

If Beau was involved with her, what did that mean? She didn't know Beau well enough to consider the possibilities, and she was past making assumptions. But Luc would have some ideas. CoCo glanced at her watch—she had less than ten minutes to meet Luc. She pushed to her feet. "I don't know what to say, other than I'm very sorry for your loss."

"Do you still want me to represent you?" He stood.

"That depends. What did the sheriff say?"

"That he'd look into the situation." His eyes blinked with honesty. "Now I'm a suspect in Beau's murder, so I under-stand if you don't want to keep me on."

Chances were he was just as innocent as she and Luc. "No, I think I'll keep you." She smiled. "I hope the sheriff finds the truth about what happened to your sister. I'll be praying for you."

His smile reached his eyes. "*Merci.* I appreciate it."

CoCo moved to the door.

"I received notice that Beau's will is being read after his funeral Saturday. Once we know who owns your property, we can contact their attorney."

"Who" would probably be Luc. Since they'd called a truce, would he drop the eviction? What if Beau had left it to his brother? Justin would evict them just as Beau had intended. Unless…her grandmother did say he'd had a crush on her.

"I'll let you know as soon as the court notifies me."

"*Merci.* Again, I'm sorry for your loss." She slipped from the conference room, wiggled her fingers in a wave at the receptionist, then rushed to her Jeep.

She cranked the engine and flipped the air conditioner on high. How, exactly, was she going to tell Luc his grandfather may have been romantically involved with a woman so young, not to mention he might have had a hand in her death?

Dear God, what should I do? Luc's had so much pain inflicted on him and his family. He doesn't need more grief. Yet, I have to tell him the truth. We agreed to work together. CoCo let out a heavy sigh. *Just show me what You want me to do, God. I'll follow Your lead.*

Her cell phone chirped, startling her. CoCo dug in her purse until she found it. "Hello."

"Where are you?"

CoCo's heart skittered at his voice, his tone…everything. She laughed. "I'm on my way now. Be there in less than fifteen minutes."

"Good. I was scared you'd stand me up."

The urge to retort "like you did me at the altar" felt strong, but she bit her tongue. Maybe she needed to let go of the past, once and for all. "Nope. I'll see you soon."

Flipping the phone shut, CoCo waited for the traffic to clear so she could merge onto the street. She would forgive and forget. She would move on. She would be able to handle being around Luc again.

If only her heart would listen to her pep talk and not thud as if it had a mind of its own.

THIRTEEN

Focus, he had to focus. Luc stood leaning against the rail of the veranda as CoCo rushed toward him. Her curls looked springier than normal, falling around her shoulders like long, black spirals. The green in her eyes glimmered.

She smiled as she stepped onto the porch. "I talked with Dwayne."

All business, that was his CoCo. His? Whoa! She wasn't his anything anymore. He'd better control his emotions before he totally scared her off. "Want to come inside?"

Her gaze darted to the swing and she gripped her bottom lip between her teeth. "Why don't we sit out here? I'd rather not be overheard when we discuss this."

Uh-oh. He nodded and let her take a seat on the swing while he plopped into the adjacent chair. "What'd you find out?" He steeled himself for whatever she had to say.

"Well…" She hesitated, concern blinking in her eyes.

His stomach knotted. "Just tell me."

"Let me start at the beginning." She twisted her hands together in her lap and relayed all she'd learned that morning.

Luc had opened his mouth to voice his thoughts, when the disgusting implication slammed against his chest. Bayou life was complicated if nothing else.

"You think my grandfather was involved with this woman? He was old enough to be *her* grandfather." Disgust, or something akin to it, wrestled against logic.

"I didn't say that." CoCo shook her head slightly. "I'm just saying…isn't it possible that could have happened? Beau Trahan wouldn't have wanted such a thing to get out—it would have killed his reputation."

"No." He shoved to his feet and leaned over the railing, letting his mind wrap around the plausibility. "No, Grandfather wouldn't have done such a thing. He wouldn't have gotten involved with a woman so young." However, Grandfather *did* like trophy-type women. "He was too savvy for such a thing."

"You're sure?" Her voice was soft, but the accusation sat in her tone.

Could Grandfather have been involved with a woman the family didn't know about? A woman so young? Luc had never kept up with his grandfather's comings and goings, never felt there was a reason to do so. If anyone would know about Grandfather's social life, it would be his brother. He'd have to ask Uncle Justin. In the meantime….

"Luc, is it possible?"

He raked a hand over his face and turned to stare at her. "Anything's possible, but it's highly unlikely." He focused on her face, hoping she could read the honesty in his eyes. "Come on, CoCo, you knew Grandfather. If they were involved, and he asked her to quit, he'd have helped get a new job for her."

"Unless he didn't want anyone to connect them." She moved to stand beside him at the rail. "Didn't reputation mean everything to your grandfather, Luc? Everything?"

She was right—he knew it all too well, had it drilled into his head since he could walk. *The Trahan name is gold, boy, gold.*

Don't smear our good name. The lectures replayed in his mind, his grandfather's stern voice tormenting him from the grave.

"Luc?"

He jerked out of his reverie and sighed. "I suppose it could have happened. But Grandfather would have said something to *someone,* if only to brag about having such a young girl-friend. I'll ask Uncle Justin. Maybe I can get a glance at Grand-father's checkbook register that Bubba has. If he was seeing her and she was hurting for money, he would have helped her."

"Do you think Justin will tell you?"

"Why wouldn't he?" Luc peered into the depths of CoCo's eyes. Compassion and concern stared back at him. His heart thumped. No, he couldn't allow himself to get caught up in her again. She might have changed, but not in the really im-portant ways.

"I don't know." She shrugged, her hair flipping over her shoulder. Just enough to remind him of how it felt to dig his fingers into the silky thickness.

He steadied himself against the onslaught of memories. He'd sure been down memory lane a lot lately—Dad, Grand-father and CoCo. *Lord, what am I missing here? What are You trying to tell me?*

"I just think, maybe, Justin might not be as forthcoming as you'd hope."

"Why not? He's been a rock throughout this whole ordeal." Another memory rammed his mind—his uncle holding him in his arms and crying with him, Justin's sobs loud and un-abashed. "Just like he was when Dad died."

Her mouth tightened into a straight line.

Way to go, Luc, ol' boy. Size thirteen in the big, fat mouth. He laid his hand over hers atop the railing. "I didn't mean to imply anything other than Uncle Justin is the glue that holds this family together." As he said the words, he knew they were true but he'd never realized it before. Why hadn't he seen it wasn't Grandfather who kept the bonds tight, but Uncle Justin?

CoCo smiled. "I know." She slipped her hand out from under his and crossed her arms over her chest. "He just rubbed me wrong the day we found the gun."

"He was only trying to defend me."

"I know." She pinched her lips closed tight, as if afraid she'd say more.

He wanted to hear her opinion—her full opinion—but Felicia chose that moment to bump her wheelchair against the threshold. "CoCo!"

All smiles, CoCo turned and yanked open the screen door. "Felicia." She leaned over and hugged Luc's sister as soon as the wheelchair cleared the way. "I've missed you, *Boo*."

He cleared his throat. "CoCo, would you like a glass of lemonade or iced tea?"

Felicia turned to him, her blue eyes shooting icicles through his chest. "Luc Trahan, where have your manners gone? She's been here in this heat, and you're just now offering her a cold drink?" She rolled her eyes at CoCo's bemused smile. "You go on and fetch us a drink." Her mumbling continued under her breath.

Tossing CoCo a teasing wink, he headed into the kitchen.

"Sit down, sit down." Felicia motioned with one hand while she pushed the control of her wheelchair with the other. "It's been too long."

Easing onto the swing, CoCo felt the guilt push tears to her eyes. Once she'd called Felicia one of her nearest and dearest friends, but then Luc had dumped her…and she just couldn't face Felicia. The memories of the fun times shared together would have robbed every ounce of her hard-earned strength. The weeks—no, the months following the break-up had been unbearable. Only by turning to God and lying in His loving arms had she been able to pull herself up and keep going. One day at a time, that had been her mantra. Still was.

"I didn't mean that like I was condemning. I wasn't. I understood." Felicia's bright blue eyes glistened. "I didn't exactly come a-calling, either."

Gratitude filled CoCo's heart until she thought it would burst. "I know. It was just…hard."

"You're here now, yes?" Hope shone on Felicia's face brighter than the noonday sun.

The reason why she was here returned to her. "I'm so sorry about your grandfather."

"I should be upset. I should be grieving. I know this." She lowered her voice. "I'm not. I'm still mad."

"Mad? Whatever for?"

"Angry with Grandfather for what he did to Frank. Or, what he tried to do to our relationship. Mad at the way he blew up at Luc."

"That's natural."

"You think?" Felicia shook her head. "I'm not so sure." She leaned forward and whispered. "I think I'm glad he's dead."

How many times had she thought the exact same thing? CoCo grabbed Felicia's hand. "It's perfectly normal to feel that way, *Boo*. You're human. Allow yourself to feel—anger, sorrow, grief…whatever emotion hits you."

"You know this how?"

CoCo hauled in a deep breath. "Been there, done that, T-shirt doesn't fit anymore."

Felicia stared at her a long moment, then her infectious smile appeared. A single dimple dug itself into the corner of her mouth. "You're bad, CoCo LeBlanc." She laid her other hand over CoCo's and squeezed. "And I've missed you something terrible."

"I've missed you, too." Her voice cracked, but CoCo didn't care. She loved Felicia, and it was true—she *had* missed her.

"So, what've you been up to? Fill me in."

"Work's going well. Hopefully the Wetlands Preservation Center will approve my current grant and approve an increase. That'll give me the funds to expand my gator-tracking equipment."

"That's wonderful." Felicia grinned. "Are you dating anyone?"

Pain, as raw as that fateful night two years ago, swarmed across her chest. CoCo swallowed. "No."

"I'm sorry." Felicia's voice quivered and her eyes filled with tears. "Sometimes I can be thoughtless, yes?"

CoCo forced herself to smile. "It's okay. Tell me about this Frank character."

Felicia talked about her boyfriend, her eyes lighting up brighter than the stars over the bayou on a clear night. Had she been that enthralled? So in love with Luc that she'd practically glowed when she talked about him? Surely not. Then again, the ache of how she'd felt about him just about ripped her heart out…again.

Luc's sister wound down her relay of Frank's wonderful attributes and peered at CoCo with prying eyes. "Now, tell me what's new with you. Come on, girl, surely there's something important you can tell me, yes?"

"There *is* something important that's happened to me." CoCo smiled at her friend.

"What?" Felicia leaned forward, her sole focus on CoCo's face.

"About a year and a half ago, I accepted Christ."

Felicia's eyes went as wide as a gator's jaw. "Well, praise God!" She laughed. "I must say, I prayed for your salvation daily."

CoCo leaned over and hugged Felicia. "And I thank you for each and every prayer you ever sent to the throne on my behalf," she whispered before pulling back.

"You've told Luc, yes?"

Shaking her head, CoCo lowered her gaze. "It doesn't matter."

"You haven't let Luc know? Oh, CoCo. Being a Christian will make all the difference in the world to Luc. You know his biggest struggle was that you were a…"

CoCo laughed at the horrified expression on her friend's face. "You can say it, a voodoo priestess."

Felicia covered her mouth with her hand. "I did it again. I'm such a *cooyon*. I'm sorry."

"Don't be. I was." She let out a sigh. "If I could do it all again, I'd never have turned to voodoo. I would have listened to Luc. I would have run to Jesus a lot earlier than I did."

"What about your family? Your grandmother?"

CoCo laughed, but the vibration came out flat. "She's still the same old Grandmere. I just keep praying for her." She stopped smiling. "And Tara, too."

"Tara? What's wrong with her?"

"When I accepted Jesus, I told Grandmere I wouldn't follow in her footsteps of learning her ways anymore." CoCo swallowed back the guilt. "Since Alyssa had already moved out, Grandmere began teaching Tara."

"Oh, no. How horrible."

"It's a mess." The smile she forced nearly hurt. "I just don't understand why God won't help them see the light."

"One thing you'll have to learn, my friend, is that salvation is all in God's timing, not ours, yes?"

How had this woman become wise beyond her years? "I know, but it's hard. I mean, it happened to me almost in a flash. I just...*knew,* ya know?"

"I do. Luc and I had been praying for your salvation for a long, long time. It may have happened fast to you, but it was slow for us. Still, it was perfect—it was God's timing."

Why couldn't she just accept that? "I just don't have much patience. I want Grandmere and Tara to know this feeling."

"That's natural. We want to share the happiness our loving God gives us, yes?" She cocked her head to one side. "Thus the term *witnessing,* spreading the Good News."

CoCo laughed. "I guess I never thought about it that way."

A breeze tiptoed over the veranda, carrying the scent of magnolias. CoCo inhaled deep. It'd been a long time since she'd sat with Luc's sister, chatting and enjoying her company.

"CoCo, you're wrong if you think telling Luc won't make a difference." Felicia's tone was somber.

"I don't think so. Back then, the main thing that split us apart was his belief I defended something that killed his father." CoCo tossed a weak smile to Felicia. "Killed your father."

"I think that's plain silly. Daddy's death tormented Luc, all of us, but he didn't blame you."

"Yes, he did. He might not have told you that, but he told me. Looked me right in the eye and said if I hadn't been interacting with the gators in that part of the bayou, his father would still be alive." The words cut to the bone to this day.

"Oh, CoCo. That was just his grief talking."

She pushed aside the tears. "No, he meant it, Fel. Trust me, one thing I do know about your brother is he says what he means."

"Now…so much time has passed. He looks at it logically. He knows you weren't to blame at all."

"What's done is done." If only her heart would believe that.

"It's not too late. You can tell him you're a Christian now. It'll make a difference. I'm positive." Such hope sparkled in Felicia's face.

CoCo hated to let her friend down. The truth, no matter what, was that Luc Trahan and CoCo LeBlanc would never have another chance. She couldn't trust him with her heart again.

"Believe me, I know my brother better than most anyone else. Besides you."

"I wish that were true, I really do. Telling Luc is a moot point. Too much water under the bridge and all that."

"I think you're wrong. I think this is exactly the thing Luc needs to hear."

"No." The last thing she needed right now was for Felicia to play matchmaker. "Please, I beg of you, don't tell Luc. Please."

Felicia's gaze darted past her. CoCo shifted in her seat to see what had caused the mortified expression to cross her friend's face.

She froze.

Luc's hot stare pinned her to the seat.

"Don't tell me what?"

FOURTEEN

The uneasy feeling settled across Luc's shoulders again. They'd just begun to build a working relationship, and already CoCo kept secrets from him. He shook his head and glared at her. "CoCo, what don't you want Felicia to tell me?"

Her eyes, those sable brown expressive eyes that haunted him in his dreams, blinked. "It has nothing to do with the investigation. It's private."

"Private? Yet you told my sister?" He crossed his arms over his chest.

"Luc," Felicia interrupted, "let it go."

"I heard you say that whatever it is, it's just what I need to hear." He narrowed his eyes at CoCo. "So, I'm going to ask you again…what aren't you telling me?"

The mistrust could be cut with a knife.

She huffed to her feet. "It was a mistake to come here, to even think you and I could work together on the same side of an issue." CoCo bent and gave Felicia a hug. "I'll call you later, Fel." With a returning stony glare, she pushed past Luc and bounded down the stairs.

He started to call after her, but she jumped into her Jeep, revved the engine and peeled out of the driveway before he gathered his thoughts. He could only stand there staring at the dust clouds chasing her vehicle.

"Way to go, Ace. Run her off right after you finally get her here." Felicia's harsh voice broke through his thoughts.

Luc wheeled around and faced her. "What're you talking about? You know how I feel about keeping secrets. Especially with CoCo." He shook his head. "We were supposed to be working together."

"You're my brother, and I love you dearly, but sometimes, Luc, you're just a man."

"She's the one keeping secrets, not me."

His little sister crossed her arms over her chest and nailed him with a piercing stare. "Oh, really? I suppose you've told her that you didn't mean to blame her for Daddy's death? You've done that, right?"

Her words merged with his own conscience and he found his tongue tied in knots.

"I didn't think so." Felicia let out a sigh and softened her tone. "Luc, when are you going to learn that communication is key?"

He peered into his sister's soft eyes. When did she grow up on him and become so knowledgeable in the matters of relationships? She and Frank must be moving toward the happily-ever-after scene. His heart longed for a woman by his side, a home to share, children to enjoy, but the woman in his dreams was CoCo. Always CoCo.

Luc groaned and lowered himself into a porch chair. "Felicia, I don't know what's wrong with me."

"You're in love with her—always have been, yes?"

Since he'd just harped on the whole honesty thing… He sucked in a breath and exhaled slowly before dropping his head into his hands. "I am."

"Then why aren't you going after her, *cooyon?*"

He jerked his head to stare into his sister's eyes. "Even though I love her, it can never work between us. We never had a chance."

"Why?" The light in her eyes flickered.

"Number one, because we have too much in our history. Dad's death…let's just say I took things out on CoCo that I shouldn't have. It's too late to say I'm sorry."

"It's never too late to offer a heartfelt apology, Luc."

Did she have to echo the Holy Spirit nudging against his heart? "You're right. I do owe her one for the accusations I tossed at her."

"And?"

"And what?"

"You said 'number one' was how you'd treated her after Daddy's death, yes? What else is keeping you two apart?"

Why did she ask the question? She knew the reason. "Felicia, I know you mean well and all, but her not being saved and being a voodoo…a person who practices voo—"

"Voodoo priestess. It's okay to say it." A smile crept into her face.

"Whatever." CoCo's unbelief and lack of salvation still etched deep cuts in his heart. Maybe if he'd not broken up with her, he could have witnessed more. Could have done more to show her the path to God.

"What's your point, Luc?"

He shook himself out of the guilt. "I can't do it again, *Boo.* I just can't let myself love her when I know it's not meant to be."

"If you love her, and I'm pretty certain she still loves you, how can you know it's not meant to be?"

"Felicia." He fought to keep his tone void of the anguish

ripping his heart in two. "It's not meant to be because it's not ordained by God."

"My, my, my, I'm impressed. You know the will of God now?"

He clenched his jaw. "You know what I mean. I can't love someone and make a life with her if I won't see her in heaven."

"And you know for a fact she won't be in heaven?"

Why would his sister do this to him? Couldn't she sense the pain he endured? "I know enough to realize I'm not cut out to be unequally yoked." That fact alone is what caused loneliness to wake him in the middle of the night.

"What if you weren't unequally yoked?" She pressed on, disregarding his tone to end the discussion.

"We are. She's a voodoo priestess and I love Jesus. Enough said."

"You sure about that, Luc?" Her tone came out sharp.

He stared at her, reading the mischievousness flashing in her eyes. What did she know? Wait a minute. CoCo had been confiding in her. Could it be? "Felicia, are you trying to tell me something?"

His sister laughed and nodded. "I'm just suggesting you talk with her."

"Has she ac—"

Felicia waved him off. She pulled open the screen door before glancing over her shoulder. "If you want any more information, you should talk to CoCo. Some things, well, some secrets are meant to be shared."

The door clanked shut behind her. The motorized wheelchair hummed. Luc ignored all the noises. Had Felicia just told him in a roundabout way that CoCo had accepted Christ?

Reaching into his pocket, he withdrew his keys. His feet barely touched the wooden stairs as he hurried toward the SUV. If what Felicia hinted at was true, they had a chance. A real chance. Hope pushed him into the vehicle and down the road. He'd find CoCo. He'd get answers. And then he'd see where his heart sat.

"*Cooyon!* The man is nothing more than an infuriating *cooyon.* I should have known better," CoCo muttered under her breath as she marched up her driveway. Why hadn't she just told him she was a Christian? *Because then there'd be nothing keeping him from pursuing me.* If she were honest with herself, she'd admit she was scared. Hopelessly scared that if Luc knew, he still might reject her. It smashed her heart into smithereens.

She started for the stairs, then stopped. No sense letting Grandmere and Tara see her so agitated. That wouldn't speak well of her faith or her mental state.

Turning, she headed toward the Confederate rosebush, its petals perky under the midday hot sun. She touched a flower, the satiny finish warm on her fingers. CoCo pushed aside the bottom leaves, staring at the ground. No metal glittered. No coin was exposed by the recent rains.

She let out a sigh and straightened. Her gaze drifted over the yard. Nothing glimmered under the sun's penetrating rays. A fluke, that's what it was. She wondered who the gentleman who found the other coin recently was, where he lived. Maybe it if was close to her place… Determined to find the answer to at least one of the problems clogging her mind, CoCo strode to the backyard. She couldn't help but smile as she glanced at the kitchen doorframe. The blue paint was fresh, not peeling and chipping like the rest of the house. Grandmere must have called Toby recently. The smile turned to a frown. Blue—to keep the evil spirits away.

Stomping up the stairs helped spend her frustration. And anger. And hurt. That's what was the worst of it all. Luc's lack of trust in her simply hurt. Not that she could blame him, really. After all, she'd turned a deaf ear to him for two years. Two years, he'd tried to lead her to God, tried to show her the path to salvation. What had she done? Laughed in his face and continued to blaspheme with voodoo.

"What's all that ruckus about, *ma chère?* You're making enough noise to raise the dead." Grandmere met her at the kitchen door. "And why are you coming in the back way?"

"I just felt like it." She jerked out a chair. It scraped against the floor, sounding like someone dragging fingernails down a chalkboard.

"Child, the heat has you as prickly as a palm this afternoon." Her grandmother poured tea over a glass of ice and passed it to her. "Cool off a spell."

Spells. *Cunjas.* Hexes. *Gris-gris.* She wanted to run away from it all. How had she ever been so blind? "I'm sorry, Grandmere. Just having a lousy day."

Her grandmother lowered herself into a chair opposite CoCo. "What's on your mind, *cher?*"

"You knew Beau Trahan, right?"

"I suppose. Why?"

"Do you think he would have gotten involved with a girl younger than his grandson?"

Grandmere ran an absentminded finger over the old kitchen table. "Beau Trahan always did have a fondness for the younger ladies."

"That's what I thought."

"Why're you asking?"

CoCo shrugged. Now wasn't a good time for a replay of the debate she'd had with Luc. "Just something I heard."

"Now, Justin…" Grandmere chuckled under her breath. "That man would chase anything in a skirt that moved. Old, young, it didn't matter."

"Grandmere!"

"It's a fact, *cher.* He never dated the same woman more than a couple of times."

"He never wanted to marry and have a family of his own?"

"That's not for me to say."

That's right. He had a crush on her grandmother. CoCo shivered.

"Cooling off?"

"Yeah." She stood and pushed the chair under the table, quieter this time. "I think I'm going to run out to the bayou for a while."

"Uh-oh." Grandmere struggled to her feet.

"What's that supposed to mean?"

"Whenever you run to your boat and go playing in the bayou, that means something's stuck in your craw." She laid a gnarled hand on CoCo's shoulder. "I'm here if you want to talk about it later, *ma chère.*"

"*Merci.* I appreciate it." She cast a smile at her grandmother before slipping back out the kitchen door.

Murder, confederate coins, strange relationships…and Luc. So many things occupied her thoughts, yet led to nothing but more questions. She chewed her lip and kept walking.

CoCo rounded the house, making a beeline to her airboat. A squeal of brakes brought her up short. She shielded her eyes with her hand, then her stomach and heart collided.

Luc.

Anger temporarily forgotten, she marveled that he'd come

after her. To…wait, what *was* he here for? Her temper returned as she made quick strides to face him as soon as he stepped on the ground. "What're you doing here?"

"I came to apologize. I had no right to jump to the wrong conclusion and try to demand something from you."

His tone and words were so sincere… No, he had to be doing all this to find out what she'd kept secret. "*Merci* for coming all this way to tell me that." She deliberately set her chin.

"CoCo…"

Now his voice took on the deep baritone which once made her heart flutter. Once? Who was she kidding? His voice still had that effect on her. She lifted her gaze to meet his stare. Mistake. Big mistake. The depth of his feelings flickered in those hazel orbs.

She. Could. Not. Trust. Him.

She took a step backward.

"I need to apologize for so much more."

"Like?" She hated that her voice cracked on a single word.

He moved closer, invading her personal space. Yet, she didn't step back. The spicy scent of his cologne hit her. So familiar, so comforting, so safe. She almost sighed, but dared not risk it.

"CoCo, I'm sorry I accused you of having anything to do with my father's death. And my grandfather's. It was an accident, and I was way out of line the way I spoke to you, treated you."

Her hands trembled. How many nights had she awoken with the dream of this exact moment fresh in her mind? Now that the moment was upon her, she couldn't think of one intelligent thing to say. "Luc, you need to understand how important my job is to me. Working to protect the wildlife of the bayou is part of who I am, not just what I do."

His gaze still focused on her, Luc closed the remaining distance between them and laid a hand on her shoulder. "I'm sorry. I was a jerk. My behavior was unforgivable."

She stiffened her back. "Let's just forget it and move on." She needed to restore balance, give herself a chance to regain her composure. "I'm about to make a run. Wanna come along?"

FIFTEEN

The airboat drifted on the bayou. Luc felt surprisingly calm.

"I wonder who killed your grandfather." CoCo spoke the words softly, but they proved to him their thoughts were on the same wavelength. It was almost scary how she could always pick up on his emotions.

"You say you believe Dwayne Williams wouldn't have. That he'd intended to get revenge with my grandfather by exposing him, yes?"

She made another entry in her log. "I know it's hard to hear, but I really believe him. I think he wanted to publicly bring Beau down a couple of notches, not murder him."

"Okay. That rules him out."

"You said there's no way Frank would have killed him because it would hurt Felicia."

"Right." He tightened his hold on the seat as she fired up the fan. "That brings us back at square one—your family and me as primary suspects."

"There has to be someone we're missing. Someone with an axe to grind."

"As Uncle Justin said, who didn't want Grandfather dead?"

"I don't know." CoCo ran her fingers through her hair. The simple gesture made him clench and unclench his fists. She steered the boat toward the LeBlanc plantation. "There has to be someone who threatened him in some way."

She expertly banked the boat and hopped to the ground.

Luc pushed to his feet, energy pumping through his muscles. "The casino sent over some boxes of Grandfather's personal belongings. Why don't we go through them? Maybe we'll find something there."

"That's a good idea. It can't hurt." She tied her boat around a stump, then led the way to the house.

"Allons."

"Let me tell Grandmere I'm heading out." She pushed open the door, leaving him alone on the porch.

He took note of the paint flecking off the wood. The place needed some heavy repair work, he thought as he glanced over the loose boards and skewed gutters. With precise movements, Luc moved to the side of the house and gripped one of the swaying gutters. Tall enough to reach, he tried to pop it back into place.

It didn't hold.

With more strength, he tried again. The gutter clattered against the side of the house. Then two wood planks fell, hitting the ground with a plunk. Followed by tings as bits of metal hit the porch rail on their descent.

"What're you doing?" CoCo pulled the door closed behind her. Her eyes widened as she strode to join him.

He faced her, watching the emotions cross her eyes. "I noticed the gutter hanging, so I tried to snap it back in place. I'm sorry, it pulled out a couple of boards, too. I'll fix it this weekend for you."

She didn't answer. Her gaze wasn't even focused on him. She stared over the rail to the ground below.

He looked to see what caused her face to pale so. And gawked.

Old coins, about six to ten of them, littered the dry and dying grass.

Jerking his gaze back to her face, he gently touched her arm. "CoCo?"

"Confederate coins," she whispered.

"What?"

She didn't answer. Instead, she bolted off the porch and knelt in the grass. It crunched under her knees. She grabbed the coins and inspected them. "All of them. Confederate coins."

Luc joined her. "What're you talking about?"

She stood and held out a coin. "They're Confederate coins. Valuable."

He flipped one over in his palm and ran a finger over the raised design. Sure, he'd seen pictures of them in books, but never personally. They had to be fakes. "They're probably replicas."

"They aren't."

"Honey," he said as he handed her back the coin. "I know it's nice to think we've found a fortune in our own yard, literally, but that rarely happens."

"I have." She stared at him, excitement lighting her face. "I know. I found one under the rosebush and thought the same thing—it's fake. I took it to a coin appraiser just to prove to myself I wasn't caught in silly dreams. I was wrong. It was…is…a genuine Confederate restrike coin."

"Are you sure these are just like the one you found?"

She studied them for a few seconds, before meeting his gaze. "Yes. I'm positive they're exactly like the other one."

"Can I see it? The one you had appraised?" Maybe there was some minor difference, something to set them apart.

"I put it in a safety deposit box, per the appraiser's suggestion."

"Smart thinking." That still didn't offer any explanation.

"Any idea how these got behind those planks of wood?" He glanced up at the side of the house, but couldn't make out anything unusual from where they'd fallen.

"Grandmere says during the Civil War several families hid their silver and money in the house and buried them in the yard."

"Here?"

"She said several families hid out here from the Yankees."

The magnitude of the find hiked his pulse. "Are there more?"

"I don't know. I looked over the yard briefly, but didn't find any." She glanced at the fallen planks. "I would've never thought to look behind the wood."

"So, there could be more?"

"I suppose." She narrowed her eyes as she studied him. "We're not tearing apart my house to see if there are more coins hidden."

"I didn't say that." A fortune could be within these very walls. A fortune that could belong to his family, if Beau really had held the deed. Money for Felicia to get the medical treatments Frank told her about. For his mother, to build herself a life. As long as he was a suspect, anything his grandfather had left him would be tied up in court for a long time. Did Grandfather leave anything to Felicia or his mother? His grandfather had never been keen on giving a woman anything when a man could hold the purse strings and control. Luc tightened his lips into a thin line. According to the Louisiana police, if anyone in the will is a suspect, the settling of the estate can be held up for quite some time, which would put the Trahans in a financial bind, as their grandfather was the sole supporter of Felicia and her mother.

CoCo continued to scrutinize him with those deeply dark eyes. "You thought about it, didn't you?"

Not even an hour back on even footing, and she could

already read his mind again. He hung his head. "It crossed my mind, yes."

Her penetrating glare brought his head up.

"It also crossed your mind that if my grandfather signed over the deed of this house to your grandfather, these coins might belong to you, yes?"

Guilty as charged. Did her voodoo training give her the ability to read his thoughts? "I would never d—"

"Has it ever occurred to you that if my grandfather did sign over this house, maybe Beau tricked him in some way?"

"What? Grandfather was a shrewd businessman. He wouldn't have sunk to something so underhanded."

"Are you certain about that, Luc? Really positive?"

There were a lot of things about his grandfather he didn't know, Luc realized. He swallowed hard, keeping his mouth closed.

CoCo rested a hand against his forearm. "Luc, we're working together. I'll add these coins to the safety deposit box." She let out a heavy sigh. "If, and that's a big if, the court says you own this house, then we'll discuss the coins."

"I—"

"Technically, your family never lived here, never had possession of the house. So, I think all the contents would belong to my family."

She had a point. But courts and lawsuits? No, that wasn't what he wanted. Still, he couldn't disregard his sister's very real medical needs, either.

"Luc." Her voice came out so wistful it tugged on his heartstrings. "I don't want to be at odds with you anymore. It's been a hard two years for me." Her eyes glistened with unshed tears. "I can't do it again. I can't." Her words were barely a whisper.

He pulled her into his arms, trying to give her as much

comfort as humanly possible. "Why don't we wait and face that obstacle when we have to?"

She pushed away from him, reestablishing distance between them. "Let's go look at Beau's things."

CoCo climbed out of the vehicle, smiling at Luc. Her emotions were in a tangle, but she couldn't take time to analyze them. The raging confusion about the man she walked alongside pushed her determination into full swing. If they could just figure out who'd killed Beau, she wouldn't have to communicate with Luc every single day, and maybe she could finally put the past to rest.

"Mom said she had the boxes put in the study." He pushed the door open and motioned her inside. "Do you want something to eat or drink before we get started?"

She glanced at her watch—1:50, and she hadn't eaten since breakfast. "I could use a little something."

He smiled, so warm and gentle that her heart cracked. "I'll see if Mom can throw some sandwiches together." Luc moved toward the door. "You still like ham and cheese with lots of mayo?"

"Dripping is better."

Chuckling, Luc headed down the hall. A soft whistling of a popular Zydeco beat reached her ears. CoCo wrapped her arms around herself. She'd missed hearing Luc's music.

"So, he brought you back, yes?"

CoCo glanced to the doorway and found Felicia there, her face wreathed in a silly grin. "Yeah, he brought me back. We're going to go through your grandfather's belongings to see if we can find anything."

Felicia moved into the room and clucked her tongue. "And that's it?"

"That's it."

Felicia's smile widened, if that was possible. "And you two are…?"

"Are trying to figure out who killed your grandfather."

The younger woman's face drew somber. "I can't believe you and Luc are on the suspect list. That's just ridiculous."

Loyalty. Such a rare character trait these days. "I know. We're hoping to find something in these boxes." CoCo waved her hand over the four cardboard boxes stacked neatly in the corner of the room.

"What're we waiting for?" Felicia wheeled herself nearer to the stack.

"You don't have to do this, Fel." Luc's little sister could be described as emotional at best. "Luc and I will handle it. He's just grabbing us some sandwiches first."

"I'm not helpless, even if I am in this wheelchair."

Horrors upon horrors. CoCo drew herself up. "I didn't mean it that way."

Felicia sighed. "I know, and I'm sorry for being snappy. I just want to help. To do something, anything."

Understanding Felicia's need to be a part, CoCo nodded and lifted the first box from the top of the stack. She set it on the floor before reaching for the next, which she set on the chair beside Felicia. "How about you take this one, and I'll start on that?"

Two sandwiches, three boxes and seventeen paper cuts later they'd found nothing useful. Not one single clue.

CoCo stood and stretched, lifting her arms well above her head. With an absentminded hand, she rubbed at the knots in her neck. Luc moved behind her. His strong hands pushed hers out of the way and kneaded the bunched muscles. CoCo sighed and closed her eyes.

"Now, that's what I like to see."

CoCo snapped her eyes open and stared at Felicia, who grinned like the cat caught in the cream. "What?"

"You two. Together. Knowing what each other needs."

Heat fanned CoCo's face and she dropped her gaze.

"She's just being sassy because Frank proposed," Luc said before planting a peck on the nape of CoCo's neck.

She sucked in air and moved out of range of his touch. How could a single kiss send her heart into such a tizzy? Hadn't she made a vow not to let him get under her skin again? She needed to solve this murder mystery and get him out of her daily life before she took total leave of her senses.

"That's right. I know true love when I see it, yes?" Felicia winked at CoCo before turning a cocky expression toward her brother.

"Brat." CoCo laughed and winked back at her friend, her heart still racing. "Have you set a date yet?"

"Of course not! He hasn't even given me a proper ring." Felicia giggled.

Luc clapped his hands together. "Last box, y'all, let's knock it out."

CoCo squeezed in between brother and sister, drawing from their teasing and obvious love for one another. She missed that terribly with Tara and Alyssa. If only Tara would listen to reason. And if Alyssa wasn't so…well, Alyssa.

"Oh, my."

Jerking her gaze to Felicia, CoCo watched her friend's face pale as she read a piece of paper.

"What is it?" Luc asked, but leaned behind CoCo to read over his sister's shoulder.

"A letter. I can't believe this."

CoCo strained for a better view. The letter was typed on regular copy paper, but the creases were smudged, indicating that it'd been folded and unfolded several times over.

Beau Trahan,

Does your hypocrisy know no bounds? You claim to be a supporter of all races, yet members of your own family were involved with the KKK. Proof of your brother's rogue Klan activities were in the possession of Marcel LeBlanc, a fellow brother of the Klan. The evidence still exists. I will find it, and expose you for the fake you are. To prove I know the evidence is there, check out the etching at the bottom. Recognize this as identical to the one found there, Beau? I think you'll discover there are many things hiding in the LeBlanc house along with the coins. Your reign of dominance is over. I'll tell everyone about you, and your family. Let's see if you can save your precious name this time.

CoCo took note of the header—no date and no indication of the sender. There was no closing, no signature. Most importantly, she recognized the pencil etching in the bottom right hand corner.

A Confederate coin.

Just like the ones she'd found at her homestead. Just like the one the appraiser told her the Klan stockpiled.

Could it be?

SIXTEEN

Considering they'd found more Confederate coins mere hours ago, the context of the letter couldn't be more timely. Coincidence? No, Luc knew better. God's fingerprints were all over the situation. Now he needed to figure out what to do. He studied CoCo. "Had my grandfather been to your house recently? Where he could have found a coin?"

"Not that I'm aware. Just when he served that stupid eviction notice." She chewed her bottom lip, a sure sign her mind was working overtime.

Luc read the note again. "This letter implies Grandfather knew the coins were in your house." He raked his hand over his face. "How else could he have known? Maybe he didn't."

CoCo's mouth hung slack as she read the letter again, then lifted her gaze to his. Her eyes were bright, as if a light had come on behind them. "The coin appraiser told me a gentleman had been in the past month with a genuine Confederate coin. It was probably Beau." She snapped her fingers. "Somehow he knew. *That's* why he served the eviction notice. He wanted the coins. If the appraiser told him about the connection between the Klan and the coins, well, that would be even more reason for Beau to want my house."

Surely his grandfather wouldn't stoop so low. Then

again… "We don't know that. This letter could have been sent a long time ago."

CoCo pulled the paper from Felicia's slack hands and scanned it yet a third time. "No date." She straightened. "Don't you see, Luc? He wanted the coins. That's why he served the eviction notice now and not years ago." CoCo waved the letter. "And he wanted to find whatever evidence this person implies is hidden in my house. The one that would defame his reputation."

Felicia finally found her voice. "Would one of y'all please explain what's going on here?"

Luc tapped the letter. "That image right there is of a Confederate coin. Someone laid this paper over a coin and rubbed the paper with a pencil, thus making a copy etching here to prove they knew the coins were in CoCo's house. We think more are hidden there." He pinched the bridge of his nose. "This is proof that someone knew the coins were in the LeBlanc house, so it stands to reason they'd know of other things, this so-called evidence that would hurt Grandfather, being hidden there as well." He pierced CoCo with a hard stare.

"You can't think I would send Beau this letter!" The green flecks of her eyes flashed with anger.

The memory of his accusing her of being a party to his father's death, Grandfather's murder, flashed against his mind. "I'm not saying that. How would someone know what's hidden in your house?"

"I don't know." She crossed her arms over her chest. "I can assure you that no one in my family would have written Beau that letter. It implicates my own grandfather of being in the Klan. Why would we want that exposed? Not that I believe it's true for a minute."

"This letter could be from when Grandfather was in office," Luc said.

"I don't think so." CoCo ran a finger along the crease. "This was opened and folded back several times over. If your grandfather had it for that long a time, the creases would've already split." She laid the letter in Felicia's lap and stared directly into Luc's eyes. "Besides, the paper's still crisp. And think about it—this is a perfect reason why Beau served us an eviction notice. He'd recently been told about the connection between the coins and the KKK."

"I don't understand," Felicia said.

"Follow me for a minute, okay?" CoCo stood and paced. "Someone found the coins and this supposed evidence in my house. Beau must have known the coins were there. I'm thinking he probably found out about them and then started legal proceedings to serve us the eviction notice. When he got this letter, with this rubbing of the Confederate coin, it was proof someone else knew things are hidden in my house." She turned and stopped. "If they knew about the coins, then Beau would probably assume the evidence was also legitimate."

"What does this have to do with Grandfather's murder?" Felicia asked.

Luc raked a hand over his face. "It's possible that whoever wrote this letter might have killed Grandfather."

"Whatever for?" Felicia paled.

CoCo laid a hand on her shoulder. "What if Beau found out who'd written this letter and confronted him?"

Both Felicia and Luc chuckled. Luc shook his head. "Come on, CoCo. Grandfather would never resort to violence. You know that. He'd have turned them in to the police amid quite a fanfare where he'd look like a hero, but never would he have gotten into a physical confrontation. His years in politics taught him well."

"What if the writer planned on blackmailing Beau with whatever he'd supposedly found in my house and then found out that Beau was trying to take possession of my place? That'd be motive to kill your grandfather. Not getting the evidence to be able to blackmail him."

Felicia shook her head. "Grandfather would never pay a blackmailer. Ever." She waved a thin arm through the air. "Besides, this accusation of Klan activity is so long ago. It wouldn't have made that much of a difference to Grandfather."

Felicia stared at CoCo. "Who else has access to your house?"

"Me, Grandmere, Tara and Alyssa." She tapped her finger against her bottom lip. "A young grandson of a neighbor who does odd jobs for Grandmere. One of Tara's friends, maybe."

"About as many people who had access to Grandfather's gun cabinet," Luc said with a sigh.

"I say we first have to figure out if this letter is recent or not, yes?" Felicia asked.

"Maybe Bubba can run some tests and determine its age. We need to turn it in to him anyway, as evidence or something." Luc took the letter, read it a final time, then folded it again. He glanced at his watch. "If we hurry, we can get it to his office before he leaves."

"Allons." CoCo gave Felicia a quick hug.

"Let me know what the sheriff says," Felicia hollered behind them.

Luc opened the door for CoCo. He slipped behind the steering wheel of the SUV. "I hope he's still there. It is Friday."

"Me, too." CoCo blew her bangs off her forehead and stared out the window.

He punched the accelerator and headed down the driveway. Gravel spun and popped against the undercarriage with little pings.

"Do you have any clue who could have written that letter?" She peered back at him.

"I can't even begin to imagine."

The tires hit the blacktop, zinging in the heat. The sun teased the tips of the trees. All too soon, July would fade in the Louisiana heat and August would be upon them.

CoCo licked her lips. "He never said anything about this letter to you?"

"Not a single word." He gripped the steering wheel tighter, despite feeling as if the leather would melt against his hands. "You know, Grandfather didn't actually confide in me much, now that I think about it." Much? How about never? With all that had been uncovered, Luc couldn't help but replay every conversation he'd shared with his grandfather. Upon doing so, he realized Grandfather hadn't ever, not once, opened up to him. So much for strong family ties.

"Let me guess, he confided in Justin."

He cut his gaze to her, held her stare for a moment, then focused back on the road. "They are brothers, you know."

She let out a long sigh. "I know. I just don't think your uncle likes me very much."

"He likes you. He never said anything against you while we were…"

"Together?"

"Yes, together."

Her laughter filled the vehicle and set his heart on fire. "I wouldn't think he would. That would be bad, now wouldn't it?"

He joined her with a chuckle of his own. "Shows how much you know about Uncle Justin. Trust me, if he didn't like you, he'd have let me hear about it."

"Really?" Her laughter ceased.

Luc felt her stare before he turned to meet it. "Yeah. He's pretty outspoken about his likes and dislikes."

"Oh." She leaned her head against the headrest, her hair splaying over the tan leather.

Here she sat beside him, and he had to force himself to concentrate on driving. How long had he dreamed of having her back at his side? He needed to figure out a way that they could prove their innocence.

She sat upright and dug around in her purse. "Can you run me by the post office right quick? I need to mail this." She waved a large envelope.

"If it's that important, of course."

"It's my grant proposal to the Center."

His mouth went dry.

"Look, I know this is a sore subject with you, Luc, but it's important to me. It's who I am."

She was right—it was who she was. "I know." He flipped on the blinker to turn in to the post office.

"Merci," she all but whispered.

They made the rest of the drive in a comfortable silence. Luc's every sense was acutely aware of CoCo—her breathing pattern, her nervous gesture of chewing her bottom lip, her wiping her palms against her shorts. If he tried hard enough, he could even pick up the sweet smell of coconuts clinging to her hair. He slammed the vehicle into Park with a jerk.

She snapped to look at him. "Something wrong?"

"Just ready to get some answers," he said and stepped from the vehicle.

Once again his luck held. Bubba's cruiser sat outside.

He opened her door and helped her out, then kept his hand on the small of her back as he led her into the sheriff's office. The air-conditioning felt nice against his skin, which heated from the contact with CoCo's back.

Missy smiled when he leaned over the counter. Then her

gaze drifted to CoCo standing close by his side. Missy's smile slipped. "What can I help you two with?" Her stare darted between them.

"We need to see the sheriff."

"I see." She lifted the receiver to her ear and whispered into it, all the while staring at CoCo as if she had a piece of cabbage stuck in her teeth. Missy let the phone drop back on its cradle with a thunk. "He'll be right out."

"Thank you," CoCo said smiling sweetly.

Luc recognized that smile—as fake as Missy's platinum hair color. He pressed his lips together and turned to watch Bubba stride to the counter.

"Luc! What brings you by so late again?"

CoCo moved toward the sheriff. Bubba's eyes widened. "And CoCo. What're you doing here?"

Although Bubba didn't say it, his eyes finished the question—what're you doing here with him? Luc laid his hand in the small of CoCo's back again, guiding her toward the swinging door, but the thrill he got from touching her didn't dissipate. "We have something else to show you."

Bubba led the way as he had before. Luc could feel the heat from Missy's stare. He knew that within five minutes, most of the townspeople would know he and CoCo LeBlanc had come to the sheriff's office together. The knowledge brought a smile to his face. Maybe he should send Missy a thank-you card.

"So, whatcha got?" Bubba asked as soon as they were seated. Luc handed him the folded note.

"Another letter?" Bubba took the paper, unfolded it, read it, then set it on his desk. "Any idea who it's from?"

"Not a clue. This is the first time I've really seen, up close, the animosity my grandfather invoked in people."

The sheriff turned his scrutiny to CoCo. "What do you know about this?"

"I found some Confederate coins on my property." She squirmed in her seat, glancing quickly at Luc before giving her full attention to Bubba. "I had one appraised. They're authentic." She nodded toward the letter. "They match the etching on the bottom of the page."

"Uh-huh. I see." Bubba grabbed an empty water bottle to hold his tobacco juice. "So whoever wrote this letter knew those coins were at your place."

"I believe so, yes." She swallowed, looking away from the revolting bottle.

Luc didn't blame her. It was disgusting. He cleared his throat. "Obviously my grandfather knew the coins were there, too. If this person knew to use that as confirmation of knowing what was in the LeBlanc house."

"Which is why he served my grandmother an eviction notice as soon as he found out about the coins. He wanted to get his hands on them." CoCo lowered her voice a notch. "And whatever proof is hiding in my house. Proof most likely connected to the Klan."

"We don't know that," Luc interjected, throwing a hard look at her.

She met his stare and lifted her chin. If he weren't aggravated with her accusations, he'd find the gesture cute and endearing.

"Okay, it's *probably* why." Defiance wrinkled into her face. "It's the only thing that makes sense. The trigger to serving the eviction notice. I mean, isn't it odd that he serves his eviction notice and then the next day he's murdered?" She shook her head when Bubba opened his mouth. "Isn't that entirely too convenient to point the finger at my family?"

"I'll follow up on this as soon as I can." Bubba pushed back his chair. "Is there anything else? If not, I need to get home."

Luc scrambled to beat CoCo to her feet. She won. He shook Bubba's hand. "Let me know as soon as you have anything."

"As much as I can." The sheriff nodded at CoCo. "You, too."

CoCo stared through the windshield at the setting sun. Purplish-orange hues streaked the Louisiana sky.

"Are you hungry?" Luc's voice interrupted her observations.

She turned her head and looked at him. "Kinda. Why?"

"You didn't eat much for lunch. I thought we might grab something."

She arched a brow. "Are you asking me to have dinner with you, Luc Trahan?"

His cheeks reddened. Ah, she'd forgotten about his blushing. It had always been such an endearing sight to her. Still was, so she steeled her will. "I don't think that's such a good idea."

"Come on, you gotta eat." His dimples cut into his tanned face. She swallowed, not able to remember how many nights dreams of those dimples had awoken her with such a sense of loss. "And we need to form a plan."

He had a point. They couldn't just wait on the sheriff to figure things out. Right now he seemed bent on them as the primary suspects. Especially her. "Okay. Just dinner."

"The diner okay?"

"It doesn't matter. I'm starved."

He whipped into the lot and parked, then rushed to open her door. They went inside, her heart hammering. He'd always been such a gentleman—opening doors, sending flowers, ordering for her.

No, this was a working partnership. Nothing more.

They slipped into a corner booth, and the waitress appeared with glasses of water and menus. After taking their order of chicken-fried steak with mashed potatoes and lots of lard-based gravy, she scuttled off behind the counter.

CoCo rested her elbows on the table. "So, what have we learned?"

"You're beautiful," he whispered.

Her heart fluttered. *Beautiful.* He used to call her that all the time. No one had since. Her insides felt like grits. "Luc…"

"Sorry, but you are. Even more now than before." His eyes darkened.

Oh, yeah, she could see the emotions were still there. Her entire being shot to attention. He still loved her. Despite all the tragedies and pain between them, Luc Trahan still loved her. The knowledge sent her senses reeling. How could she have missed it?

"I'm not trying to sweet-talk you, ya know."

She chewed her bottom lip. "You're doing it so well."

He laughed, the loud, honest laugh she'd missed. The one that could make her believe in the happily-ever-after part of fairy tales. Then she remembered they weren't even close to that part of their story. Time to get the discussion back on track—back to a safe topic for her emotional well-being. "Seriously, your grandfather found out about the coins in my house before I even knew they were there. You have to admit that's only logical."

Luc sobered. "You're probably right."

"Admit it, that's most likely the reason he served us the eviction notice."

He let out a heavy sigh. "Probably."

"We're going to find out the truth, no matter what. Right?"

"Right." His eyes still reflected sadness and confusion.

For now, that was enough. It would have to be, as the

waitress returned with their soft drinks and plates. She set them down with a clatter and turned away, not even bothering to ask if they needed anything.

"Merci," CoCo called out after her.

Luc chuckled and handed her the pepper. "If I remember correctly, you bury your food in this."

She took the shaker with a grin. "Can't eat without it." CoCo sprinkled pepper over her food until darkened. She cut off some of the steak and slipped it into her mouth. Her taste buds sang their approval.

Luc chuckled and shook his head. "Glad to see some things never change."

She swallowed. "Such as my addiction to pepper?"

"That and your delight in food."

With emphasis, she jabbed another bite into her mouth. Luc grinned over his glass.

"Okay, we know your grandfather knew about the coins at my place before I did. They're what made him serve us the eviction notice. My question is, how did he know?"

He swallowed. "I don't have a clue. You haven't any idea?"

"None." She took another bite. "He wouldn't exactly have come callin' to see Grandmere."

"He had to know the coins were there for the threat of the letter to be effective."

How did Beau know those coins even existed? Come to think of it, nobody ever really came to visit. Most of the locals who employed Grandmere's services met her at her outbuilding, never the house. Even when CoCo had been practicing herself, her grandmother had told her never to bring it inside. The spirits wouldn't approve.

"What?" Luc took a gulp of his drink, his eyes studying her over the rim of the glass.

"I can't think of anyone who's been in my house in the last month or so."

"No friends of yours or Tara's?"

Her mind raced. Tara did bring friends over a lot. But, if Tara had found a coin, CoCo or Grandmere would've known about it.

Luc tossed a couple of bills on the table. "You know, your house probably holds a lot of answers to the questions we've been asking. Why don't we go see what we can find?"

She stood, her legs still wobbly from the emotional tidal wave that had ransacked her heart. "Sounds like the best idea we've come up with all day. *Allons.*"

SEVENTEEN

CoCo spied her grandmother dozing on the couch. She took two steps in that direction. Grandmere's eyes opened wide. "Oh, CoCo, it's you."

"I'm home. Where's Tara?"

Grandmere mustered herself into sitting straight. "Out." Her eyes widened again as she caught sight of Luc filling the doorway. "Luc Trahan, what're you doing here?" Her gaze darted back to CoCo, questions shimmering in her fading eyes.

Motioning Luc to join her, CoCo sat on the edge of the couch. "Grandmere, I need to tell you something. Something important." She took her grandmother's hand, rubbing her thumb over the paper-thin skin covering the bent knuckles. "We've found some Confederate coins here recently. Hidden in the wall outside and under the rosebush. Do you know anything about them?"

"Coins…" Her grandmother wore a faraway stare.

CoCo squeezed her hand slightly. "Think, Grandmere. Anything."

"Now, I do remember Toby finding a doubloon back when he came to touch up the doorframes." She shook her head, the long gray hair moving like straw. "Paint's always chipping and peeling."

"A doubloon?" CoCo couldn't afford to let her grand-mother become sidetracked. This was too important. "Did you see it when Toby found it? What'd you do with it?"

Grandmere's eyes focused back on CoCo. "He showed it to me. Said it fell out when he was putting a nail in the frame." She shrugged. "Looked like a Mardi Gras trinket, so I told him he could keep it."

CoCo chewed her bottom lip. Toby couldn't be more than twelve, thirteen at the most…he wouldn't have recognized it as being real. "Think, Grandmere. When was this? When did Toby find the coin?"

"A couple of weeks ago, maybe a month at most." Recog-nition dawned in her eyes. "It was real? A real coin?"

"A real Confederate coin. I've found several others." CoCo sucked in a deep breath and let her thumb massage her grandmother's hand. "I think there may be more. But…" She tossed a glance over her shoulder and met Luc's stare.

He cleared his throat. "Mrs. LeBlanc, we found a letter in my grandfather's things that implied he knew the coins were here. Had he been here in the past month or so?"

"Not hardly! Your grandfather thought I was a mad woman." Grandmere chuckled under her breath. "He was scared of what I could do to him."

Seeing the hardening in Luc's eyes, CoCo tugged her grandmother's hand. "That letter also said there was proof of Justin Trahan's involvement in the Klan." CoCo swallowed hard. "And Grandpere's."

"Not my Marcel. No! He would never have been involved in the Klan." Grandmere jerked her hand away, raising the gnarled knuckles to her mouth. "Not Marcel," she whispered more to herself than to them.

"The letter could be all lies, but we just want to check it out." Luc's deep voice held a calming note.

Grandmere let out a long breath. "No, I'll not believe it." Tears glittered as she stared at CoCo. "You can check it out. All of your grandfather's personal things are in the trunks in the attic."

She patted her grandmother's leg, then stood and gave a quick jerk of her head to Luc. "We'll go see what we can find."

"CoCo," Grandmere said, "if you do find something about Marcel's involvement, I want to know."

"Of course." CoCo led Luc down the hall until they stood under the pull-down steps to the attic.

A long string allowed her to reach. She tugged, and the folding stairs descended. A blast of steamy air hit them square in the face.

"It's gonna be hot up here, even though it's night." CoCo unfolded the stairs and pushed the feet to the area rug.

"I'm ready for answers, no matter how hot it is."

She nodded, then ascended the steps. At the top, she jerked another string, spilling light into the attic. Cobwebs hung on the rafters and dust coated every surface, like some gruesome movie. CoCo sneezed as she moved to allow Luc access.

"Wow, this place hasn't been visited in a while," he said.

"I don't think I've ever been up here." She ducked to miss hitting a rafter and headed to the far end of the attic.

Two large trunks sat side-by-side under a window. CoCo struggled to open the window, but it wouldn't budge. She leaned over farther, pushing aside boxes with her foot, and put all her upper strength into the movement. It still didn't move.

"Let me." Luc's hands reached around her and popped the sill. The window slid open with a couple of catches. He breathed in over her shoulder. "Fresh air."

CoCo turned around and faced him. His hands were still braced against the window, entrapping her in his embrace. Her heart pitter-patted wildly. Her mouth felt as dry as the ground in August. She licked her lips, but it brought no relief.

His gaze dropped to her mouth, lingered for an eternity-filled moment, then traveled back to her eyes. The love she'd recognized in them earlier returned. Full force. With only the slightest hesitation, Luc leaned into her as he wrapped his arms around her. His head bent and she closed her eyes.

His lips grazed hers…soft, gentle, like a whisper. Her body quickened as she gripped his biceps. Then logic tapped her on the shoulder. She pushed away from him.

"I told you we were just working together and that's it." The thudding of her heart weakened her knees.

"There's so much I want to say to you, need to say to you, but n—"

"No. I can't do this again, Luc. Please."

The muscles in his jaw popped, but he nodded. He dusted his hands on his jeans and turned to stare at the attic. "Fine. You take that trunk and I'll take this one."

Luc's heart zinged every time he glanced over at CoCo. He'd seen the love glimmering in her eyes when he'd kissed her, even when she'd pushed him away. It was wrong. He knew their love didn't stand a chance—never had.

"Oh, my, check this out." She stood and placed a white hat with a wide brim on her head, tilting it slightly.

"You look good in hats." He swallowed. CoCo looked good in everything. Even the walking shorts and camp-style shirt she now wore. A sheen of perspiration dotted her upper lip. The lip he'd kissed a few minutes ago. The one he wanted to kiss again. He'd missed their emotional connection for years.

She laughed, dispelling the intense thoughts running through his head. "I'll have to give it to Alyssa next time she's here. Maybe she can use it for her United Daughters of the Confederacy meetings."

"How *is* Alyssa?" He pulled out old photo albums from the trunk.

"Fine. Still living up in Shreveport, working as a reporter. Every free minute she has, she's doing something for the UDC."

He stopped from flipping the pages of the album. "I detect a note of hesitation in your voice. What's wrong?"

She lowered her head, but not before he'd caught the hurt in her expression. "Tara. She's Grandmere's new student."

Luc nearly choked. "Of voodoo?"

She nodded.

"Why?"

"Because I refused to learn anymore. And Alyssa's been gone for so long." She pushed her bangs off her forehead. "Grandmere feels she must teach one of us, and by process of elimination, only Tara's left."

His heart flipped. "Why aren't you learning from your grandmother anymore?"

"Luc…" Her voice cracked. "Luc, less than a month after you—after we broke up—I finally realized I'd been wrong."

"About?" Borderline joy sung in his heart.

"About God. Jesus. Voodoo. My life. Everything." Fresh tears stung her eyes.

"And?"

"I accepted Jesus into my heart. I confessed my sins and turned from them."

His eyes pooled. Tears ran down her face. Time stood still.

Then, he moved forward and drew her into his arms. Held her tight. Kissed the top of her head.

She shook her head and moved away from him. "Anyway, Alyssa had run to another town after college to get away from Grandmere's ways. Thought I was a regular heathen." She let out a half sigh, half snort. "I guess I was. Anyway, now that Grandmere's teaching Tara, Alyssa blames me."

"How can she blame you?"

"Because I allowed it to happen. I turned my back, therefore, Grandmere started teaching Tara. She's the baby, so Alyssa and I are supposed to protect her." Tears snuck from her eyes. "I'm not doing such a grand job."

He set the album on the dust-covered floor and stared, afraid to move toward her. "It's not your responsibility."

She lowered her head.

Luc put a finger under her chin and lifted until her eyes met his. "You can't be responsible for someone else's actions."

She blinked. "I have to lead her to Jesus, Luc. You know that."

His heart did, because he'd felt the exact same emotion. "You know, I learned a really hard lesson two years ago. A painful lesson."

Panic crept across her face.

"No, not what happened to my father and between us."

Uncertainty pushed the fear aside.

"I learned that I can plant a seed of salvation, but it's each individual person's choice to accept it or not." He dropped his hand, but her gaze stayed glued to him. "I learned that beating someone over the head with my Bible isn't going to make them decide to accept Christ. If anything, it can make them run farther away."

"What do I do?" Her tone was void of hope.

He stiffened his spine. "You let God do the miracles. We're only human, CoCo, but God's still in the miracle business. Trust Him."

Her eyes filled with tears again, but he could tell these were tears of relief. Of letting go of a burden she never should have carried. "Thank you."

It was enough for the time being. "Now, get back to work."

Luc's words had lightened her load, made her spirit free. He was right—she had to leave it all in God's very capable hands. *Stepping out in faith.*

CoCo cut her glance to him. He sat cross-legged on the floor, a tattered old photo album open in his lap. Light caught the dust dancing in the air every time either of them moved. She smiled and went back to digging in her trunk. If she had to go through one more plantation crop record book....

He let out a low whistle and jumped to his feet. Particles filled the air.

"What?"

"Let's get this under better light." He moved toward the hanging single bulb to hold the album right under its glow. "Check this out."

She rushed to his side. Her arm brushed against his as she peered at the book. She squinted her eyes and studied the picture he had illuminated under the light. Her heart contracted, and it had nothing to do with Luc Trahan's close proximity.

The photograph depicted two men in their midtwenties, smiling as they stood together, their arms slung around each other. Both men wore white robes with the Ku Klux Klan emblem emblazoned.

CoCo swallowed. "Is that Grandpere and Justin?"

Luc let out a rush of air. "I think so."

She pulled the photo free from the corner-holders and moved the picture closer to her face to make out the details.

"It is them. At this house." She shook her head. "I would never have believed Grandpere was a member of the Klan. Knowing how Grandmere feels…"

He grabbed a yellowed sheet of paper from the album. "Looks like some type of journal entry."

"That's Grandpere's handwriting." Her breath caught in her throat as she read.

I confess now that I was involved in the KKK, deeply. I did unspeakable things, horrible things that I never want to remember. But remember I must. I hid these albums up in the attic because I couldn't burn them— wouldn't. I need the reminder of the sins I've committed. I can only pray that when my time comes, the Lord has mercy on my soul.

The ache stripped against her very heart. "Poor Grandpere. I never knew." CoCo shoved away the tears. By the tone of the letter, she could assume he'd accepted Jesus and now sat in heaven. She sighed and ran a finger over the shed caught in the background of the picture. "That's Grandmere's workshop."

"I thought she didn't know about the Klan involvement."

Her heart hammered so loud she could hear her pulse in her head. Had she been fed lie after lie and gobbled up every one of them? "Let's go ask her."

They descended from the attic single-file. CoCo led the way to the living room, gripping the picture and letter tight. Her grandmother may be a lot of things, but she'd never lied to her or her sisters. At least not that she knew of. CoCo's stomach burned with the thought.

Her grandmother sat on the couch, a void look on her face as she stared out the front windows.

"Grandmere?"

Her grandmother jerked, clearly startled. "You frightened me, *ma chère*. I was woolgathering."

CoCo sat on the couch, Luc sitting beside her. She held out the picture to her grandmother. "We found this in one of the trunks."

Grandmere took the picture and glanced at it. "What have we here?"

With a sigh, she lifted the glasses she wore on a chain around her neck and perched them over the bridge of her nose. She sucked in air. Her hands trembled. The photo drifted to the floor, like a dried leaf caught on an autumn breeze.

"Grandmere!" CoCo's insides shuddered and goose bumps pricked her skin. She wrapped an arm around the older woman, guilt for her earlier accusing thoughts settling in her heart.

Her grandmother's face turned ashen. "Not Marcel. In the Klan?" Her voice quivered.

"That photo was taken here, on this land. You didn't know?"

"Of course not! My traditions come from Haiti, *ma chère,* you know that. I would never have allowed Marcel to be so prejudiced against something I value so deeply. Never."

"Then who took this picture?" Luc asked, lifting the photo from where it had landed on the hardwood floor.

"I know not." Grandmere's entire body shook.

With a trembling hand, CoCo passed the letter to her grandmother. "We found this as well."

Grandmere shook as she read, her eyes filling with tears.

Luc pushed to his feet. "I think it's high time I talk to Uncle Justin and get some answers."

"I don't think now's a good time," CoCo said.

"Why not?" Irritation sat in his features. "I'm tired of getting the runaround. It's time for the truth."

"Wait until after tomorrow, Luc."

"Why?" Impatience hovered in his tone.

"Because tomorrow is your grandfather's funeral."

EIGHTEEN

It didn't seem right for the day to be bright and beautiful when they were going to bury a man. The blue jays tweeted and sang outside. CoCo stood at the window in her bedroom, staring out over the bayou. Funerals—hadn't she endured enough of them in her life already? Mom and Dad, Grandpere, Luc's father, now his grandfather. If she closed her eyes, she could still see her parents' coffins, side by side. She avoided their graves with the single headstone. It hurt too much.

Lord, help me to understand. I can't see why death keeps kicking me in the face. Please, Father, give me strength.

"Are you going to his funeral?" Tara asked from the doorway.

CoCo turned to her sister. "I am."

"Grandmere told me Luc was here with you last night." Tara's eyebrows arched into her forehead. "Guess you two kissed and made up?"

"Not really. We're just working together to try and find out who killed his grandfather."

"Nothing more?"

"No. I just want our family name cleared."

Her sister laughed. "Me thinks thou doth protest too much."

She shrugged. "Hey, if he's the one who'll make you happy, I'm all for it." She took a couple of steps into the room. "His grandfather is a whole other story. If you want my opinion—"

"I don't." CoCo set her chin.

Tara snorted. A most unladylike snort at that. "I say you should have let the gators keep him."

"Tara! That's a horrible thing to say about another human being."

"Some human he was." Tara crossed her arms over her chest. "He was perfectly willing to throw us out, and you know it."

CoCo chewed her bottom lip. *Lord, help me out.* "You know, there's a lot more going on here than the obvious. I didn't personally like Beau, but I respected his life."

"Good. You go respect. I'll stay here with Grandmere."

She managed to hold back the sigh. No sense getting into yet another argument with her sister. They obviously didn't see eye-to-eye, probably never would. Until God touched Tara's heart anyway.

"By the way, Alyssa said she's calling you tonight." Tara threw the departing slam before leaving.

Oh, happy day. Joy and rapture. Another scathing call from her sister. Her *younger* sister. As if today wouldn't be hard enough. Then again, last night had been pretty tough. She had never seen Grandmere break down and sob so. It nearly broke CoCo's heart. Grandpere's letter, in his own words, had reinforced the witnessing she'd been trying with her grandmother. Maybe God's timing would come around quicker after all. She prayed so.

She grabbed her purse from the dresser and glanced in the mirror to give herself a once-over. She'd coerced her curls into a tight bun. The hairstyle made her eyes appear darker against her tanned skin. At least she had a clear complexion. The plain black dress with gold buttons all the way down the front would have to suffice. Her skin itched against the panty hose. Good thing the church she'd been attending across town allowed pants. Getting all gussied up in hose, dresses and pumps left a lot to be desired. A whole lot.

Her heels clicked as she made her way down the stairs. The robust aroma of fresh coffee met her as she stepped into the foyer. She marched into the kitchen.

Grandmere turned, offering her a cup. "Thought you might need this, *cher.*"

"*Merci.*" She took a cautious sip and savored the strong French Roast.

"I can make you some breakfast."

"*Merci,* but no. I don't feel much up to eating right now." CoCo took another sip of coffee, studying her grandmother over the rim. "How're you feeling this morning?"

"I'm right as rain, *ma chère.* I talked to the spirits last night, and I know my Marcel's at peace."

The spirits? CoCo chewed her bottom lip. Would it never end? She'd been so sure she'd gotten through to her grandmother. What more could she say? She sure didn't want to beat her over the head with the Bible like Luc said.

"You'd better get a move on. You don't want to be late."

"Right." She took a final sip of coffee before setting the cup in the sink. China rattled against porcelain.

Her grandmother smiled, softening her pensive expression. "*Ma chère,* I may be old, but I can see the look of love on both of your faces."

"Don't be silly. He broke off our engagement. We're just working together to figure this out, that's all." Were her emotions that obvious to everyone?

"I guess it's not much of my business, yes?"

CoCo stared at her grandmother for only a split second before pulling her into a hug. "I love you."

"I only want you to be happy, *cher,*" her grandmother whispered and returned the hug.

"I am." CoCo straightened. If only she could believe her own argument.

Grandmere ducked her head. "Now, get."

The heat pressed down, nearly suffocating CoCo as she walked to the Jeep. She stumbled as she picked her way amid rocks and uneven ground. Stupid heels. How ever did working women wear them every day, all day? She slipped in the driver's seat and hopped, the leather so hot against the back of her bare knees. Why didn't men ever have to undergo such torture?

Trees passed by in a blur as she drove, even though she kept the speed five miles below the limit. No one rushed to bury the dead. Not in Cajun country anyway. In Vermilion parish, the folks liked to draw out the mourning, the burying and the grieving. It was just the Southern way. Unlike the Yankees, who did quick memorial services and went on about their normal lives.

Her heart pounded as she pulled up to the cemetery. Justin and Luc had opted to have the service at graveside, knowing so many in the area would attend and the church building wouldn't hold everyone. She killed the engine and stared at the people picking their way across the ground toward the big tent. Luc would be here already. The family had a private viewing earlier this morning and planned to come straight to the graveside immediately afterward. CoCo shook as she remembered the last funeral she'd attended. She'd gone to that one for Luc, too. The day they'd buried his father. The day he'd turned to her with eyes as cold as the Antarctic. The day he'd broken their engagement. And her heart.

CoCo shook off the memory. She and Luc had come full circle.

Luc stood head and shoulders above most of the other men. Her heart leapt to her throat. He looked so strong as he accepted handshake after handshake. Like a pillar.

She made her way toward him. He caught sight of her when she was halfway there. He smiled—a smile reserved only for her. A secret smile of dreams. Her heart thudded.

He bent to whisper in her ear. "I'm glad you're here."

That's all she needed to hear, all she needed to know for this short moment. She faced his uncle sitting in the last chair in the front row. His eyes were glazed over, glued to the coffin on the stand over the open grave. She took the few steps to stand before him. "I'm very sorry for your loss, Mr. Justin."

He jerked his gaze to her, but the glazed appearance stayed. "What're you doing here?" He spoke loud and sharp.

His words were as effective as a slap across the face. She stumbled a step backward and hit a wall. She spun around and met Luc's stern expression. He was the wall she'd hit.

"Uncle Justin, CoCo's here because I asked her to come." He laid an arm around her shoulders. "For me."

His uncle stared at Luc's face for a long minute, then he gave a curt nod. "So that's how it is, huh?"

Luc let a slow breath hiss between his teeth. Justin's gaze dropped to CoCo's face. His scrutiny caused heat that had nothing to do with the hot sun to sizzle in her spine. She lifted her chin and met his stare. He narrowed his eyes and then let out a little chuckle. "I like your spunk, girl." He stood and nodded. "Thank you for coming."

That was about as sincere as she was going to get. She smiled and offered her hand. "I am very sorry for your loss,

Mr. Justin. I know how it feels to lose people you love." Her words softened.

So did his eyes. "I remember, young lady." His voice cracked. He gave another nod before moving to a group of older people standing in a semicircle off to the side of the chairs.

CoCo let out the breath she'd been holding.

"See, he does like you."

She gave a snort similar to the one Tara had earlier. "Yeah, that's why he demanded to know why I'm here, because he likes me so much."

"You're a suspect, and he's grieving. He backed off."

"Only because you practically threatened him with the tone of your words." She caught sight of Toby standing by himself, away from the rest of the crowd. "I'll be back in just a minute," she told Luc before heading toward the teen.

"Hi, Toby."

The boy jerked his head to stare at her. The surprise on his face faded back to normal when he recognized her. "Hiya, Ms. CoCo."

"I didn't know you knew Mr. Trahan."

"My dad made me come."

"Oh." She glanced around, but didn't see anybody watching Toby. This was the first she'd heard of the boy's father. Toby lived with his grandmother, his deceased mother's mom. Where had the father come from? "I planned to call you. We need some more repairs done around the house."

The boy's eyes lit up. "Cool. Maybe I can find another doubloon."

Her heart pounded loud, drowning out the conversations around her. "About that doubloon—do you still have it?"

"Nah, my dad's boss said he collected old doubloons and wanted it for his collection. He paid me twenty bucks for it."

Twenty bucks for a coin worth five thousand. She chewed her bottom lip. "Did you tell him where you'd gotten it?"

"Yeah. He said he'd buy any more I found, too." The teen's eyes sparkled.

The hairs on the back of her neck stood at attention. Someone else knew the coins were in her house. "Toby, who is your dad's b—"

Luc took a gentle hold of her elbow. "Let's take our seats. Looks like Preacher's ready to get started." He led her toward the chairs, then froze. "What's he doing here?"

She followed his line of vision, which stopped at Dwayne Williams's feet. "I'll go see," she whispered as she made her way toward her attorney.

Dwayne stood behind the crowd, his tight afro shining in the sun. She nudged up beside him. "What are you doing here?"

"I came to pay my respects."

"Dwayne, you can't be serious." She darted her gaze around the area where people were milling toward the tent. "I know better."

"Look, I'm a suspect in his murder just like you are. Nine times out of ten, the murderer shows up at a funeral. I'm just keeping my eyes and ears open." He gave a slight jerk of his head. "Just like the cops there. Keeping an eye on everyone."

Sure enough, Sheriff Theriot and two deputies hovered near the entrance to the cemetery. Until Beau's murder was solved, she remained under the microscope. Right alongside Luc and Dwayne.

Luc jerked the knot loose on his tie. He tossed the offensive article of clothing across the back of the bedroom chair. Its silky texture couldn't catch on the tapestry so it slipped to the floor. He left it there, refusing to pick it up. His day couldn't have been much worse. What was it about burying the dead that left the living feeling guilty for still breathing?

"Luc, your grandfather's attorney is here." His mother's voice floated up the stairs and down the hall to his open door.

"Be there in a sec." He wished CoCo could have come to sit beside him. Funny how he, a grown man, wanted someone to hold his hand. He sure as shootin' couldn't look to Bubba for support. Not today. His childhood friend was present in an official capacity at the reading of Beau Trahan's last will and testament.

Luc's stomach roiled. He'd just seen his grandfather's body lowered into the ground, and now he'd have to face some lawyer to hear Grandfather's last wishes. It just seemed… wrong.

What else could he do? He unbuttoned the top button of his white Oxford with a sigh and clunked down the stairs. Several voices reached him before he entered the study. His grandfather's study. He didn't miss the irony.

"There you are, *cher*," his mother said as she patted the seat next to her on the couch. "Come sit so we can get started. Mr. Milton is a busy man, I'm sure."

Luc sat beside his mother and stared at the man sitting behind the desk. His grandfather's desk. The man had thinning gray hair, glasses thicker than Bubba's and a paunchy belly, yet his eyes shone as he looked at Luc's mother. She patted her hair in response. Luc fidgeted, glancing over his shoulder to the other people in the room.

Felicia's wheelchair sat next to the couch, on the other side of his mother. He worried about her. She'd cried at the funeral, but Frank had consoled her. Too bad Frank couldn't be here now.

Uncle Justin sat in Grandfather's recliner, his face ruddy, his expression serious. He'd sobbed at the funeral, too, but in a manly sort of way. Luc couldn't imagine losing a sibling—he'd be devastated if something happened to Felicia. The thought of her recurring medical bills flashed across his mind. Maybe Grandfather had a stipulation in his will for her continued medical care. He prayed it was so.

Sammy Moran? What was he doing here? The acting casino manager sat stiff-backed in one of the chairs facing the desk. He'd shed no tears at the funeral. Matter-of-fact, he hadn't shown one iota of emotion period. Luc couldn't believe his grandfather would have left him something.

A couple of old dogs, as Grandfather had called them, reclined in chairs brought in from the living room. Luc couldn't put names to faces, but he recognized most of them from Grandfather's politician days.

Finally, Bubba Theriot stood in the back of the room, his arms crossed casually over his chest, but his eyes as sharp as a hawk's. Luc's gut clenched. Bubba probably assumed the murderer stood to gain something from Grandfather's death. Luc swallowed hard. He hoped his grandfather hadn't left him much of anything.

CoCo plopped down on the bed and stared up at the ceiling. The fan rotated clockwise, humming at the high speed. Something felt off inside her spirit, as if peace hid from her. What was it? What was she missing? She closed her eyes and replayed everything since Beau's murder like a movie rewinding frame by frame.

Being served the eviction notice had to be triggered by Beau finding out about the coins hidden here in the house. Hiring Dwayne as her attorney. Finding the body—she fast forwarded over that segment. The sheriff's visit, followed by Luc's. A small shiver crossed her spine. She shoved away the distraction of Luc's handsome face and returned to her thoughts. Meeting with Dwayne and giving her statement to the police. Luc's apology. She smiled, but pinched her eyes shut tighter. Discovering the letters and then the picture in the attic.

Her heart thumped, and she bolted up on the bed. She widened her eyes while her mind reeled.

Dwayne had said he'd been investigating Beau. Of course, she knew now that was in regard to his sister. If he'd been digging into the past, maybe, just maybe, he knew something about Justin's involvement with the KKK. She could get a lead on who had written the letter found in Beau's things.

Moving to the edge of the mattress, CoCo lifted the phone receiver on the bedside table. She punched in the number for Dwayne's office, realizing he'd probably gone straight home after the funeral, but determined to try anyway. After three rings, she got his voice mail. Apparently Dwayne had a life. Imagine that. She left a message and hung up the phone. A couple more days and she could ask. It might be a long shot, but right now, anything was better than what they had to go on…nothing.

She looked up to find Tara hovering in the doorway. "Problems?"

"Nothing I can't handle." CoCo sighed and moved to the vanity table. She lifted her makeup remover. "How're you?"

"I'm fine and dandy." Tara flopped on the bed. "How was the funeral?"

"Standard funeral." She daubed the lotion on her eyes with a tissue.

"I see."

She finished removing the mascara and eyeliner, then stared at her sister in the mirror. "Hey, you know Toby?"

"The kid who does stuff around here?"

"Yeah. That's him. I know he lives with Ms. Mason. Do you know his last name?"

Tara twirled a lock of hair around her finger. Oh, what CoCo wouldn't give to have straight hair like her sister's.

"That's his grandmother. I don't know him by anything other than just Toby. Why?"

CoCo shrugged and then wiped her face with a moist cloth. "I saw him at the funeral today. He mentioned something about his father."

"I didn't even know he had a father on the scene. He's always with his grandmother. Why so curious?"

Again, CoCo shrugged. Tara was entirely too astute for her own good. No sense raising her suspicions. "I asked him to come around to do some more light repairs. I just thought I'd call him and follow up."

"Grandmere has the number on the icebox."

She tossed the cloth in the trash, thankful to have the makeup gone. Her face couldn't breathe under all that gunk.

"How was Luc?"

CoCo turned and faced her sister. "Good." She licked her lips. "Considering."

NINETEEN

Something was wrong, very wrong. She could tell. The restaurant's soft glow added a mysterious ambiance, not that she didn't already feel something uneasy settling over their table. CoCo sat across the table from Luc, dreading whatever it was he had to tell her.

Please, God, don't let him try to persuade me to give us a second chance. I know I should just pray for Your will, but I love him. Always have, always will. And I'm not strong enough to withstand him breaking my heart a second time.

Her mind knew God had her best interests at heart, but she really wanted to be able to resist the temptation Luc brought to her door.

"You're beautiful." Luc's eyes caressed her as softly as his spoken words.

Heat marched across her face and she could only imagine the blush, but she just blinked and stared back at him.

He chuckled. "You are. Even when you're turning four shades of red."

She laughed and lowered her gaze.

"I need to tell you something."

CoCo's heart skipped a beat. All traces of laughter fled from his voice. She swallowed hard.

"In the reading of the will today…" His words trailed off.

Her gut knotted. She'd only eaten a couple of pieces of bread and a salad, yet her stomach felt loaded with lead. "Yeah?"

He wouldn't meet her eyes. Her heart joined the lead in her stomach.

"Grandfather left the deed to your property to Uncle Justin. And the lawyer assured me that it's legit. The transfer of ownership was just never filed."

She didn't have much fight left in her. "I guess that's the way the coons run."

Now his gaze did touch hers. "The only issue is the delay of transferring of ownership filing. That's what Dwayne will argue in court to try and sway the judge to let you keep your house." He took a sip of tea. "CoCo, Uncle Justin's going to evict you if the court decides in his favor. I asked him. Tried to talk him into just letting things go on as is. He doesn't need your house, but he wants it. Says he owes it to Grandfather to carry out what he started."·

Fury coursed through her veins faster than her airboat over the bayou. She spoke between clenched teeth. "I told you he didn't like me."

"Aww, CoCo, it's not that. I don't know. He's got a bee in his bonnet to get your house." He reached across the table and laid his hand over hers. "He was adamant."

Chewing her bottom lip, she recalled the look in his eyes at the funeral. She hadn't detected hate after Luc had stood up for her. It was more like…fear. Yes, that was it. Something about her scared Justin Trahan. Or, could it be…

"Luc, did you tell Justin about the picture we found in my attic? Or the coins?"

"No. I didn't think the funeral would be the right time or place."

"Right. What if he knew that picture was up there? Wouldn't he want it back, so that nobody would know about his involvement? Could he have been the one to find out about the coins? And knowing about the picture, pushed Beau into serving us with an eviction?"

"Why would he care? Unlike Grandfather, Uncle Justin has never given a flip about his reputation." Luc gave a wry laugh. "Matter of fact, he enjoys having people talk about him."

"Hmmm." He had a point. Justin's past wouldn't come up and bite him, not like Beau's. Why would it have bothered him? She sighed. It wouldn't have. Unless...

"Luc, is it possible someone's blackmailing Justin?"

"What?"

She held up a finger. "Just follow me, here. Beau gets the letter we found, threatening to expose him. What if the author of the letter went further? Sent another letter, one demanding money?" CoCo leaned over the table with its pristine white tablecloth, her words practically tumbling on top of themselves. "If that person threatened your grandfather, why not Justin, too?"

He ran his fingertip over the lip of the glass. "Uncle Justin wouldn't care."

"Unless they threatened to expose his past to hurt his brother. Wouldn't that have fired up Justin? Someone using his past to hurt Beau?"

Luc pressed his lips together and his eyes widened. He gave a slow nod.

"So, if someone tried to blackmail both him and Beau, it stands to reason Justin would want the house to get those pictures."

"But," Luc shook his head, "now that Grandfather's dead, Uncle Justin could care less about his past coming out in the open. There'd be no point in blackmailing him anymore. So why is he still bound and determined to evict you?"

And therein his statement laid the flaw in her scenario. "I don't know." She chewed her bottom lip.

"What's going through that beautiful head of yours?"

"The teenager who does yard work for us found one of the coins. Grandmere told him he could keep it. He said his father's boss bought it for twenty bucks and offered to buy any more he found."

Luc narrowed his eyes. "When did you find this out?"

"At the funeral. The young man I was talking to just before you saw Dwayne."

He pressed his lips together and then shook his head. "I can't place the kid." He let out a puff of air. "Who does his father work for?"

"His father's never been in his life before, as far as I know. He lives with his grandmother. Maybe the father just got back in town or something. I don't know, but I intend to find out. Soon."

"How does this figure with Justin still planning on evicting you?"

"What if he knows about those coins in my house? And that's why he wants possession of it."

"I don't know. I'll try to find out." He squeezed her hand tighter. "We'll figure it out. Something's gotta give."

"I hope so. The sooner the better."

The waitress delivered their plates of *étouffée*. The enticing aroma of crawfish and cayenne wafted to CoCo's senses, and she discovered she did have an appetite after all. The waitress refilled their glasses with sweet tea, then left them alone. Luc said grace over their food and then they began to eat.

* * *

The night air crackled with heat from the squelching Louisiana temperatures—or the emotional bond between them. Luc couldn't tell. He did know one thing for sure— he wanted to spend the rest of his earthly life with CoCo LeBlanc. Now that he knew she was a Christian, well, there wasn't really anything keeping them apart. Except that she didn't trust him anymore. He had only himself to blame for that. He should have had more faith that God would call CoCo to Him.

In his mind's eye, he could already see their wedding. Their home together. Their children. It was enough to make him push down the lump in his chest. He would work on winning his way back into CoCo's heart.

He opened the SUV door for CoCo, and she slipped inside. His heart ached as he rounded the vehicle and got behind the wheel. Not much longer, and he could concentrate on their relationship. On *them*. "Do you mind if I just drop you off at your house?"

"O-okay." Her eyes went wide and surprise teased the irises.

He laughed. "A lot of what you supposed tonight made sense. I'd like to talk to Uncle Justin, ask him about the picture and hear what he says. Also, see if I can find out if he knows about the coins."

"And you can't do that with me there?"

He didn't want to hurt her. "I just think Uncle Justin will feel more comfortable if I go alone."

"I understand." She worried her bottom lip.

"I'll call you and let you know what I uncover." He grabbed her hand and brought her fingers to his lips. He planted a light kiss against the tips.

She jerked her hand back to her lap and sat in stony silence.

After pulling into her driveway, he shifted to look at her. "I'll call you."

She smiled and jumped out of the vehicle. He watched her climb the stairs and open the screen door. She tossed him a wave before ducking inside.

He let out a long breath. Backing up, Luc turned around and drove in the direction of his uncle's house—where, hopefully, he'd get some answers.

"CoCo, is that you?" Tara bellowed from upstairs.

No, it's the Ghost of Christmas Past. Who else would be coming into the house? "Yeah, it's me."

"You missed Alyssa's call." Tara hovered at the top of the stairs, her menacing glare caught by the overhead light. "She was ticked."

"Hmm, I imagine." *Ticked* was probably a mild word to describe Alyssa's reaction to her not being home.

Tara took the steps two at a time. "I think she's overexaggerating like she normally does, but she's threatening to come down next weekend."

CoCo refused to voice the groan caught on her tongue. She set her purse on the buffet and faced her sister. "Where's Grandmere?"

"She went to bed early. Seemed upset." Tara narrowed her eyes at CoCo. "You wouldn't know anything about that, would you?"

"She found out something about Grandpere last night that upset her, but she seemed fine this morning."

"What'd you say, CoCo?" Tara popped her hands on her slim hips, one of which she cocked out.

"I didn't say anything. I just showed her a picture and something he'd written I'd found in the attic. In Grandpere's things."

"What kind of picture? I didn't know we had anything up there except for Mom and Dad's stuff."

Just hearing their names scraped against CoCo's heart. She licked her lips. "There're two trunks that were Grandpere's. Photo albums and such."

"Grandmere has all the photos down here." Tara waved her hand toward the bookshelves lining the living room. Several scrapbooks and photo albums lined the bottom shelves, and framed photos cluttered every free space.

"No, these are ones that were private to Grandpere. Grandmere didn't even know about them—only that the trunks were there."

"About what? Just tell me, yes?"

"Grandpere and Luc's great-uncle were in the Klan together." Tara gasped. "No way!"

"It's true. We found a picture."

"I want to see." Tara's bottom lip protruded.

CoCo weighed her decision. If she refused, Tara would simply explore the attic as soon as she was alone. "Come on. I need to see if there's anything else up there of any importance." She and Luc had cut their search short before going through both of the trunks completely.

Tara smiled, eagerness and curiosity battling in her eyes.

Up the folding stairs they trekked, dust stirring as they moved. Tara sneezed, but shrugged off CoCo's *God bless you*. At least the window remained open so some fresh air drifted in. CoCo made her way to the trunk Luc had been going through. "Here's what we didn't finish looking through."

Together they knelt and began pulling items from the trunk.

A bundle of letters tied with an old piece of twine fell apart as soon as Tara touched it. She looked at CoCo. "I didn't break it."

CoCo smiled. "I know you didn't. It's so old it's disintegrating." She peered at the top envelope. "Can you make out what they are?"

"Let me see."

While Tara gently tugged yellowed paper out, CoCo turned her attention back to the trunk. She pulled out a cigar box. She lifted the lid and smelled the distinct aroma of Cuban cigars, the kind Grandpere had smoked for as long as she could remember. Her lips curled into a smile at the memory. Peering inside, she found buttons and....

Two Confederate coins.

She lifted them, held them in her hand. They felt just like all the others. Grandpere had known the coins were here. Her heart faltered. And they were connected to the Klan, just as the legend had said. She pushed them aside and lifted a photo that was turned facedown.

Tara glanced over, tears streaking her face.

"What is it?" CoCo set the box on the floor.

"There are love letters between Mom and Dad." She shook her head, then wiped her nose on her sleeve. "They were really and truly in love with each other."

CoCo hugged her sister. "I know," she whispered. She gave Tara a final squeeze and backed away.

Tara sniffled and wiped her nose on her sleeve. "I want to finish reading them."

"Okay. I want to read them when you're done." She went back to the cigar box sitting on the dust-covered floor and lifted the photo again. In the dim light, she couldn't make out the photograph's subject. CoCo held the photo up close to the single lightbulb.

Her heart stalled. Bumps pimpled her arms. The hairs on the back of her neck stood tall and erect.

"Oh, no," she whispered.

She glanced over to her sister, totally emerged in love letters from the past. CoCo swallowed and stared at the picture again.

Lord, please don't let this be what I think it is.

Grandpere and Justin Trahan stood together again. This time they'd lost the robes and hats. This time they held guns. And a man had been hanged in a tree between them. On the back in her grandfather's handwriting were the words: *The man Justin and I killed.*

TWENTY

The phone's shrill sound jerked CoCo's attention from the photo. She rushed down the stairs, the photo tight in her hand, hoping the call didn't disturb Grandmere.

"Hello." She panted, struggling to even her breathing.

"CoCo? It's Dwayne Williams. Is it too late to call?"

She glanced at the clock over the mantle—8:10. "No, not at all."

"Is this a bad time? You sound out of breath."

"I was in the attic."

"Oh. I got your message on my answering service and wanted to call you back. Has something else happened?"

Yeah, she could say that. "Actually, yes. At the reading of Beau Trahan's will today, Justin was left the deed to my property."

"Any chance he'll drop the eviction case?"

She snorted. "Not hardly."

"We'll just proceed as planned then. I'll go to the courthouse Monday and file another motion."

"Dwayne, there's something else I need to tell you."

"Yes?" His voice remained even, but she detected the hesitation in the single word.

"We found a letter in Beau's things. A letter threatening to expose Justin as a member of the KKK, to ruin Beau's reputation." She hesitated for but a moment before rambling on. "You said you were researching Beau before you took my case. Did you ever find any hint of Justin's KKK involvement?" Because if it was widely known information, the list of murder suspects had just grown.

"Probably just a threat. Did you turn the letter over to the sheriff?"

"Yes, but it's not just a threat. Luc and I found a picture of Justin and my grandfather, in full KKK robes." And a picture of them with a hanged man, with a written confession by Grandpere, but she didn't want to say anything about that just yet. Not until she'd had a chance to talk with Luc. "Did you know about the KKK involvement?"

A long pause thundered over the connection.

"Dwayne? Are you still there?"

"I'm here." The sigh he emitted nearly cracked CoCo's eardrums. "The sheriff will follow the leads on that. It's late and I need to go. I'll file the motion Monday morning." He disconnected the call before she could say goodbye.

A nagging sensation struck her—he never answered her question.

She glanced down at the photo still gripped in her hand and her heart took a tumble. It wasn't just a suspicion of blackmail that lay hidden in her house. Now there was motive for murder.

Plopping down on the worn couch, CoCo thought it through again. Supposing the person who knew about the coins also knew about Grandpere's and Justin's involvement in the Klan and used that information to blackmail Beau. Why would that person kill him? It didn't make sense.

"CoCo?" Tara rounded the corner, her eyes red and puffy.

"Did you find something else?" She sat upright, tension drawing every muscle taut, and shoved the picture in her pocket.

Tara dropped the stack of letters onto the coffee table and sat beside CoCo on the couch. "No, just the letters." She dabbed at her eyes. "They loved each other so much. Why'd they have to be killed?"

The question she'd asked God many times over in the last two years. CoCo caught her bottom lip between her teeth.

Lord, help me out here. I need the words to give testimony to You.

"*Boo,* I can't know the whys. No one can. We just have to trust there is a reason. Even if we never understand it this side of heaven, we have to accept it."

Her sister's eyes went cold. "Your god let them die. How can you sit there and defend him? Talk about trusting and accepting. That's wrong."

Fire sizzled in her spine. "It's better than believing they did something so wrong that the spirits retaliated against them."

Tara gasped. Her eyes bugged. "I—I—I can't believe you'd say that."

"Isn't that what Grandmere's *traditions* teach? That untimely deaths are a result of the person's bad karma and the spirits intervening?"

"Th-that's not true."

"Isn't it?" CoCo jumped to her feet and shot up an eyebrow. "I was trained much longer than you, remember? That's what the traditional teachings of voodoo state."

Tara stood, her body trembling. CoCo could see the raw fury in her baby sister's face matching her stance. "Mom and Dad did nothing to deserve dying so young."

"That's right, they didn't." CoCo crossed her arms over her

chest. "And maybe that's what helped me see that Grand-mere's traditions are wrong."

"It's okay to believe your god allowed this to happen to them?"

"Knowing that they're in the loving arms of Jesus is what I believe."

"You don't know that."

"Yes, Tara, I do. Wait here, and I'll prove it to you." CoCo marched up the stairs to her bedroom. She grabbed the Amplified Bible from her nightstand and rushed down the stairs. Just holding the patented leather grain against her chest soothed her anger. She handed the Bible to her sister. "Open it and read the first page."

With a sigh Tara sat up and did as she was told. Her eyes grew wider as she looked from the page to CoCo. "This was Mom's?"

"Yes. There are notes and passages underlined and highlighted all through it. Notes of her and Dad praying certain Scriptures over us as babies. They were practicing Christians, Tara." She sat beside her sister. "So I do know they're in heaven now."

Tara flipped through the Bible. The fluttering of pages filled CoCo's spirit with a deep sense of calm, of peace. She laid her hand on Tara's forearm. "You can take it to your room and read it if you'd like."

For a moment, she feared her sister would toss the Bible on the couch and storm out. But she didn't. Instead, she closed the Bible gently and grabbed the love letters from the coffee table. She clutched them to her chest. "I'll give it back to you tomorrow, yes?"

She helped Tara to her feet. "That's fine." She planted a kiss on her sister's temple. "Good night, *Boo.* I love you."

Tara nodded and headed toward her room. CoCo watched her climb the stairs.

Thank You, God, for at least opening her mind enough to consider the truth. Lead me to continue witnessing so that glory may be brought to Your name.

It was a good night for getting answers. For getting the truth.

Luc parked in his uncle's driveway and stared up at the stars. Despite the recent storms, the temperatures had been reaching into the high nineties, even breaking a hundred a time or two this past week. Not a cloud blocked the view of the moon beaming down over Lagniappe.

He directed his attention on his uncle's house. A single light shone through the living room window. With a sigh, Luc got out and ambled up the stairs. "Uncle Justin, it's Luc." He didn't want to be met at the door with a shotgun this time.

No footsteps dragged against the floor. No television sounded from inside. Luc rapped the door with his knuckles. "Uncle Justin?"

Nary a sound. He waited, listening for any signs of movement from inside the house. Nothing. So much for getting answers tonight. Uncle Justin may have gone down to the tavern.

Luc got back into the vehicle, but didn't turn over the engine. He should go home, check on his mother and Felicia. Something deep inside him churned. He needed an emotional release, too. Grabbing his cell phone, he then flipped it open and pressed the speed-dial number he'd assigned to CoCo.

"Hello." She answered on the first ring. Just the sound of her voice caused his heart to stutter.

"Hi, there."

"Luc! Are you finished talking to Justin already?"

"He isn't home."

"Oh. I finished going through the trunks in the attic." Her voice hitched.

He was almost afraid to ask. "Did you find anything else?"

"Luc, can you come over?"

She must have found something serious. Now he was scared. "I'm on my way."

He closed the phone and turned over the ignition. She'd discovered something that had distressed her. What could be worse than finding a picture of their grandfathers in KKK robes?

Worry pushed his foot harder on the accelerator as he drove to her house. He paid no heed to the fleeting countryside or the cars he passed. His sole focus was on CoCo and whatever more she'd found.

A siren blasted into his thoughts. A quick glance in the rearview mirror and he saw the flashing blue lights. He dropped his gaze to his speedometer and sighed. Sixty-five in a forty-five. Now he'd get a ticket on top of everything else. Just what he didn't need. Not today.

Luc slowed down and veered to the edge of the road, careful to avoid the dramatic drop. They didn't have shoulders this far south, but there wasn't much traffic anyway. He moved the gearshift into Park, then rolled down his window. Even after nine o'clock, the heat still rushed in.

"Where's the fire?" Sheriff Bubba Theriot bent to stare into his face.

"Sorry, Bubba. I wasn't paying attention to my speed." He glanced at his old friend and gave a shaky smile. "I've been a bit distracted today."

"I can understand that." Bubba glanced over his shoulder. He leaned down even more and stared into Luc's face. "Look, I shouldn't even be telling you this, but Luc, I don't think you had anything to do with your grandfather's death."

Icy chills held Luc captive. He nodded, but didn't speak a word.

"However, the results came back today. The gun we found in the bayou? It's Beau's. And its butt matches the imprint from the gun cabinet."

Could his day get any worse? "What's that mean?"

Bubba's eyes dimmed. "It means I'll have to officially bring you in for questioning on Monday."

Luc's heart crashed at his feet. "Question me about what? I've already answered all your questions. What more is there to tell?"

"It'll be an official questioning regarding your possible involvement in Beau's murder."

The words vibrated against Luc's chest, pressing so tight against his lungs he couldn't breathe.

"I thought I should give you a heads-up."

"I—I appreciate that."

"If you can think of anything that will help you, Luc, you need to find it before Monday morning. The judge will be available to sign the paperwork at nine."

Nine. Paperwork. Official questioning. Murder.

"You okay, Luc?"

"Yeah. *Merci,* Bubba."

"Just find something to clear your name, okay?" Bubba clapped him on the shoulder and then sauntered back to his cruiser.

Luc sat still, every muscle in his body tensed to the point of a too-tight spring. His head echoed the blood pulsating through his veins.

A short burst of a horn behind him shook him from his fearful thoughts. He glanced in the side mirror. Bubba had turned off the twirling, flashing light, but flashed his high beams at him. Letting out a long breath, Luc put the vehicle in gear and edged back onto the road.

Should he tell CoCo? They'd racked their brains trying to find the answers. He didn't think they could do any more than what they'd already done. Maybe Uncle Justin could provide some answers. He'd definitely track him down, tomorrow at the latest. He had a deadline now. And didn't like it one bit.

He pulled into her driveway and noticed CoCo waiting on the front porch. He rushed to her, anxious to just be near her. As if that would make all his worries take flight.

"Luc, what's wrong?"

There she went again, reading his mind. He should have known he couldn't keep something from her. It was probably for the best. If he was going to win her back, he didn't want to keep secrets. Not from her, not anymore. "I got pulled over on my way here."

"Speeding?" She made a grimace.

"Yeah, but I didn't get a ticket."

"You caught a break. Good. You need one."

"Bubba pulled me over and gave me a bit of information."

Her eyes probed his. "What kind of information?"

"The results came back on the gun you found in the bayou. It's Grandfather's and it matches the missing one from my house."

Her almond eyes widened, and she grabbed his hands. "Oh, no!"

Might as well get it all out and over with. "Come Monday, they'll be hauling me in for official questioning."

Her bottom lip caught between her teeth and tears filled her eyes. "I'm so sorry, Luc. If I hadn't found the stupid gun…"

"It's okay." He pulled her against his chest to comfort her, but he drew strength from the embrace. "Bubba said if I could find anything to prove my innocence, I'd better hurry."

She looked up at him, and pushed away from his embrace. "The letters aren't enough?"

"Obviously not."

"I may have something that can help. It will definitely give rise to some uncomfortable questions."

His heart smashed against his gut. "What have you found?"

She pulled something from her shorts pocket. She glanced at it for a moment, seeming to battle something within herself before handing it to him. "If you want to use it, that is."

"As if I wouldn't?" He took the object. A photo.

He ran a hand over his hair. Another picture. What heartache would it cause this time? He sucked in air and then let it all out at once. No sense in avoiding now—his own freedom was at stake.

Luc stared at the photo and the notation. A queasy sensation roiled in his gut, stomach acid churning. Uncle Justin and Marcel LeBlanc…hanged a man?

He lifted his gaze to CoCo's and saw the same concerns reflecting in her eyes. While their grandfathers were dead, Justin wasn't. What would happen to him if this picture got out? Was this the proof referred to in the letter they'd found of his grandfather's things? If so, how did whoever wrote the letter know about this picture? A worse scenario pushed against his mind—what if this wasn't the proof? What if the proof was actually much worse?

What could be worse than a racially motivated murder?

TWENTY-ONE

Sure would be nice to know what clicked behind his eyes. CoCo could detect the shock and hurt, naturally, but the rest of what he felt stayed hidden. She touched his elbow. "Luc?"

His Adam's apple bobbed. "I just...I just can't believe it." He shook his head, his gaze dropping back to the photograph. "I'm looking at it, it's real, but I can't believe it."

"I know," she whispered. Her heart ached to take away the pain in his face, yet she swallowed the pity. "What do you want to do?"

He leaned against the porch railing. "I haven't a clue. This just—it just floors me."

She glanced out into the darkness. *Why, God? Why is this so hard? All we keep finding, all the decisions...what're we supposed to do?*

"Okay, let's try to think about this logically."

"All right." She dropped to one of the rockers. "Let's hear it."

"We know Grandfather got a threatening letter from your lawyer."

"Right, but I don't think he's involved with any of this. It's all about his sister. I don't think he'd have killed Beau over that." She thought about Dwayne, his actions and his motivations. "I think he would have rather exposed Beau if he'd found out anything."

"That brings us to the next letter, but we don't know who wrote it."

"Someone who knew that picture was in my house. Knew the coins were here." She tapped her finger against her bottom lip. *Think. Concentrate.*

"Who?"

"The only people who have access to the attic are me, Grandmere and Tara. Today was the first time Tara had been up there, and the first time I'd been up was with you. I don't think Grandmere could even climb those rickety steps."

"Someone has to know." He raked his hand over his face, a scratch sounding when his fingers brushed his five o'clock shadow. "Could your grandfather have told someone before he died?"

CoCo considered the idea. Then immediately ruled it out. "Why? From the entry we found, he felt horrible about it later. Begged for forgiveness. Would punish himself by looking at the pictures. I can't see him telling anyone. I think he'd be too ashamed."

Luc nodded. "I think so, too." He rubbed his head, fast and rough. "That leaves Uncle Justin..I can't see him telling anyone, either. I mean, he's kept it secret for all these years, why spill the beans now?"

"Right." Confusion clouded her thoughts. "No one else could know."

He snapped his fingers. "Except the person who took the picture."

Her heart jumped. "We have no clue who that is."

"Yes, but at least three people know the picture exists. One is dead, so that leaves two. Uncle Justin and the photographer."

Another thought forced itself to the forefront of her mind. "Luc, how does that person know the picture still exists?" She stood and leaned against him, using his strength to fortify herself. "Most of the people who were active in the Klan burned all their stuff years ago, back when it became an embarrassment to have ties to the KKK."

"You're right."

She took a step backward and stared into his face. "So, what do we do?"

"Beats me." He took one of her hands in his and refused to let go even when she tugged. "We'll just pray and see where God directs us."

"Speaking of God, do you want to go to my church with me tomorrow?"

"You don't want to go with *me?*"

How could she explain? "I thought maybe you'd like a break from being on display. With your grandfather's death and funeral and all." Besides, she wanted him to meet her preacher and her small church community.

"I think I'd like that." He smiled. "What time should I pick you up?"

"Nine."

"Then I guess I'd better go." He turned, keeping hold of her hand and pulling her to him.

With a slowness she thought would kill her, he lowered his head to rub his lips against hers. Soft...sweet...and entirely too brief. Before she could say or do anything else stupid, she shoved him back a space.

He smiled at her. "I'll see you in the morning."

She watched him walk away, pressing her fingers against her mouth, recalling his lips on hers. With a sigh she turned and headed into the house, already knowing her dreams would be filled with images of Luc Trahan. So much for a restful night's sleep.

The morning church service had been nice. CoCo's preacher gave a good sermon. Luc had enjoyed himself, which surprised him. Sure, the church was located farther out of town than his, but the service fed his spirit. Maybe he should consider changing.

CoCo gasped as he turned into her driveway. An old Lincoln sat parked behind her Jeep. "Whose car is that?"

"My lawyer's. Dwayne's." Her face registered several emotions, but surprise carried the load. She opened her door and hopped out before Luc had a chance to turn off the engine.

Luc rushed to catch up with her as she stopped in front of the tall dark man leaning against the front of his car. "Dwayne, what're you doing here?" She tilted her head to the side, that cute way she had of sizing up someone. He moved to stand next to her.

The attorney didn't look too happy to see Luc with her. Too bad. He'd just have to cope with it. Luc was in her life and had no intention of going anywhere.

"I realized I was a bit rude with you on the phone yesterday." Dwayne straightened, his gaze right on CoCo.

"That's okay."

When had she talked to Dwayne? Luc turned to gape at her. Had she told her lawyer about the picture?

She must have felt his stare because she gave a brief shake of her head. Just enough to let him know she hadn't said anything. There she went again, reading his thoughts before he could voice them.

"There's, uh, a reason I was short with you." Dwayne stared at the tips of his shoes.

CoCo's tone softened considerably. "You can tell me, Dwayne."

"The thing is, my sister's diary…"

Luc held his own breath, not wanting to draw attention to himself.

"Her diary?" CoCo prompted.

"My sister came back to Lagniappe with one goal in mind—to find out what happened to our grandfather."

CoCo shook her head. "I'm not following you."

"She moved here from California to find out what happened to our mother's father." He lifted his gaze to stare at CoCo. "Remember I told you my mother's people were from here? My grandfather was a civil rights attorney and he was here, in this town, when he disappeared back in the mid-1950s."

"Disappeared?"

"Without a trace."

"And your sister was trying to find out what happened to him?"

"Right. She'd made some progress. At least, according to the diary she had."

CoCo softened her tone. "What kind of progress?"

"She'd discovered Justin Trahan and your grandfather were linked to the KKK." His face screamed that he didn't want to accuse her grandfather of such nastiness.

The strong woman that she was, CoCo took it in stride. "She had proof of this?" Her voice didn't waver. Even lifted her chin a bit. Pride rose in Luc's chest.

"She wrote in her diary that she'd gotten proof." Dwayne's voice lowered so much that it was hard to hear him over the ruckus of the crickets and tree frogs singing for more rain. "When she quit her job, I…I told you she became a drug addict." His face tightened. "I think one of the men she was involved with got her hooked. She was too proud to ask for help. Even from me. Maybe it was stubbornness."

If it were possible for the earth to swallow a person whole, Luc imagined the person would look pretty much like Dwayne did at that exact moment.

Both Luc and CoCo remained silent. Luc sure didn't want to rush the man. He could only imagine how he'd feel if it'd been Felicia in Dwayne's sister's place.

"According to her diary, Beulah was seeing two men. One she referred to as her 'Friday Night Special.' One night after one too many whiskeys, he let it slip that he'd had ties to the Klan back in the day." Dwayne scuffed the ground with the toe of his loafer. "Said he knew of some members who had gone rogue, hanging the men they caught."

Luc's heart skidded to his knees. He gulped in air.

"Go on." CoCo's voice came out calm, although Luc knew she had to be thinking the same thing.

Dwayne cast a glance at her. "She was following up on that lead, searching this man's house when he'd pass out cold. She recorded everything in her diary at night."

"And?" Luc couldn't stop the question.

The lawyer tossed him a glare, but continued his tale anyway. "Near the end of her diary, she wrote that she'd caught the SAM character she'd been involved with at the casino reading her research notes about our grandfather, which she kept in a spiral notebook. She'd gotten mad and he'd ended up smacking her upside the head. She fell to the ground and must've hit her head because she lost time. When she came to, the SAM guy was gone. Along with her spiral notebook."

"This SAM knew the man she saw on Friday nights was aware of the rogue Klan members years ago?"

"Not only that, she believed he was one himself." Dwayne shifted his weight from one leg to the other. "She writes about going to her 'Friday Night Special' man and telling him what she'd written in her notebook about him."

CoCo gasped. "What happened?"

"She only made one entry after that. Wrote she was scared. She knew one of the men was going to kill her. All her evidence was gone so she was putting her diary in the mail to me." His last word carried out on a sob. Dwayne sniffed, then cleared his throat. "Beulah was dead four days from the date of her last entry."

"I'm sorry." CoCo's words were as soft as the edges of the bayou.

"Thank you." Dwayne lifted his gaze again. "That's what made me decide to stay here and open my practice. To find out what happened to my sister. They said she'd injected too much meth, but I know better. She would've never done that—she was terrified of needles." He jerked his stare to Luc.

The stare felt hard enough that Luc fought the urge to squirm.

"I didn't hurt your grandfather. I just wanted to get him to confess to encouraging my sister to quit, which started the downhill spiral that led to her death. I truly believe he was one of the men seeing her and wanted to protect himself. I think he gave her cash, which would explain why she could afford the drugs. Had I found any solid evidence, I would have taken it to the police." The man's eyes were honest. "I think your grandfather and SAM were one and the same man."

Luc offered his hand. "I have a little sister, so I can understand your pain. I'm very sorry for your loss, but SAM can't be my grandfather. He abhorred violence, so there's no way he would have hit a woman."

The lawyer gripped his hand, firm and solid, like an honest man's handshake.

"Dwayne," CoCo interrupted, "I'm wondering if your sister's diary implied that these two men in your sister's life knew each other, or of each other."

"By the contents, I think the SAM guy knew about the Friday Night Special, but I don't know about vice versa."

She laid a hand on his. "Thank you for coming by and telling me all this." Her smile spoke volumes of compassion and empathy. "I have to ask, though. Why didn't you take her diary to the police?"

Good question, thought Luc, and waited for the answer.

"Come on, CoCo. We may be in the twenty-first century and all, but do you really think the police were that concerned about the supposed drug overdose of a barmaid?"

"I guess not." CoCo's face enflamed in a blush.

"What do you think?" CoCo faced Luc, having waited until Dwayne left and they were comfortable in the rockers on the porch before she asked.

He ran a hand over his face. His smooth face—no whiskers darkened his chin today. "I don't know. It's a lot to take in. Especially considering the photos we've found."

"Any idea who the men are—code names SAM and Friday Night Special?" He rested his elbows on his knees. "I know Dwayne thinks SAM is Grandfather, but I just have trouble picturing it. He would never have hit a woman. Ever."

"I'd have to say this Friday Night Special could be our photographer. The man who took our grandfathers' pictures."

"I was thinking the same thing. Could that man have

been the one writing Beau and threatening to expose Justin's involvement?"

"Probably."

She recognized the agony in his expression. Knowing what was right, yet wanting to protect his family. She cast a glance over her shoulder at the open door. She could understand; she wanted to protect her family, too. "Luc…"

He pulled the barrette from her hair, letting all the curls tumble against her face. "Shh…don't ask."

"We need to decide what we're going to do with the pic—"

"Not now." He cupped the nape of her neck and drew her to him.

His kiss was as light as the moonbeams. Her heart skittered from her chest into his. She relaxed against the sweet kiss, lifting a palm to rest against his cheek.

"Ahem."

CoCo jerked to her feet two seconds before Luc hit his. Toby stood at the foot of the stairs, avoiding eye contact. "Ms. CoCo, you told me you needed some work done around here?"

She wiped her cheeks, as if that would remove the telltale blush. "I did."

"I thought I'd mosey over and see if you wanted me to work for you this afternoon." He finally lifted his eyes to hers.

He was such a good kid. Sweet and reliable. Especially considering he'd grown up without a father on site. "Actually, I need the grass mowed. Ever since we got rain the other day, I believe the grass has grown two inches."

Toby chuckled, then sobered as he stared at Luc. "Mr. Trahan. I'm sorry about your granddaddy."

Tingles started in her toes and worked all the way up to her fingers. This was her perfect opportunity.

"Thank you, son."

CoCo smiled again. "You said your daddy knew Mr. Beau, Toby?"

The teenager nodded, his cropped hair not moving one iota. "Yes, ma'am. He works for Mr. Beau. Well, he did."

She held her breath, fighting to keep the excitement from coming out in her voice. This was it, she could feel it. "Toby, I'm sorry that I've never asked, but who is your daddy?"

He gave her a strange look, as if she'd sprouted two heads. "It's okay, Ms. CoCo. I only met him for the first time about six months ago. My daddy's name is Sammy. Sammy Arthur Moran." Toby puffed his chest out with pride.

TWENTY-TWO

CoCo's heart beat double-time as she waited for Toby to fire up the lawn mower. Once its roar filled the air, she grabbed the sleeve of Luc's shirt and twisted the fabric into a tight wad. "Did you catch it?"

Wearing a look of utter confusion, Luc spoke slowly. "Grandfather knew the coins were here because Toby sold the one he'd found to him."

"Right. And if Toby showed it to Beau, it only stands to reason that Sammy might have seen it as well." She tightened her grip on his shirt sleeve. "Could Sammy have been trying to blackmail Beau?"

"To what means? What would Sammy have to benefit? There were no large amounts of money missing from Grandfather's accounts."

An idea popped up in her mind. "What if he blackmailed Beau, but not for money?"

"Then for what?"

"Maybe to get Beau's endorsement for casino manager after he retired?"

Luc stiffened and widened his eyes. "That could be it, Sammy had talked to me several times, knowing I didn't want to work there. He'd encouraged me to tell Grandfather." He closed his eyes for a moment. "Told me I should stand up strong for my beliefs."

"Knowing you wouldn't take the job, Sammy intended to blackmail Beau to get his endorsement."

"Only one problem with that, beautiful."

Her heart took another fall. "What?"

"We know how Sammy and Beau knew about the coins. If Sammy was the one who wrote that letter to Beau, getting ready to set him up to blackmail him for an endorsement, how could Sammy know about the KKK stuff in your attic?"

Yep, his logic was a major problem in her theory. She chewed her bottom lip and stared out over the bayou. The gentle breeze wafted the smell of water and soil across the porch. She closed her eyes and inhaled, drawing the comforting scent in deep.

God, we could use a little guidance. We're missing something. What?

Her heart crushed against her lungs. Her breaths came in forced pants. "Wait a minute. Sammy Arthur Moran. S. A. M." She shot her glance back to Luc, her knees turning to mush. "It wasn't a code name in her diary—it was the man's initials."

The lawnmower rumbled from the backyard. Luc spun CoCo around like a man gone wild. "Don't you see? Sammy knew about the pictures because he was the man Dwayne's sister was involved with at the casino. Not my grandfather."

The dots all connected in her mind. "Sammy saw the notes Beulah had in her notebook. He broke off their relationship because he realized he had enough to blackmail Beau. And he took her notebook."

He nodded, smiling like a big loon, and her heart followed the way of her knees. Excitement lit his entire face. "She must've had enough information that implicated your grandfather and Uncle Justin. Sammy realized he could use that to get to Grandfather."

Anticipation built in her chest. "He knew Beau knew about the Confederate coins because of Toby, so he made the coin rubbing to prove to Beau that he made a legitimate claim."

"Right. Knowing Grandfather, he wouldn't put up with blackmail. Maybe he found out Sammy was the one who sent him the letter."

"Would Beau have confronted Sammy?"

Luc shook his head. "No. He would have taken the evidence to the police and exposed Sammy."

"Maybe that's what he intended, and Sammy had to kill Beau to stop him from turning him in for blackmail."

"Sounds like Grandfather." Luc pulled CoCo to him.

She barely registered his head bending before his lips were on hers.

He let her go so suddenly she lost her balance. She clutched his forearms and regained her footing.

Luc gave a little chuckle. "We need to tell Bubba. This gives Sammy Moran strong motive for murder."

Something was still off. Hovering just outside the edges of her reasoning, so close she could touch it. "Hang on, let me think for a second." She chewed her bottom lip, rewinding all they'd discovered.

Luc leaned against the rail and let out a long breath.

Her mind's fingers finally grasped what she'd been overlooking. "The pictures."

"What?"

"How did Dwayne's sister know about the pictures in my attic?"

He ran a hand over his face. "I don't know. Dwayne said that her notebook was gone. Maybe she'd gotten curious about the coins and found out about the link between them and the Klan. Let's just assume she did know."

"Okay. It's enough that Sheriff Theriot can look into it."

Another thought slapped her mind. "Dwayne says he knows his sister was involved with the man at the casino who encouraged her to quit. I just wonder…what if Sammy set her up from the beginning—once he found out what she knew?"

"That's a thought. I can ask Bubba to check that out." Luc planted a kiss on the tip of her nose. "Speaking of, I should run out to Bubba's and fill him in on what we've learned."

"Are you ready to do that just yet?"

"Why wouldn't I? I only have until tomorrow morning to get off the main suspect list."

"Will you tell the sheriff about the pictures we've found? One implicates your uncle in murder."

"What do I do, CoCo? Protect Uncle Justin or myself?"

"I'd say you, but that's because the truth needs to come out."

Luc's laughter brushed against her face. "I don't want to turn in Uncle Justin until I've had a chance to talk to him." He shrugged. "He might feel just as bad as your grandfather did. I'd like to give him a chance to explain."

"Then what do we do?"

"What if I just give Bubba the first picture? The one we found of them in the KKK robes?"

"And not the other one?" No, Luc—the upstanding man who had a strong sense of morals and values, a strong Christian—wouldn't withhold evidence in a murder investigation.

"Just for now. Just until I can talk to my uncle. A day or so at most." He narrowed his eyes and lowered his voice. "I'll pray about it first."

So would she. Now. *Dear God, what would You have us do? A man was murdered…by my grandfather and Luc's uncle. We have the evidence. Do we turn it over now, or hold it a day? God, I don't know what's right.*

Luc's eyes met hers, and her heart melted into a pool. She knew what to do. Her heart told her, loud and clear.

Luc pulled out of Sheriff Bubba Theriot's driveway, heading toward Uncle Justin's place. The afternoon sun beat down, giving Lagniappe no reprieve. Bubba had been most receptive to his and CoCo's theories, and had promised to start looking into things as soon as he finished his lunch, which Luc had so rudely interrupted.

A twinge of guilt snapped against his chest. He hadn't told Bubba about the second picture. The *other* one. CoCo had told him to wait until he'd talked to Justin—that he owed his uncle that much. He was thankful for her understanding. Now, he just needed the truth and he could tell Bubba the rest of the story. He groaned—his thoughts sounded like Paul Harvey.

Turning into Uncle Justin's driveway, Luc's heart hammered. How exactly should he start the conversation? *Hey, Uncle Justin, I found a picture of you as a member of the KKK and you murdered a man. How're you doing?* His mouth went dry. Nope, that wouldn't work.

Heavenly Father, I come to You for Your wisdom and guidance. This is most difficult for me, and I pray You'll guide my words.

He'd made it to the second step when the door swung open and Justin stood at the threshold, this time brandishing a rifle. He lowered the barrel as soon as he recognized Luc. "What brings ya by, boy?"

Luc swallowed hard. "I need to talk to you, Uncle Justin."

"Come on in." His uncle moved aside to let him cross. "If

it's about me droppin' the eviction on your girlfriend, ya can forget it."

"No, it's not about that." Luc dropped onto the couch. "It's about the past."

Uncle Justin rested the rifle on the floor, propping it against the wall. "The past?"

"This is really hard for me, Uncle Justin."

"Just spit it out. Can't be no worse than tellin' me someone murdered my brother."

"CoCo and I were up in her attic…" Luc stopped when he saw the fear cover his uncle's eyes. He touched Uncle Justin's knee. "Are you okay?"

Uncle Justin shook his head. When he refocused on Luc, all traces of fear were gone from his eyes. "I'm fine. But if your gonna tell me about your love life with that gal in her attic, I'd rather not hear about it." He chuckled.

"No, not about my love life." He rubbed his hands against his khakis. Funny how a layer of sweat had instantly coated his palms. "We found a picture in her attic. Of you and Marcel LeBlanc."

Uncle Justin's eyes became guarded. "Now that could be. He and I were friends when we were younger."

"I know." Luc swallowed again. Why did his throat feel as if it'd been stuffed with cotton? "In this particular photo, y'all were wearing robes. With the KKK emblem."

Dropping his gaze to the floor, Uncle Justin shook his big head. "I never wanted you to find that out, boy. You've been like a grandson to me since I never had any children of my own. Matter of fact, you're my sole heir, boy. I never wanted you to know that about me."

Relief filled all of Luc's senses. His uncle regretted his past, just like CoCo's grandfather had. *Thank You, God.* If there was no repentance, well, that would have been hard for Luc to take.

"We were kids, you understand. Back then it was a different time. I don't expect you to understand." Uncle Justin never lifted his head, but spoke to the floor.

"I do understand. We all have things in our past we wish we could change."

Like breaking up with the woman you love because you didn't trust God enough to come through.

Uncle Justin snapped his head up and stared into his eyes. "I'm glad ya understand. I'd rather just forget all 'bout that time in my life."

Only thing, Luc couldn't let it drop. Oh, how he wished he could. He inched to the edge of the couch. "I understand, but I can't let it go, Uncle Justin. As much as I'd like to, I can't."

"Why not?" His uncle's eyes hardened in a flash.

Chills trickled up his spine. "Because we found another picture, too." Luc licked his lips with a dry tongue. "A picture of you and Marcel standing beside a hanging black man. Marcel wrote on the back that you and he had killed the man. Murdered him."

TWENTY-THREE

CoCo banked the airboat before jumping to the soggy ground. She tied the boat off on the oak tree, then slowly made her way to the mailbox. Her heart tripped as she recognized the return address of the Wetlands Preservation Center. She dropped to the dried grass, her pulse thundering in her head. This was it. She'd either get the grant approval or not. If she didn't get it, she'd be out of a job with no income. And she'd need all the money she could get to fight Justin Trahan to keep the house.

With a shaking hand, she tore open the envelope and withdrew the letter. Her eyes moved faster than her brain could keep up, until she came to the second paragraph. The one that told her she would receive her grant, along with the increase she'd requested. CoCo leapt to her feet, let out a whoop, and jogged to the house.

Tara stood on the front porch, a cell phone in her hand. "This is Luc's. He left it here on the porch rail."

"Okay." CoCo climbed the stairs.

"Sheriff Theriot's been calling like crazy."

"On Luc's phone?"

Tara set the cell in CoCo's hand. "Yep. I told him Luc had left the phone here by accident. He asked for you. Said for

you to call him as soon as you got back, that it was urgent."
She shook her head. "Grandmere was about to send me out
in the pirogue to find you."

"Merci." She tuned her sister out and scrolled through the
calls listed on Luc's phone. She found the one marked Bubba
and pressed the call button.

"Luc."

"Sheriff, it's CoCo. Luc's not back yet."

"Where'd he go? Do you know?"

"He was going to see you first." A frisson of danger crept
between her shoulder blades. "Why? He didn't make it to
your place?"

"He was here." The sheriff let out a long breath. "Told me
your theory about Sammy Moran."

She bit her bottom lip. Hard enough that she tasted the
coppery tang of blood. "And?"

"I did some checking and talked to Mr. Moran as soon
as Luc left."

Chills pricked her skin despite the hot afternoon. "Were we
right?"

"Partially." His sigh hung heavy over the phone. "Look, I
probably shouldn't tell you all this, but I need to talk to Luc.
I'm on my way to Dwayne's now."

"Tell me what's going on."

The sheriff remained silent.

"Please. I love Luc and need to know." As she said the
words aloud, she knew she had to give Luc another chance.
Had to give *them* another chance.

He grunted. "Sammy admitted he'd written that letter to
Beau a few weeks ago. He'd been involved with Dwayne's
sister, just like you suspected. He didn't go through her
notebook thoroughly until last month."

"Okay." Fear knotted in her heart.

"You were right about the coin, Toby's supplying it and all. Sammy admitted he'd edged Dwayne's sister's out the door. He didn't want her talking to Beau and letting it slip she knew about Justin and Marcel's involvement."

"He set her up?"

"Yes." He sighed again. "Sammy swears he didn't kill Beau. He has some pretty hot evidence pointing the finger at Justin."

CoCo hissed in air.

Justin. Murdered his brother?

"Are you still there?"

"Yes. What evidence?"

"According to the notebook Sammy showed me, Dwayne's sister was sleeping with Justin every week. One night, after a bit too much whiskey, he told her about rogue Klan members who were killing black men. Hanging them. I guess he wanted to shock her."

Her stomach heaved. She gagged, but pushed it back.

The sheriff kept talking, not noticing her reaction. "Dwayne's sister felt like Justin just might have been the one responsible for her grandfather's disappearance so many years ago. She made notes of what he told her. Documented it in her notebook that Sammy turned over to me. I need to collaborate the notebook with her diary, which is why I'm heading to Dwayne's now."

It was too much. The pieces fell into place, making CoCo's blood turn cold. "We found a picture, an incriminating one. I have it. Sheriff, Luc was going to see his uncle…"

The sound of brakes squealing broke over the line. "Luc's at Justin's?" The sheriff let out a litany of curses under his breath. "Why didn't you tell me?"

"I didn't know it was important."

"I'm heading there now. I'll get there as quick as I can."

Luc. With his uncle, a murderer twice over.

If looks could kill....

Luc stared into Uncle Justin's eyes. Eyes filled with a rage Luc had never seen before.

His uncle lumbered to his feet. "It's real unfortunate ya found that picture, boy." He paced in front of the couch. "I told Marcel to get rid of it, but nooo, he needed it. For his repentance, he said."

All of a sudden, the room seemed much smaller to Luc. He could feel the walls pressing in against him. He jumped to his feet. "I know, Uncle Justin. We can—"

His uncle shoved his shoulder, hard. Luc fell back onto the couch. Faster than Luc imagined the older man could move, Justin grabbed the rifle and stuck the barrel against Luc's chest.

"Uncle Justin, it's okay. We can go to Bubba and—"

Justin shoved the gun harder into Luc's chest. "Shut up." He cursed under his breath. "Who else knows about the picture, huh?"

"I took it to the sheriff after CoCo and I found it." That wasn't really a lie. He did take a photo, just not *that* one.

Another stream of curses. Justin wiped his forehead.

"I don't understand..."

His uncle's glare stopped him short. "Ya couldn't figure anything out. Not like my brother."

Luc dared not move.

"When did ya give it to the sheriff?"

"Less than an hour ago."

Justin sat on the edge of the coffee table, but kept the gun digging into Luc's chest. "For decades I get away with it, and now…" He glared back at Luc. "You're just too nosy for your own good, ya know that?"

"I really don't understand, Uncle Justin." *Just keep him talking, keep him calm.*

The laugh his uncle gave was more of a snort, riddled with an evil Luc had never heard before. "I woulda gotten away with it all if it hadn't been for Beulah, that little conniving, thieving, wh—"

"Who?" Luc could've swallowed his tongue for the look Justin gave him.

"The little girl who warmed my bed every Friday night."

Friday Night Special. Luc's gut twisted. Dwayne's sister.

Justin studied him through narrowed eyes. "Ah, I see ya know 'bout her, yes?"

"She's Dwayne William's little sister."

"Well, I'll be da—"

"You didn't know?"

"Nope. News to me." Justin loosened his grip on the rifle just a fraction of an inch and rubbed his head. "No matter, though." He pushed the gun back digging into Luc's chest, right over his heart. "She got me to tell her things I'd done in the past. Too much whiskey. Didn't even think too much about her until Beau came over last week."

Every nerve tangled in Luc.

Justin nodded. "Yeah, he came by to show me that Confederate coin. Knew it'd come from your little swamp thang's house, too.

"He'd talked to a coin appraiser who'd filled him in how our local Klan had accumulated quite a bit of them and what they were worth. That's why he was gonna evict them, to get his hands on those coins. He always was too greedy for his own good. And he told me 'bout a letter someone had written, telling him there was evidence of my Klan activities hidden in that house, too."

Luc pressed his back as far into the couch as possible. His uncle was a much older man than he, but built like a middle linebacker. Besides, he had a gun. Luc could watch for an opening…an opportunity to get the upper hand. Maybe if he got his uncle on a roll, he'd get a chance. "Which there was."

"I didn't know that yet, but I knew ole Marcel might've kept some mementos. 'Course, I thought he mighta gotten rid of everything right before he died since he seemed to find Jesus and all that hoopla."

"You weren't sure?" Anything to keep him talking.

"It was likely there'd still be somethin' over at Marcel's. I'd tried to cozy up to Marie after he died, but she would have none of it."

"Marie didn't like you?"

Justin skewered his face into a grimace. "Woman didn't know what she was missin'—I'll tell ya that."

Luc crossed his ankles, providing himself a means of shifting a bit to the edge of the couch. He needed to be ready to make his move.

"Beau…he comes over here all het up because of that letter and what he learned about the coins linked to the Klan. My own brother tells me if he finds any evidence about me being in the Klan, he'd turn me over to the police himself." He let out a long huff. "Can ya imagine?"

"He didn't know for sure?"

"Of course not! He had that eviction notice going, and I knew it'd only be a matter of time before he found something Marcel left behind."

Luc stiffened, every muscle in his body tensing. "What happened?"

"I tried to explain, but noooo, not to my brother, Mr. Up-standing and all. He was bound and determined to prove to everyone he upheld the law. Even if it meant turning in his own flesh and blood."

Justin shook his head. "I've outlived them both—Marcel and Roger, our other true brother of the Klan who'd taken the pictures. Both of 'em dead for years now."

Justin jumped to his feet suddenly, pushing the gun up to Luc's neck. "Ya know, we need to go. That sheriff, *cooyon* that he is, could be on his way here right now." He jabbed the barrel into Luc's arm. "Get up."

Luc stood, sizing up his uncle.

Justin rammed the gun into his side. "Don't be gettin' no ideas, boy. I'll shoot ya dead just like I did your granddaddy."

Luc's heart and stomach flip-flopped. "You killed Grand-father? Your own brother?"

Laughing, Justin shoved him toward the back door of the house. "With his own gun, ain't that a kick in the bucket?"

Once he stood on the ground, Luc asked, "You shot him and set me up?"

"Had to, boy. Don't ya get it? There's no statute of limitations on murder. That picture is proof I killed a man, with that note on it." Justin shoved him forward with the barrel. "Don't be stupid. If ya give me any problems, I'll go kill that swamp witch girlfriend of yours as soon as I kill ya." He let out an evil laugh.

Hot rage swarmed Luc's logic. He fisted his hands at his sides.

Uncle Justin shoved the gun to Luc's face, right under his nose. "I said not to try nothin', ya hear?"

Dear Lord, he's gonna kill me just like he killed Grand-father. I don't care about that, God, I really don't. If You're ready to call me home, then I'm ready to come. But, God, please keep CoCo and her family safe. I pray You put your hedge of protection around them all.

Tires crunched on the gravel driveway.

Justin jabbed the rifle into Luc's back. "Keep your mouth shut. I mean it, boy."

Luc pressed his lips together even as he heard a banging on the front door.

"Justin! Luc! Open up. It's Sheriff Theriot."

"Not one word," Justin hissed in his ear. He shoved Luc toward the edge of the bayou backing up to his land.

He's gonna put me in the water and shoot me. They may never find my body. An alligator could get me. Luc's chest constricted. *Just like Dad.*

CoCo shut off the trolling motor of her airboat. She grabbed the palms lining the edge of the bayou and pulled the boat as close to the mounds of plants as possible. The sharp edges of the stalks dug into her hands, like multiple paper cuts. She didn't cry out. Her entire being focused on the two men standing no more than fifty feet from where she hid.

Justin had a gun pressed against the small of Luc's back. She sucked in her bottom lip and caught it between her teeth.

God, please protect Luc. Please, God, save him.

She could hear Bubba yelling from the front porch. When she'd hung up the phone with him, she'd rushed to her airboat, knowing she could get to Justin's house faster on water. And she'd made it in time. Could she save Luc?

CoCo lifted her binoculars, focusing on Justin's face. She took in every wrinkle lined with rage, the way his eyes were weighed down with fury, the firm set of his jaw. Lowering the field glasses, she realized Justin Trahan had gone off the deep end. The very deep end.

Justin pushed Luc to his knees at the water's edge. He pressed the end of the rifle at the base of Luc's skull.

The sob rose from her chest without warning. She would not watch someone she loved be taken away from her. CoCo jumped from the boat and crept toward the men.

"Justin! Luc!" Bubba's voice drew nearer.

From the corner of her eye, she caught the sheriff's movement around the side of the house.

Justin mumbled curses, lifting the butt of the rifle and brought it down on Luc's head. The cracking sounded just before Luc toppled face-first into the bayou.

Luc's uncle tossed the gun into the undergrowth beside the water and then turned and jogged up the incline. "Why, Sheriff Theriot, what're ya doin' here?" His voice didn't even hint at the horror of what he'd just done to his great-nephew.

Keeping in a crouched position, CoCo made her way toward Luc. She glanced over to the men at the side of the house before breaking out of her hiding behind the mounds of palms. The sheriff had a stern look on his face, but CoCo couldn't worry about him. Besides, the sheriff was younger and stronger than Justin, and Luc's uncle was now unarmed.

She tugged Luc's shoulders until she pulled him on dry land and held his head in her lap. Water rivulets covered his face, splats fell across her legs. "Luc, wake up," she whispered and tapped his cheek. "Come on, please wake up." She shot a look at the sheriff and Justin, still seeming in benign conversation. She gazed at Luc.

His eyes were open, focused on her. "CoCo? What—"

"Shh." She laid a finger against his lips. "I need to get you back to my boat before the sheriff and Justin get finished talking."

Luc sat up and rubbed the back of his head. "No.

CoCo, Uncle Justin is the one who killed Grandfather. He told me so—"

"I know," she hissed. "Keep your voice down. The sheriff knows, too. He's just distracting him because he doesn't know where you are. Now hush and follow me." She crouched and made her way to the mound of palms, then motioned him to follow.

Out in the open, he froze. His gaze locked on his great-uncle.

"Luc," she whispered.

He turned and looked at her.

"Please. Come on."

He stared back at the men.

"Please, Luc. I love you."

Luc jerked his stare to hers. He blinked several times.

Then a gunshot shattered the tranquility of the bayou.

TWENTY-FOUR

CoCo screamed. Luc rushed to her, gathering her into his arms. Together, they both turned.

Sheriff Theriot holstered his sidearm, before slapping cuff ties on Justin's wrists and tightened them. "Luc," he hollered. Justin laid on the ground moaning in pain from the shot to his foot. "Shouldn't have charged me, Mr. Trahan."

"Luc's okay," CoCo yelled. Her entire body quivered.

Luc tightened his hold on her and approached the men. "Bubba, he confessed. He killed my grandfather."

"I know. I figured that out." He gave a nod toward her. "Because your lady told me what else y'all had discovered."

Luc tightened his hold around her shoulders. She snuggled against him. "He needs to have his head checked out, Sheriff. I saw Justin hit him with the butt of the rifle."

"I'm fine." Luc waved off the sheriff's offer to take him to the hospital. "At least, now I am," he said, and leaned to kiss her.

"I'm just glad both of you are safe," CoCo's grandmother announced.

A small group sat on the LeBlancs' veranda. Felicia and her mother would soon arrive, completing the group. Tara sat on the arm of her grandmother's rocker. CoCo perched against the porch railing, Dwayne sat in the other rocker, and Luc leaned against the wall.

"I still can't believe Justin killed Beau." Marie LeBlanc made a clucking noise.

"It's all unbelievable," Dwayne said as he rubbed his head.

"God watched over us." CoCo's eyes met Luc's as she spoke.

Pride rose in his chest. He watched everyone's reactions. Tara dropped her gaze to the floor. Her grandmother stared with sharp eyes. Dwayne smiled, understanding. And something else hit against Luc's spirit. He glanced over and saw the question in CoCo's eyes. He gave a slight nod.

CoCo went into the house, then came out within seconds. She held a picture in her hand, which she offered to Dwayne. "Do you recognize the man in the middle?"

The lawyer took the picture and stared. His chest heaved and tears lined his eyes as he looked back to CoCo. "This was my grandfather, Jimmy Jones."

CoCo wrapped an arm around the big man's shoulders. "I'm so sorry, Dwayne. So sorry for my grandfather's actions. I don't know what else to say. I'm so ashamed."

"Me, too," Luc said as he moved to grip Dwayne's shoulder. "I can't say how sorry I am."

Dwayne looked from Luc to CoCo. "You just did. You solved the mystery of what happened to my grandfather." He glanced at the picture again. "And my sister," he mumbled under his breath. "Sheriff said Justin admitted to injecting her with an overdose of drugs."

"I'm sorry," CoCo whispered.

"May I have a copy of this?" Dwayne held up the picture. "I'd like to let my mother know. He was a civil rights attorney, did you know that?"

"I know." CoCo's voice was soft and even.

"You know what, I don't want a copy," Dwayne said. "I'd rather Mom not ever see this."

CoCo took the picture and shoved it into her shorts pocket. "I understand. I'll take this to the sheriff this afternoon."

Luc couldn't stand it any longer. He took CoCo's hand. "Can I talk to you a minute?" They'd barely had a second alone before they had to rehash the story over and over again. He excused them, then led her down to the bayou beside her airboat.

"What's wrong?"

"Uncle Justin told me something before he went ballistic."

"Oh, yeah?"

Luc smiled. "Told me that I was his sole heir."

"That impresses you?" She cocked her head.

He bit back the smile. "Not really. But see, if he's in jail for murder, chances are pretty good that he'll never get around to evicting you."

She grinned, sending his heart racing. "Is that a fact?"

"I think I can arrange for that to fall through the cracks." He stared at her, love burning in his chest. "Back there, did you mean what you said?"

Her face turned a delightful shade of red. "That I love you?"

His heart thundered. "Yes."

"Yes. *Je t'aime*."

His heart exploded with love and joy. He tugged her to him, planting kisses along her face before settling on her mouth. She murmured against him, then broke away from the kiss.

"I love you, too," he whispered.

"I know." She smiled. There she went again, reading his mind. Only this time, she read his heart.

Dear Reader,

Welcome to Cajun country! Having been born and raised in the state, I have Louisiana in my blood, and as such, this book is near and dear to my heart. I wanted to share with you the diverse and intriguing culture of the Cajun people and their unique customs. While Lagniappe doesn't really exist, the flavor of the Deep South seasoned into this story does. Weaving in the beautiful culture of the area has been so much fun. I hope you enjoyed journeying through the Louisiana waterways.

The Trahans and LeBlancs are so similar to many families in the Deep South—strong heritage, strong culture, strong people. Writing about these empowering families was like going home for me, and I thank you for traveling with me.

I love to hear from readers. Please visit me at::
www.robincaroll.com and drop me a line.

Join my newsletter group…sign my guestbook. You can mail me at:

P.O. Box 242091, Little Rock, AR 72223.

I look forward to hearing from you.

Blessings,

Robin Caroll

QUESTIONS FOR DISCUSSION

1. CoCo's family didn't believe in God, which caused her great pain. How do your family's and friends' beliefs affect your faith walk? Like CoCo, how might you be the "salt of the earth?"

2. Luc and CoCo's past relationship failed for many reasons, but primarily because they were unequally yoked. Have you ever had a relationship with a nonbeliever? How did this relationship affect your spiritual life?

3. Justin Trahan went to extremes to protect secrets from the past. Have you ever done anything you knew was wrong to protect yourself? How did you reconcile your actions with God?

4. Beau Trahan had a controling personality, which made those who loved him uncomfortable at times. Have you ever had to deal with someone you loved who tried to control you? If so, how did you handle the situation?

5. Luc had to learn about unconditional forgiveness. Looking into your own experiences, has there ever been a time when forgiving someone really pushed your faith?

6. CoCo learned that the salvation of others can't be pushed, that it comes in God's timing. Have you ever wanted instant salvation for someone? How did you come to terms with the frustrations over this?

7. Luc and CoCo called a truce in order to solve the murder, yet both had issues with trust. How has your lack of trust ever influenced your relationship with someone? How did you overcome the issue?

8. CoCo loved the bayou, looking at it as one of God's masterpieces, yet others were leery. How do you view nature?

9. Some of the issues Luc and CoCo faced in their relationship had to do with generations-old issues. Has something or someone in your family's past ever caused you concern in a current relationship?

10. CoCo was very comfortable in her own skin, knowing she was a child of God. How at ease are you with yourself and with life?

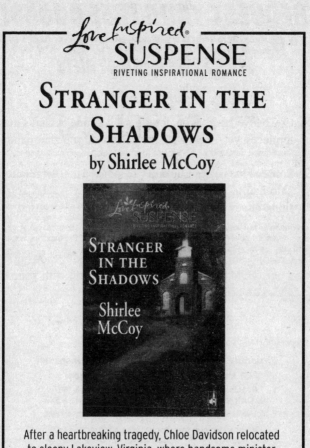

Love Inspired®

Celebrate Love Inspired's 10th anniversary
with top authors and great stories all year long!

Look for

Giving Thanks for Baby

by Terri Reed

A Tiny Blessings Tale

**Loving families and
needy children continue
to come together to fulfill
God's greatest plans!**

Single mom Trista Van Zandt
enrolled in a Christian singles'
Web site hoping to find a friend.
But love might lurk closer than
she thought in the shape of new
assistant pastor, Scott Crosby,
who had already made a great
impression on Trista in real life.

HEARTWARMING INSPIRATIONAL ROMANCE

Love Inspired®

Giving Thanks for Baby
Terri Reed
A Tiny Blessings Tale

Steeple
Hill®

*Available November
wherever you buy books.*

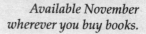

Love Inspired
SUSPENSE

TITLES AVAILABLE NEXT MONTH

Don't miss these four stories in November

A CHRISTMAS TO DIE FOR by Marta Perry
The Three Sisters Inn
Tyler Dunn came to Rachel Hampton's inn seeking justice
for a decades-old crime. She wanted to trust the handsome
architect, but his inquiries opened up old family secrets and
turned her Christmas season amid the Plain People into a
hazardous holiday.

STRANGER IN THE SHADOWS by Shirlee McCoy
After a heartbreaking tragedy, Chloe Davidson had relocated
to sleepy Lakeview, Virginia, where handsome minister
Ben Avery had welcomed her. Yet Chloe had an inkling that a
stalker was waiting to strike. Had her place of refuge turned
into a dangerous hideaway?

THE PRICE OF REDEMPTION by Pamela Tracy
There was a body in his shed, but Eric Santellis had an alibi.
He'd been wrongfully imprisoned when the murder had
occurred. When the body was identified as police officer
Ruth Atkins's long-dead husband, Eric knew he had to help
Ruth—who'd fought to see him exonerated—catch the real
killer.

CRADLE OF SECRETS by Lisa Mondello
A shocking secret about her birth sent Tammie Gardner
across the country on a mission to find the truth.
Dylan Montgomery had reasons of his own for wanting to
solve the mystery. But the answers they uncover lead to
deadly consequences neither of them are prepared for.

LISCNM1007